Check into the Pennyfoot Hotel . . .
for delightful tales of detection!

Room with a Clue

The view from the Pennyfoot's roof garden is lovely—but for Lady Eleanor Danbury, it was the last thing she ever saw. Now Cecily must find out who sent the snobbish society matron falling to her death . . .

Do Not Disturb

Mr. Bickley answered the door knocker and ended up dead. Cecily must capture the culprit—before murder darkens another doorstep . . .

Service for Two

Dr. McDuff's funeral became a fiasco when the mourners found a stranger's body in the casket. Now Cecily must close the case—for at the Pennyfoot, murder is a most unwelcome guest . . .

Eat, Drink, and Be Buried

April showers bring May murders—when one of the guests is found strangled with a maypole ribbon. Soon the May Day celebration turns into a hotel investigation—and Cecily fears it's a merry month . . . for murder.

Check-Out Time

A distinguished guest plummets to his death while trying to balance on a balcony railing. Now Cecily has to juggle her plans for the Midsummer Ball while solving a deadly acrobatic puzzle . . .

GROUNDS FOR MURDER

KATE KINGSBURY

BERKLEY PRIME CRIME, NEW YORK

GROUNDS FOR MURDER

A Berkley Prime Crime Book / published by arrangement with the author

PRINTING HISTORY
Berkley Prime Crime edition / August 1995

ISBN: 0-425-14901-3

Berkley Prime Crime Books are published by
The Berkley Publishing Group,
200 Madison Avenue, New York, NY 10016.
The name BERKLEY PRIME CRIME and the BERKLEY PRIME CRIME
design are trademarks belonging to Berkley Publishing Corporation.

PRINTED IN THE UNITED STATES OF AMERICA

10 9 8 7 6 5 4 3 2 1

CHAPTER

1

October drew to a close in a rash of blustery winds and chilling showers in the year of 1908. In anticipation of the winter storms that would roar in from the North Sea, the staff of the Pennyfoot Hotel in Badgers End battened down the windows of the upper floors, emptied the window boxes on the front terrace, and replaced the windshields on the chimney pots.

Warm and secure inside the stalwart walls, the planning committee feverishly worked on the arrangements for the Guy Fawkes Ball, destined to take place on the Fifth of November.

The festivities were not the only cause for excitement, however. Gertie Brown was expecting her baby to enter the world within the next week or two, and the betting on the correct date had reached fever pitch.

Even Michel, who usually disdained such womanly goings-on, cast an anxious eye now and again at the pregnant housemaid. Occasionally he went so far as to forget his lofty stature of hotel chef and offered the housemaid a helping hand with the heavy cauldrons of steaming hot water, all the while pretending to ignore the smiles of gratitude from the hefty young woman.

Mrs. Chubb, whose arduous duties as housekeeper kept her own hands busy, was pleasantly surprised by this unexpected chivalry. "It really is amazing," she told Gertie, who stood in front of the cast-iron stove warming her backside, "just how much a baby can change people's attitude."

"Well, it's bleeding changed mine, I can tell you," Gertie said, massaging her aching back with both hands. "I'll be bloody glad when it's all over and I can get this lump of lard out of me belly. I'm tired of carrying it around with me. It's like lugging around a blinking sack of potatoes all day."

"You should make the most of this time," Mrs. Chubb said briskly. "Once the baby's here you won't have time to enjoy it. It will keep you hopping, mark my words."

Gertie groaned. "All I can say is it'll be bleeding lovely to hop anywhere after this lot."

"And you will be hopping around, my girl. Now that Ethel has left you'll have to take over her duties in the dining room."

Gertie's face turned red with indignation. "What, me? Bloody cheek! What's wrong with that new girl, Doris? Got a wooden leg, has she?"

"You know very well that Doris doesn't have enough experience to work the dining room. I'll need her here in the kitchen where I can keep an eye on her." Mrs. Chubb took a pile of serviettes out of the sideboard and flipped through them with expert fingers, checking for creases. "It will be up to you to teach her what she needs to know."

"Well, someone will have to do the dining room once the nipper arrives. Or am I supposed to go back to work as soon as it pops out?"

"There's no need to be impertinent, my girl." The housekeeper thrust the serviettes at her, then folded her arms across her ample chest. "Now, take these into the dining room. And you'd better look sharp and get that silver cleaned before we have to lay the tables for lunch."

Having put a satisfactory end to the conversation, she turned her back on Gertie's scowling face and headed for the scullery.

Behind her back, Gertie muttered, "Well, I bleeding hope it waits until after the Fifth. It would be just my blooming luck to miss the fireworks."

At the committee meeting in the library upstairs, Cecily Sinclair—the Pennyfoot's owner—found it difficult to hold the conversation to the topic of the coming festivities.

Phoebe Carter-Holmes, who was in charge of the entertainment, was certain that Gertie's baby would be a girl. "I always wanted a daughter myself," she declared, smoothing a crease from one of her elbow-length gloves. "So comforting to a woman if she has the misfortune to be left a widow, as I was. I'm afraid that my son is far too busy with his work in the church to give much thought to his mother."

"I'm inclined to agree," Cecily murmured, thinking of her own son. "Michael seems so preoccupied with running his business. Even so, I have to admit the George and Dragon is no easy operation to handle, and it's not Michael's fault his father died too young."

"Men are simply too selfish to give much thought to the

women in their lives, no matter if they have all the time in the world."

The dry comment had come from the third member of the group, Madeline Pengrath. Meeting Phoebe's icy stare, she tossed her long, silky black tresses over one shoulder with a gesture of contempt.

Phoebe bristled. Raising both hands, she gave the immense brim of her hat an unnecessary tug. "Algie has a great deal to do as vicar of this parish, and naturally his work is of the utmost importance. I should be most upset if I thought he placed me before his parishioners."

"Well, I'm sure there's no danger of that." Ignoring Phoebe's offended gasp, Madeline turned to Cecily. "Let us hope, however, that in this case the unborn baby is indeed a boy. This will be a Scorpio child, the most powerful of all the zodiac. He will have tremendous drive and ambition, as well as untiring energy. He will be creative and could be successful at anything he turns his hand to, and all of that would be wasted on a girl unfortunately."

"I don't see why," Cecily said mildly. "New and greater opportunities are opening up for women every day, thanks to the New Women's Movement."

"But not fast enough," Madeline said, shaking her head. "If I could be born again into this world, I'd want to be a man."

"Is that why you spend so much time looking for one?" Phoebe said sweetly.

Madeline's dark eyes flashed fire, and Cecily said hurriedly, "Perhaps it might be better if we concentrated on the preparations for the ball. Phoebe, do you have anything confirmed for entertainment?"

Placed in the limelight, Phoebe preened herself, while Madeline smoldered in silence at the end of the long Jacobean table.

"I have secured the appearance of a remarkable song-stress, Wilhelmina Freidrich," Phoebe announced in ringing tones. "She has graced many a stage, so I believe, and is well thought of in operatic circles."

Madeline groaned, and again Cecily hurriedly cut in. "That sounds wonderful, Phoebe. As a matter of fact, we have an opera singer staying here at the hotel this week. His name is Ellsworth Galloway. Have you heard of him?"

Phoebe clasped her hands together, her face lighting up with excitement. "Truly? Oh, how wonderful! He is a most engaging baritone. Perhaps he can be persuaded to join Miss Freidrich in a duet. Wouldn't that be absolutely divine?"

"Quite," Madeline murmured. "And perhaps we can persuade the audience to join in. A rousing chorus from *Hansel und Gretel* perhaps?"

Phoebe looked down her nose. "How awfully vulgar. But that's to be expected from one who is sadly lacking in knowledge of the finer arts."

"Madeline, have you decided on the flower arrangements?" Cecily asked, a little desperately.

Madeline yawned. "I was waiting to hear the nature of the entertainment before deciding. No doubt I shall be able to think of something to liven up the proceedings. That is, unless Phoebe has something innovative up her sleeve, like a stray snake, for instance?"

"Will you never let me forget that?" Phoebe cried, rising to her feet. "I am quite sure there have been times in your life when you have made mistakes. Ah, but then I forget, you have the dubious power to foresee any misfortunes before they arise, and can therefore avoid them."

"If that were so," Madeline said evenly, "I would not be seated at this table right now."

"Ladies, please." Cecily held up her hands in appeal. "Can't we conduct ourselves in a more peaceful manner?"

"Never mind." Madeline got to her feet and floated over to the door, her lavender cotton skirt swirling about her trim ankles. "I have work to do. I'll be back as soon as I can conjure up a flower arrangement suitable for our windy warblers."

She paused in the doorway and glanced back over her shoulder. "The moon is full this week. And All Hallows' Eve draws near. If I were you, Phoebe dear, I'd take special care to avoid offending the wrong person. One never knows what evil lurks beneath a pleasant countenance. I should hate to see you spirited away to the underworld. How we should miss your inane comments." With an airy wave of her hand, she disappeared.

Phoebe made an explosive sound. "Well, really!" Straightening her hat with both hands, she said in a plaintive tone, "I really don't know why you put up with that dreadful woman. She can be quite barbaric at times."

"Madeline might be a little unconventional," Cecily said quietly, "but people who possess creative talents very often are a little unusual. In any case, she is a good friend." She gave Phoebe a warm smile. "As you are, I would add."

Phoebe picked up her parasol and, with a rustling of her silk skirt, headed across the Axminster carpet. "Yes, well, if I were you, Cecily dear, I'd be a little more cautious about choosing my friends. One never knows if someone like that could turn nasty and do something dreadful."

Pausing halfway across the room, she turned to look back at Cecily. "If I owned a hotel such as this one, I'm quite sure I would be most wary about whom I invited to work in it. With all these rumors flying around about the gypsies being back on Putney Downs, one simply can't be too careful."

"I'll bear that in mind," Cecily murmured.

Phoebe patted the brim of her hat as she reached the door. "I must be off, in any case. Algie will be waiting for his lunch." She swept out, leaving Cecily to stare beseechingly up at the portrait of her late husband.

James Sinclair had died much too young, after a bout of malaria he'd first contracted while serving in the tropics in Her Majesty's army. There were times, even now, almost three years later, when Cecily found it hard to believe he'd gone.

The portrait had brought a measure of comfort in the early days, when the pain had been almost too intense to bear. Now the pain had subsided, and even the dull ache that had replaced it rarely bothered her. Except for the occasional bittersweet pang of remembrance, her period of mourning was over.

Even so, she still addressed the portrait at times to air her grievances and opinions. With Phoebe's words still ringing in her ears, she gazed pensively at the image of her dead husband. "James," she murmured, "I do believe I agree with Madeline. All in all, Gertie's baby might do well to be born a boy."

"Cor blimey, Doris, I know you've only been here two days, but how many times do I have to tell you the forks go in this drawer, not that one." Gertie dug her fists into her ample hips in a fair imitation of Mrs. Chubb. The gesture lost some of its effect in view of her swollen belly, but her scowl made up for that.

The diminutive girl standing in front of her looked as if she were about to cry. Despite her frustration, Gertie felt a tug of sympathy for the child. Doris didn't look old enough to be working. Her black skirt swept the floor, covering up her shoes, and she looked lost in the folds of the white pinafore apron that swamped her skinny figure.

Even her cap seemed too big for her, seated squarely on top of her head and pinned to the large knot of light brown hair. Or maybe it was just her eyes that made her face look too small. Huge eyes they were, and seemed to change color, looking brown one day, green the next.

"I'm sorry, Miss Brown, I am honestly," she whispered in her little girl voice. "I am trying, but there's so much to remember."

Gertie let out her breath on an exasperated sigh. She'd been fourteen bloody years old herself when she'd started, but she'd had more gumption in her little finger than this twit had in her entire body.

"I know there's a bleeding lot to learn, but you ain't going to learn nothing if you don't pay attention. I explained to you just yesterday about the knives and forks, didn't I?"

Doris nodded miserably.

"Then pay bloody attention. I ain't going to waste my blinking breath telling you the same things over and over again. Now you flipping listen to me, Doris 'oggins. If you don't do things right, it's me what will get the blame. I'm supposed to be teaching you. I don't want Mrs. Chubb breathing hot fumes down me bloody neck 'cause you're not listening to me."

Gertie jumped as a strident voice declared from the doorway of the kitchen, "Gertie! Whatever are you screeching about? I could hear you all the way down the hallway."

Gertie sent the housekeeper a pained look. "I'm trying to teach this little twerp how to be a housemaid, that's what. I've got to yell at her, to make her listen to me."

"As long as the child isn't deaf, there is really no need to raise your voice like that." Mrs. Chubb bustled into the kitchen, smoothing her plump hands over her hips. "We don't want the guests to know all our business belowstairs, now do we? You know how madam feels about gossip."

Irritated that she should be the one to receive a reprimand, Gertie said in a tart voice, "I'm not the one spreading gossip around. I wasn't the one what talked about the gypsies being back, now was I?"

Mrs. Chubb's round face flushed. "No need to be cheeky, Gertie Brown. I had no idea that strange woman was standing behind me when I mentioned it to you."

Gertie grinned. "That Lady Belleville is bonkers, all right. Every time she comes down here to stay, she's more batty than before. I thought she was going to wet her drawers when she heard about the gypsies."

"She'd wet them for sure if she heard the latest news." An expression of dismay crossed Mrs. Chubb's face, and she shot a glance at the new housemaid, still standing forlornly by the huge scrubbed-wood table.

"Doris," the housekeeper said quickly, "would you please fetch that jug of milk from the pantry for me? It's on the top shelf in the corner."

Realizing that the housekeeper had sent Doris out on purpose, Gertie could hardly contain herself. This had to be bloody good. She could tell from the way Mrs. Chubb's eyes sparkled with excitement.

"Go on," she said when Doris had disappeared, "what's up, then?"

Mrs. Chubb put a finger to her lips and crept closer. "A murder," she whispered in a voice that sent cold shivers down Gertie's back.

"Bloody 'ell," Gertie whispered back hoarsely. "What, here in the hotel?"

"No. Up at Putney Downs. I just heard the news from Samuel, who got it from the milkman this morning. They found her in the woods at the back of the Downs."

"Strewth." Gertie clutched her right breast. "Makes me bleeding heart thump, it does. Do they think it's the gypsies?"

"I wouldn't be at all surprised, seeing as how the body

was a gypsy. At least they think so. She was wearing gypsy clothes, and they found a bag of clothes pegs lying close by."

"Well, couldn't they tell who she was? The gypsies would know her, if she was one of them, wouldn't they?"

Mrs. Chubb's face wore the look of a judge about to declare the death sentence. "They couldn't recognize her," she said and slowly licked her upper lip.

Gertie had the distinct impression that she didn't want to hear the rest of this. Little bumps were raising all over her arms, in spite of the moist warmth of the kitchen. Her curiosity wouldn't let her leave it alone, however.

"Go on," she said, swallowing hard on the words. "Why couldn't they recognize her?"

"Because she had no head, that's why," Mrs. Chubb said on a note of triumph. "It was chopped off with an axe, so I heard."

A loud crash greeted her words, and both women jumped an inch off the ground. Mrs. Chubb gave a little yelp and stared at Doris, who stood just inside the doorway.

"Bloody 'ell," Gertie said crossly when she saw the puddle of milk spreading across the tiled floor. "You almost gave me a bloody 'eart attack, you did, you little twerp."

Doris dabbed at the drops of milk running down her skirt. "I'm sorry, Miss Brown, Mrs. Chubb. I'll clean it up. I got scared, and the jug slipped out of me hands."

"Every blooming thing you touch slips out of your hand." Gertie lifted her skirt and stepped out of the way of the spreading puddle. "Hurry up and get this muck cleaned up before it runs all over the bleeding floor."

"It was my fault," Mrs. Chubb said as Doris flew to the sink. "I should have noticed she was there."

"Well, she would hear about the murder sometime." Gertie stomped over the stove and grabbed hold of the coal scuttle. "Everybody will bloody know soon. I don't know why it has to be such a blinking secret. It's not as if she's a blooming baby now, is it."

"Have a little more patience, Gertie." Mrs. Chubb crossed her arms across her heavy bosom. "You were her age once, and just as green. I remember you barging into doors, and what about the time you burned your bum on the stove when you backed into it?"

A smothered giggle from Doris brought hot color to Gertie's face. "At least I didn't drop things all the time and forget what I'd been told. Tell me once, that's all you bleeding had to do, and I remembered."

"Well, Doris will, too, in time, won't you, ducks," Mrs. Chubb said, sending Doris an encouraging smile. "Now be a good girl and get this mess cleaned up before Michel comes in here banging his saucepans around, the way he does."

Put out by the housekeeper's defense of the new house-maid, Gertie muttered, "I don't know why Ethel had to bleeding go to London to live. She might have been slow but she knew what she was doing."

Mrs. Chubb rolled up her sleeves and moved over to the sink to help Doris lift the heavy bucket of water to the floor. "Now, you know Joe went there to work after selling their farm. If your husband went to London to live, wouldn't you want to go with him?"

"I s'pose." Gertie sighed heavily. "But I don't have no bleeding husband, do I. Nor do I want one." She saw Doris's eyes grow wide as her gaze traveled to Gertie's swollen belly.

"And don't bloody look at me like that," Gertie snapped. "I was bleeding married when I got lumbered. At least I thought I was. It weren't my fault he already had a blinking wife."

Doris looked away hurriedly and dipped her hands in the hot water. Bringing up a dripping dishcloth from the soapsuds, she squeezed some of the water out of it then slapped it on the floor. "I'm sorry," she said meekly. "It's none of my business, I'm sure."

"Too right, it ain't." Gertie strode over to the back door and flung it open. "I'm going to get the coal. I'll be back in a minute, so I hope the floor is clean by then."

She stepped out into the damp, dark night and lifted her face to the sky. It felt good not to be on the bottom rung of the work ladder anymore. Now it was her turn to order someone about, and she was going to enjoy it after all the years of taking it from everyone else.

Stomping across the yard to the coal shed, she dragged her thin shawl closer around her shoulders. A cool, crisp wind from the sea brushed her cheeks and brought the taste of salt to her lips. She shivered and wished she'd worn the heavier shawl, the one Mrs. Chubb had knitted for her.

The door of the shed was stuck again, and she tugged on it, lustily swearing when it wouldn't budge. She'd complained no end of times that the door kept getting stuck. No one took any notice of her anymore. If Ian had been here, he would have mended it for her.

She took a firmer grip on the door and tugged harder. But Ian wasn't here. He'd gone back to London with the wife he'd somehow forgotten to tell her about. And now she was left here all alone, to have his baby. The baby he'd never see, she'd make bloody sure of that.

One last final heave did the trick. Groaning and creaking, the door opened, sending a shaft of moonlight through the partially open door. It caught the blade of the axe hanging from a hook on the wall, and the sharp edge gleamed with a cold, cruel light.

Gertie stopped dead, unable to take her eyes from the

silvery blade. *She had no head. It was chopped off with an axe.*

"Don't be bleeding daft, girl," Gertie muttered out loud. There had to be thousands of axes around the village, she assured herself.

Even so, she shoveled coal into the scuttle as fast as her bulky frame would allow, and as she lugged her heavy load across the yard she made up her mind that from now on Doris could chop the sticks for the fire. She wasn't going to touch that axe again if her bleeding life depended on it.

CHAPTER
❖ 2 ❖

Cecily was inclined to treat complaints about Doris with a
certain measure of restraint. "The child has had a regrettable
background," she explained to Mrs. Chubb when the housekeeper paid a visit to Cecily's suite to voice her concern.
"Doris's parents are dead. They died within a month of each
other. Pneumonia, I believe."

Mrs. Chubb clicked her tongue in distress. "Poor baby.
No wonder she has a problem concentrating. Did she come
from an orphanage, then?"

Cecily plumped up a green velvet cushion on the chaise
lounge. "No, Doris was being looked after by an aunt. The
woman was unbelievably cruel, metering out punishment

14

that would have been considered harsh even for the hardest criminal. Doris ran away to escape the abuse."

"Oh, my." Mrs. Chubb covered her mouth with her hand.

"I did contact the aunt," Cecily went on, "although Doris begged me not to. I felt it my duty to inform her of her niece's whereabouts, though of course I had no intention of sending her back there."

"So what did she say, then?"

Cecily sighed, remembering the brief note she'd received in response to her letter. "She thanked me for letting her know, and expressed relief that the child was off her hands."

"Well, then." Mrs. Chubb dusted the front of her apron with her plump hands. "In that case, mum, I shall do my best to put up with the child's bungling, and perhaps if we have patience with her she'll get the hang of things before too long."

She turned to go, and Cecily said gently, "I'd appreciate it, Altheda, if you would be patient with her. Perhaps my decision to hire Doris was based more on sympathy than on her abilities as a housemaid, but if you remember, James hired Gertie at that age for the same reasons, and look how well she has turned out."

Mrs. Chubb made a face, then smiled. "Oh, Gertie's not so bad, mum, I must say. She'll always be rough around the edges, that girl, but she means well and she's a good worker, Gertie is."

"So she is," Cecily agreed, returning the smile. "Perhaps she can help Doris learn the ropes."

"Don't you worry, mum. If anyone can lick that poor little mite into shape, it'll be our Gertie. You mark my words."

Cecily hoped profoundly that her housekeeper was right. The subject of Doris was still on her mind as she made her way down to the drawing room later. It had always been James's contention that everyone deserved a chance, and

Doris was no exception. Cecily rather thought that James would be pleased by her decision.

It was just as well a large crowd was expected for the Guy Fawkes celebrations, Cecily thought, as she entered the drawing room. Otherwise the hotel's financial situation would be even worse than it was at present. The hotel guest list was unusually short, this being so late in the year.

The considerable bills that James had run up while renovating the hotel had left formidable debts that would take years to pay back. The Pennyfoot needed a full house now and again during the off-season to survive.

Colonel Fortescue, seated on the rocking chair by the blazing fire, greeted Cecily with his usual hearty exuberance. A regular guest at the hotel, he considered himself a shade or two more privileged than the rest of the guests and often took advantage of the fact.

Cecily put up with his somewhat disturbing behavior for two reasons. In the first place, his custom was sorely needed. In the second place, the colonel suffered from a highly nervous condition brought upon by his close proximity to gunfire. Amongst other things, the experience had left him with a pronounced stutter, and what some people described as an addled brain.

Having been the wife of a military man, Cecily could sympathize with the man's condition, though at times even she was sorely tried by the colonel's strange antics.

"Spiffing!" Colonel Fortescue exclaimed, when Cecily announced that she was there to join the guests for afternoon tea. "Just what a chappie needs to brighten up this gray dismal day, what? What?"

The other guests in the room politely mumbled in agreement.

"It is indeed a horrible day out there," Lady Belleville

chirped. "Why, the wind was so fierce my poor little birds could hardly balance on my shoulders."

Colonel Fortescue looked startled. "Birds?"

The elderly widow nodded her head. "Yes, my canaries." She lifted a finger to her lips. "Hush! They don't like people talking about them. They think they are invisible, you see."

"Oh, quite, quite," the colonel murmured, obviously at a loss for a suitable answer.

Cecily could hardly blame him. Lady Belleville was well known for her eccentricities, including her conviction that her "birds" accompanied her everywhere, seated either on her shoulder or her wrist. The fact that, as yet, no one had ever seen or heard these particular birds appeared to faze her not at all.

"Yes," Lady Belleville said, "that dreadful wind would have taken my hat into the ocean with it, had I not had it pinned securely to my head."

"By George, that must be dashed painful," the colonel said, furiously blinking his eyelids.

Lady Belleville lifted a pair of diamond-encrusted lorgnettes and looked down her nose through them. "You have something in your eye, my good man?"

"What?" The colonel looked confused for a moment, then shook his head. "Oh, no, madam. Can't stop the blighters from flapping up and down. Damned nuisance. Can't keep a dashed monocle in place for five seconds."

He twirled one end of his white mustache with his fingers. "Got shot at during the Boer War, you know. Frightful scrimmage that was, what? What? I remember when—"

"Colonel," Cecily said before the man could launch into one of his horrific tales of the fighting in Africa. "Tell me, what do you make of this dreadful murder on the Downs?"

Belatedly she wished she had introduced another subject.

The murder had been uppermost in her mind, and the first thing she had pounced on when searching for a diversion.

"Why, absolutely ghastly, of course, old bean," the colonel said with relish. "Imagine, chopping off her head like that. Must have been a saber, of course. Sharp as the devil, those blades are. One slice and"—he made a squelching noise in his throat and thrust his hand sideways—"right through the neck as clean as a whistle."

"I say, must you be quite so explicit?" The little man seated next to him looked thoroughly uncomfortable. Cyril Plunkett was a salesman from London and had informed Cecily that he had chosen the Pennyfoot instead of one of the bigger hotels in Wellercombe because he detested the noise and bustle of the town.

He had discovered the charm of the hotel, he'd told her, when he'd solicited a fairly large order for his cleaning supplies from Mrs. Chubb.

Now he sat on the edge of his seat, looking as if he were ready to spring in the air like a disturbed frog if someone upset him.

The colonel glanced down at him as if surprised to find him there. "Oh, sorry, old chap. Didn't mean to offend, what? What?"

"Who's offending whom?" a bored voice asked from the doorway.

Cecily turned to see a tall, bulky man enter the room. His dark bushy beard was neatly trimmed, his mustache carefully waxed, and his full lips nestled in the center like ripe berries in a furry paw.

Ellsworth Galloway always made an entrance, and he did so now, striking a majestic pose with one hand over his heart while he surveyed the rest of the occupants in the room.

Colonel Fortescue viewed the opera singer with distaste.

"Don't think that should concern you, old chap," he said pompously. "We happened to be talking about the murder of that gypsy girl."

"Oh, is that all." Ellsworth turned to Cecily and gave her a slight bow of his head. "For a moment I thought I might have interrupted something interesting."

"You don't find a murder interesting, Mr. Galloway?" Cecily asked, raising an eyebrow. "After all, it isn't every day one hears of such a gruesome death. One does have to wonder why the murderer went to all that trouble to chop off the head and apparently hide it elsewhere, while leaving the rest of the body in full view for anyone to find."

"Er . . . do we really have to discuss this subject?" Cyril Plunkett said, fidgeting with his glasses. Tiny beads of sweat stood out on the bald patch above his forehead. "I do find it all rather disgusting, you know."

"Disgusting?" Ellsworth's laugh rumbled through the room. "My dear chap, as far as I am concerned, that's one less savage we have to worry about. Probably deserved to have her head chopped off, that's what I say. I'd like to see every last one of them wiped off the face of this earth."

"She was a human being, sir," Cecily protested. "No human being deserves that kind of treatment."

"Well, dashed if I could lose too much sleep over the little beggar," the colonel said, patting his pockets as if looking for something. "Never did like those blasted heathens running around in the woods. Spoils the atmosphere, old bean. Can't have a decent walk in the woods anymore without tripping over one of the bastards."

"I say," Cyril muttered, casting an anxious look at Cecily. "Ladies present and all that, you know."

"Well, I should think so." Lady Belleville placed her fingers on her shoulder. "Come, darlings, we shall go for a little walk. All this talk of heathens running around the woods is quite upsetting. Not at all what we want to hear, is it, my lovelies?"

Cyril's jaw dropped as he watched the dowager gently lift her empty fingers close to her face. The lace collar that bound her throat ended in a ruffle beneath her chin, and the soft fabric fluttered as she twittered chirping noises at an imaginary bird.

As if aware of his stare, Lady Belleville transferred her gaze to Cyril. "Thank you, so much, Mr. Plunkett, for coming to our rescue. Such a true gentleman, indeed." She swept toward him, and Cyril jerked back in his chair as if he'd been stung by a nettle.

"Not that I like gypsies," Lady Belleville said, leaning precariously over him to expose her bosom. "They kill the birds and eat them, you know. Perhaps that's what happened to that gypsy girl's head."

Cecily winced as she watched Cyril visibly pale.

He swallowed several times, then said faintly, "I . . . er . . . don't think so."

"Well, whatever. As long as they don't touch my birds, I don't suppose it matters." Lady Belleville crossed the room to stand in front of Cecily. "I don't think I shall stay for afternoon tea," she said, fixing her strange, intent stare on Cecily's face. "I don't care for the conversation."

"I'm sorry, Lady Belleville. Perhaps I can have a tray sent to your room?"

"Thank you. That would be most pleasant." The dowager wandered out of the door, still making twittering noises at her "birds."

"Good Lord," Ellsworth said, running his fingers through his thick, curly hair. "Is everyone batty around here? Am I the only sane one to inhabit this hotel?"

Cyril got up abruptly from his chair. "I don't think I shall stay either," he said, looking apologetically at Cecily.

"Frightened you off, did we?" Ellsworth said, with one of his hearty laughs. "Can't take a juicy murder, heh? Or perhaps you are friends with the uncivilized devils, is that it? Make lots of good sales to them, do you?"

Cyril paused in front of the sneering opera singer. "I do not deal with the gypsies, no, sir," he said quietly. "I agree that for the most part they are nothing but thieves and liars. I do believe, however, that a certain measure of decorum should be employed when conversing with ladies. I find your manner quite despicable."

He left quickly, as if aghast at his own audacity, nevertheless earning Cecily's respect. As proprietor of the hotel, she had often been forced to bite her tongue in order to avoid offending a guest, but with regards to Ellsworth Galloway, never had she been quite so tempted to tell someone exactly what she thought of him.

"Sniveling little plebeian," Galloway said with a contemptuous toss of his head. "Who does that insignificant lowbrow think he's talking to? Really, Mrs. Sinclair, you are lowering the class of this establishment by allowing such ill-bred riffraff to invade the Pennyfoot. This hotel always had such an impeccable reputation when your husband was alive."

Cecily drew in a sharp breath. "Mr. Galloway, not that it's any of your business, but I feel compelled to inform you that Mr. Plunkett works for a very prestigious firm in London. I happen to be acquainted with the chairman of the board, and he speaks very highly of Mr. Plunkett. A respected and valuable asset to their sales force, I believe were his very words."

"But working class nevertheless. Not at all the type of person I should expect to find at the Pennyfoot Hotel."

Throwing caution to the wind, Cecily said quietly, "As far as I am concerned, sir, if someone can afford to pay the price, he has every right to the product. I will not turn anyone away from this establishment on the basis of class distinction."

"Then, madam, I fear your hotel will soon lose its appeal to the more privileged among us. I for one will not associate with such ugly lowlife."

"That, sir, is your privilege."

"I say, old bean," the colonel said, obviously upset by this somewhat heated exchange, "don't take it to heart. I'm sure Galloway didn't mean any offense."

For a moment the singer looked as if he would argue the point, then he cleared his throat. "My apologies, madam. I believe I have lost my appetite." He strode from the room, and Cecily let her shoulders sag. Really, the man was impossible.

"I imagine that leaves just you and me for tea, what? What?"

Cecily glanced at the colonel, who was looking at her as if afraid to catch the backlash of her wrath. She forced a smile, saying, "Colonel, I shall be happy to join you."

"Splendid! Then I can tell you about the time I cut off the head of a chicken when I was in India. Blasted thing ran around headless for an hour squawking like a burned cat. I'm damn sure it was looking for its head. . . . "

It was going to be a very long afternoon, Cecily thought dismally.

If there was one person who could calm her shattered nerves, Cecily told herself later, it was Baxter. Ever since James had died, leaving her to face the innumerable problems of running the hotel, she had relied on her manager for guidance, support, and sympathy.

She had received all that she had asked for and so much more. Baxter had become so important in her life she couldn't imagine existing without him. And right now she needed him rather badly.

She found him bent over his desk, studying a sheet of figures with a frown that boded unpleasant news.

The minute she entered the office, Baxter straightened. Scrambling to his feet, he reached for his jacket and thrust his arms into the sleeves. "I do wish you would forewarn me of your visits," he said, scowling at her, "and allow me to prepare."

Knowing that his discomfort was due to the fact that she had caught him without his jacket, Cecily merely smiled. Baxter insisted on the proper rules of propriety. He chose to ignore the relaxed rules of etiquette that had been in evidence since Edward had inherited the throne from Queen Victoria seven years earlier.

His attitude could not be changed, no matter how much Cecily tried. He abhorred the work of the suffragettes, viewed the rapid changes taking place in society with suspicion and even alarm, and was horrified when Cecily showed signs of subscribing to the New Women's Movement.

Which was why Cecily took the greatest delight in baiting him. She leaned over the desk and peered up into his face. "Baxter, I am in dire need of one of those delightful little cigars you always carry with you. Would you please be so kind as to offer me one?"

"You know perfectly well, madam, how I feel about you indulging in such a disgraceful habit."

"Yes, I do, Baxter. And you know perfectly well that I shall insist on smoking, no matter how much you disapprove. Now, will you please light one up for me, or do I have to ask Samuel to purchase a package for me from the George and Dragon?"

Sighing, Baxter withdrew the slim package from his pocket and offered it to her.

She remained leaning forward until he had struck a match and held it to the end of the cigar, while she drew hard enough to start a glow.

"Thank you." Seating herself in a chair at the side of his desk, she let out a long sigh and watched the smoke curl up in front of her. "You have nice hands, Baxter."

"Madam?" He sounded shocked, looking down at her with both eyebrows arched.

She met his gaze steadily. "Do sit down, Baxter, please. I get a crick in my neck looking up at you like this."

"I prefer to stand, madam."

Grimacing, she repeated, "I said, you have nice hands."

"That's what I thought you said, madam."

"Not like that insufferable oaf, Ellsworth Galloway."

There was a slight pause, then Baxter said cautiously, "The gentleman upset you, madam?"

"That idiot is no gentleman." Cecily drew hard on the cigar, then puffed out the smoke. "Do you know that the back of his hands sprout almost as much hair as his chin?"

Baxter coughed. "I can't say that I've noticed, madam."

"Then you'll have to accept my word for it." She leaned over and tapped the ash from the end of her cigar into the ashtray on Baxter's desk. "We have been discussing the murder, Baxter."

"Yes, madam."

"It would seem that no one is at all upset by the death of a young girl. All that matters to them is that the girl was a gypsy, therefore of no account."

Baxter cleared his throat. "I trust, madam, that since this unfortunate act has nothing to do with the hotel, that madam will refrain from involving herself in the situation?"

Cecily raised her eyebrows in mock surprise. "Why,

Baxter, you know very well I do not concern myself with something that is none of my business."

He chose not to answer, but looked at her with such skepticism she felt like laughing. Instead she sat back in her chair, contemplated the smoldering end of her cigar, and said softly, "I would very much like to know, however, why the murderer felt it necessary to bury the head and not the body."

Baxter's groan seemed to echo around the room. "I do wonder why that simple remark strikes such a note of doom in my mind."

Cecily merely smiled. "You worry too much, Baxter," she said, and puffed once more on the cigar. "I assure you, this time I shall leave well enough alone. I have no wish to involve myself in murder again."

The words sounded confident enough, she thought. Now if only her mind would obey, perhaps this time she could, indeed, stay out of trouble.

CHAPTER

3

"Ah . . . choo!"

The sneeze was followed by the splintering shatter of glass on the tiled floor of the kitchen. Gertie spun around from the sink, a half-peeled potato in her hand.

Doris stood in the doorway of the scullery, one small hand covering her mouth. Scattered around the kitchen maid's feet lay the remains of a crystal fruit bowl.

"Bloody hell, Doris," Gertie yelled, glaring at the cowering girl. "What's the bleeding matter with you? That's the third thing you've dropped this morning."

"I'm sorry, Miss Brown, it was the cat what did it." Doris's words ended in a wail, and Gertie threw the potato back in the sink. Drying her hands on her apron, she marched across the floor toward the sniveling child.

"What cat where?" she demanded, her fists digging into her wide hips.

Doris jerked a thumb over her shoulder. "In there. Every time I see one I sneeze. They make me eyes water and me nose run, and I sneeze. I can't help it. They just make me sneeze."

"All right, all right," Gertie muttered. "Wait a minute while I chase it out. Bleeding strays ought to be shot, thieving from the pantry every blooming chance they get."

She grabbed a broom from the side of the stove and advanced into the scullery. There was no sign of a cat anywhere, but the pantry door had been left open. Probably by Doris, Gertie thought, her hands itching to wring the unfortunate girl's neck.

Peering into the tiny cupboard space, she saw a flash of black fur disappear under one of the low shelves. "Get out of there, you bloody little perisher," she yelled, stabbing at the space with her broom. Her belly prevented her from stooping low enough to be effective, and she kicked the shelf with her foot as hard as she could.

Her howl of pain blended with the frightened squawk from the cat as it dashed in between her legs, throwing her off balance. The broom fell from her hand, and her elbow sent the large crock of butter spinning off the shelf. The crash that followed seemed to Gertie like the voice of doom.

"Oo, 'eck," Doris said behind her in a voice filled with awe.

"I'll bleeding oo 'eck you," Gertie yelled, spinning around to face the startled girl. "Now look what you gone and made me done."

Doris started bawling, digging her fists into her eyes. From across the kitchen came the sound of a saucepan crashing to the floor. "Mercy *moi*," said an irate voice, "what in the 'ell ees 'appening? Someone get murdered, *oui*?"

At the sound of the dreaded word, Doris howled louder.

"It's not my bleeding fault," Gertie yelled back, stooping as low as she could to pick up the pieces of brick red pottery generously lathered with butter. "But I tell you, I'd bloody well like to murder someone around here, that I would."

"That's e-*nough*!"

Gertie closed her eyes as Mrs. Chubb's shrill voice joined in. At least the command shut off Doris's wailing.

The plump housekeeper appeared in the doorway, her face glowing a bright red. "Doris, get to the sink and finish peeling those potatoes. Gertie, I want a word with you in the passage."

Gertie opened her mouth to protest, then shut it again when Mrs. Chubb's eyes spit sparks. "This very minute, Gertie."

Doris flew across to the sink, just as Michel threw up his hands in disgust and sent another saucepan crashing to the ground. "'Ow in the world am I supposed to concentrate on my *grande soufflé* with all this racket going on? Isn't it enough I 'ave to make another apple crumble because this imbecile opens the window and it fall out? *Sacre bleu*, it is enough to give a man zee cobblewollies."

"Collywobbles," Gertie muttered as she passed him. Heaving a heavy sigh, she followed Mrs. Chubb to the door. The place was getting to be a madhouse with that twit around, she thought, scowling at the maid's skinny back. How she was going to teach the little twerp to do the work properly she had no idea. The worst thing madam ever did was hire that one, that was for sure.

Stepping out into the hallway, she braced herself for yet another lecture from the seething housekeeper.

* * *

"I do think we should hire some extra help for the ball next week," Cecily murmured as she stood with Baxter in the Pennyfoot's grand ballroom. "We usually get quite a large crowd down from London for the event, as you know."

Baxter looked down at her with an impressive expression on his square-cut face. Cecily had often envied him that inscrutable look. It covered a lot of territory.

"It is my belief, madam, that many of our clientele will be otherwise engaged on the night of the ball. I do believe a card game tournament has been arranged for that night."

Cecily raised her eyebrows. "Really! Now how did you manage to learn that, Baxter? You are not thinking of participating, are you?"

His expression remained detached, but Cecily saw him pinch his mouth. "Madam knows very well that I do not play card games."

Remembering the one and only time she had seen him play, Cecily smiled. "That's very wise, Baxter. If I recall, your efforts proved to be disastrous in the past."

"If I may remind you, madam, I was coerced into playing."

It was time to change the subject, Cecily decided, glancing at his set jaw. "What do you think of Phoebe's idea of hiring an opera singer for the night?" she asked. "Certainly a change of pace from her usual presentations, don't you agree?"

"It would seem the lady has acquired some taste at last," Baxter said dryly. "It is indeed a more palatable prospect than a disappearing python or a dancing monkey."

"You have to admit Phoebe's spectaculars are always a topic of much speculation. One never knows what to expect from her."

Baxter made a noise in the back of his throat which could have meant anything.

"I just hope she doesn't invite Ellsworth Galloway to join in a duet with Miss Fried . . . whatever-her-name-is," Cecily said, lifting her gaze to a gilt cherub smiling down at her from the vaulted ceiling. "I really do detest that man."

"I understand he has an excellent voice."

She dropped her gaze again and found him studying her with a slightly perplexed look in his eyes. "It isn't like you to take such an instant dislike to someone," he added. "Not without good reason."

Shrugging, Cecily moved toward the stage, where the huge flowerpots waited to be filled with Madeline's beautiful arrangements. "I loathe his attitude. He might well be a celebrity, but his narrow-minded bigotry appalls me. In fact, I was dismayed by everyone's attitude this afternoon. I heard no compassion, no horror or regret that a human life had been taken so violently. All I heard was relief that it was merely a gypsy who had met such an unfortunate end, rather than a 'real' human being."

"I'm sure that wasn't the general consensus," Baxter murmured, following close on her heels.

"Oh, yes, it was." She swung around to face him, almost colliding with him.

Clearing his throat, he stepped back a pace. "I beg your pardon, madam."

She looked at him for a long moment. She had rarely seen her manager dressed in anything except his uniform of black morning coat, striped gray trousers, and crisp white shirt with the stiff-winged collar.

With the silver in his hair becoming more prominent, and his gray eyes that had lost none of their shrewdness over the years, he looked distinguished and quite masterful. Yet, just once she would have liked to see him in something a little more relaxing. Such as a smoking jacket, or even a dressing gown.

"Madam?"

She blinked and collected her thoughts. "Yes, Baxter?"

"You were smiling, madam. I was merely wondering if you would care to share the source of your amusement."

For a moment she was almost tempted to tell him. Then, with a sigh of regret, she abandoned the idea. "I was thinking about Lady Belleville. One shouldn't make fun of another's foibles, but I do find her imaginary canaries laughable."

"Perhaps she should keep company with Colonel Fortescue. They would complement one another very nicely."

Cecily tilted her head to one side. "Why, Baxter," she murmured, "I do believe you are harboring romantic thoughts again. There is hope for you yet."

She regretted her provocative teasing when she saw the flush darken his cheeks. In an effort to change the subject, she added, "I must say, I wasn't too pleased with her attitude, however. She also seemed to condone the murder, and seemed not in the least put out by the gruesome details. In fact, poor Mr. Plunkett seemed the most disturbed by the news."

"If I might be permitted to say so, madam, you would do well to take care when dealing with Lady Belleville. She is most definitely troubled in the mind, and people like that can be extremely unpredictable. She may appear harmless, but one can never take that for granted."

Surprised by this unusually long speech from her manager, Cecily shook her head. "Don't worry, Baxter, I have no wish to be on personal terms with the woman. I have quite enough problems dealing with the colonel. As for Ellsworth Galloway, the less I have to do with him the better. I must say, though, that Mr. Plunkett came quite admirably to my defense when that despicable man began throwing his weight around."

"You surprise me. I would not have considered Plunkett capable of standing up to any man."

Cecily narrowed her eyes, wondering if she had detected a note of jealousy. "You seem quite put out by that, Baxter."

"Not at all, madam. Merely surprised."

Disappointed that she had misinterpreted him, Cecily murmured, "Well, Lady Belleville seemed quite taken with him, though he seemed scared to death of her. But then, he's never been married, so he tells me. That could be the cause of his shyness."

"The gentleman seems to have discussed his personal life at some length."

This time she distinctly heard the scathing tone. Feeling ridiculously pleased with herself, she looked up at him. "I think he's a nice little man."

Baxter gave her a stony stare. "In my opinion, madam, anyone as finicky as Cyril Plunkett would quite possibly drive a woman crazy."

"Finicky?"

"Finicky," he repeated firmly.

Cecily prepared to enjoy herself. "In what way do you mean that, Baxter?"

"He polishes his silverware at the table."

Taken aback, she stared at him. "He what?"

"Polishes every utensil. As you can imagine, the maids are quite put out after working so hard to make everything spotless. It is obvious the man doesn't trust our cleaning methods."

"Oh, my," Cecily murmured. "I wonder if he's found a soiled piece of silverware. I shall have to ask Mrs. Chubb to check everything very carefully. Since Doris started working here, things have not been quite the same in the kitchen."

"Well, that's not all," Baxter declared, apparently determined not to let the matter rest. "He arrived with more luggage than Lady Belleville. He actually goes to the trouble of carrying a spare set of clothes to his business meetings, in case he should get muddied on the way."

Cecily refrained from asking how Baxter knew that. "That is quite understandable," she said mildly. "After all, he drives the company motorcar. One is much more prone to being splashed with mud in a motorcar than in a trap."

Baxter gave her such a look of frustration she felt sorry for him. "Well, in any case," she added, "I prefer that quiet little man to Ellsworth Galloway and his disgusting prejudices. Unless one is born south of London and comes from a privileged family, one is considered inferior in his eyes. And as for foreigners, according to that man they are the scum of the earth and should be sent back from whence they came."

Shaking her head in disgust, she headed for the door. The sprung parquet floor beneath her feet made her feel like dancing. She had danced so much with James. She really missed it.

A fleeting vision of dancing in Baxter's arms to the lush chords of the orchestra filled her with a strange sense of longing. It was pointless to dream of such things. Baxter would never unbend as long as she was his employer. And she could hardly deprive him of his job without good reason. Even if she were to do so, she would surely lose him.

Sadly she acknowledged that it was better to accept the stilted relationship he was willing to offer than none at all. But the ache would always be with her. It was almost as bad as the ache she had felt for James. Maybe this, too, would pass. In time.

Still smarting from the dressing-down that Mrs. Chubb had given her, Gertie was not in a good mood that evening. Although there were no more than a dozen guests in the hotel, having to do everything single-handedly kept her on the trot throughout the entire dinner hour.

Ellsworth Galloway had been particularly demanding, having had her running back and forward to the kitchen because he'd changed his mind about which kind of wine to drink with his meal.

And that batty old Lady Belleville had insisted on Gertie bringing lemonade for her canaries to drink. Said it kept their feathers a nice shade of yellow.

Seated on the coal bin at the side of the huge fireplace in the kitchen, Gertie stared gloomily into the leaping flames. She missed Ethel. Not only because of the extra work and worry, but because she missed having someone to talk to and share a giggle or two.

She and Ethel used to get up to all kinds of tricks. And now she was gone, swallowed up in the muck and filth of the Smoke, while she was still stuck in the bleeding back of beyond, with not much hope of getting out. It didn't bear thinking about.

Gertie sighed and stretched her stockinged feet out to the warmth. Still, she had a lot to be thankful for. After Ian left, madam was kind enough to give her the job as well as her old room. At least she would have plenty of help taking care of the baby when it came.

And she had her health and strength. That counted for a lot. Not like that poor bleeder found up in the woods. Gertie leaned forward and grasped the poker. Giving the coals a good poke, she watched the shower of red-hot sparks shoot up the chimney.

Fancy coming across a bloody murderer with an axe in his hand. Must have been a dreadful thing. In spite of the warmth, Gertie shivered. She couldn't get the sight of that flipping axe out of her mind. It was enough to turn her off ever touching an axe again.

Not that she'd have to, now that Doris was here. Now someone else could chop sticks, though Gawd knows how that skinny liz was going to lift the bleeding axe. The twit had trouble lifting a bucket of potatoes an inch off the floor. Somehow the thought of Doris Hoggins swinging that heavy axe over her head just didn't seem possible.

Gertie sighed. She'd had to do it at that age, and now that her belly was so big, she found it hard to bring the axe down in the right place. Thinking about it prompted her to lift the lid of the kindling box. Just as well she did, because it was almost empty. It looked as if Doris would have her first go at the sticks tonight.

As if on cue, the kitchen door swung open, and Doris trudged in, looking as if she'd tramped all the way across Putney Downs and back. Gertie almost felt sorry for her. Then she hardened her heart. The kid had to learn, and eventually she'd get used to the hard work. Everyone did.

"The kindling box needs filling up," she said as the girl looked at her with dark smudged eyes. "You'll have to go out and chop some sticks tonight, so as I can start the fires first thing in the morning."

Doris passed a frail hand across her forehead. "Can't it wait till the morning?" she whispered.

Gertie shook her head. "You bring the sticks in that early they'll be damp, and I won't be able to get the fires going. You'll have to do it tonight. The axe is in the shed, and you'll find the logs piled up behind it."

Doris sent one longing look at the smoldering coals in the fireplace, then slowly turned and left the kitchen. Gertie watched her go, trying not to remember that bone-crushing weariness that could numb the very soul.

Samuel heard the faint sound of chopping as he crossed the courtyard in front of the stables. The young footman had just finished settling the horses for the night after cleaning the two traps.

The sky was clear, freshened by a stiff breeze from the North Sea, and the sound carried clearly on the cold air. At first he didn't think the noise had come from the kitchen yard. For one thing, it was too faint, and for another, the sound was uneven, ragged, not the steady chop of someone who knew what he was doing with an axe.

After closing the gates to the stables, Samuel crossed the grass to the corner of the kitchen wall and peered around it. What he saw made him softly curse, the words riding on a breath of steam.

Bathed in the light from the kitchen windows, Doris stood in front of the coal shed, a sturdy log standing on end at her feet. Using both hands, she was struggling to swing the axe, without much success.

As Samuel watched, the slender girl heaved the axe in the air. Either because of her lack of height or the fact that she simply didn't have the strength to lift it, the axe fell again before it had reached the arc. Instead of slicing cleanly through the log, it bounced off it, barely missing the legs of the exhausted maid.

With another curse, Samuel strode across the yard and snatched the axe from the startled girl's hand. "Here," he said gruffly, "stand yourself back. This shouldn't take long."

Doris started to protest, but he shut her up by saying,

"Move further back or you'll be getting a splinter in your eye."

Without another word she obeyed him.

He gave her a nod of approval, then whipped off his cap and tucked it in his pocket. Flexing his shoulders, he grasped the axe and started the swing. He could tell she was watching him, and the knowledge gave him added strength.

Again and again he swung the axe, watching the sticks fly in all directions as the axe cut through the wood.

Slowly the pile of kindling grew, until he was satisfied. "This should do it for now," he said, wiping the sweat from his brow with his sleeve.

Doris came forward, her long skirt flapping around her ankles in the chill night breeze. "Thank you, sir," she whispered. "I am most grateful, to be sure. I thought I would surely be here all night."

In the shadowy light he saw her smile. She had the prettiest smile he'd ever seen, shy and sort of sad, as if she wasn't sure what she was smiling about.

"Think no more about it. I am glad to be of help." He peered at her, trying to see her eyes more clearly. Beautiful eyes they were, huge dark eyes, like a puppy dog begging to play.

"I don't know as how I'm ever going to chop those sticks," she said in a voice so soft and low he had to strain to hear.

"You'll get the hang of it. I'll show you, if you like."

She nodded eagerly, sending warmth right through his heart.

"Tomorrow?" Already he was looking forward to seeing this fragile girl again.

To his dismay, she hesitated. "I'm not sure I'll be chopping sticks tomorrow."

Trying to hide his disappointment, he shrugged. "Very well. Another time, perhaps."

"The next day?"

He lifted his head sharply and looked at her in surprise. She laughed, a gentle, tinkling sound like water in a fountain. Confused by his poetic thoughts, he fumbled for his cap and pulled it on his head. "Ay," he said, letting his grin spread all over his face. "The next day it is."

"Fine. Then I'll look forward to it."

With a wave of her hand she hurried across the yard to the kitchen door, turning to send him another wave before disappearing inside.

"Ay," he said softly as he turned to leave. "I'll be looking forward to it, too."

CHAPTER

✦ 4 ✦

"I think banked chrysanthemums in red and gold, with perhaps sprays of mimosa and dried bulrushes," Madeline said the next morning at the committee meeting. She struck a dramatic pose and swept the air with her slender hand. "It should be quite dramatic, don't you think? A perfect setting for a prima donna."

She leaned back against the marble fireplace in the library and fixed her dark eyes on Phoebe's face, which was half hidden by the drooping veil of her enormous hat. "Now let us just hope that the songstress in question has a voice."

Phoebe, who sat at the long, polished table, tilted her head back to give Madeline an icy glare. "Of course Wilhelmina

Freidrich can sing. Admirably so, I might add. She is, after all, one of the more famous singers at Covent Garden."

"She sings in the vegetable market?" Madeline asked serenely.

Phoebe uttered a most unladylike snort. "You know very well, Madeline, that I meant the Royal Opera House."

She turned to Cecily, who sat at the end of the table watching the exchange between the two women with weary resignation. Sometimes it was easier to let them squabble until they had resolved their differences.

"Really, Cecily," Phoebe exclaimed, removing the pinked edge of a purple ribbon that dangled in front of her eyes, "it amazes me that we accomplish anything at these meetings. Yesterday's meeting was a complete waste of time, and it appears that this one is destined to suffer the same fate."

Cecily agreed, but refrained from saying so. "Perhaps we should get on with the discussion," she said, sending a look of appeal at Madeline.

"Yes, please do," Phoebe snapped. "I have to be back at the vicarage in half an hour. Lydia Willoughby is leading the choir rehearsal for the Christmas pageant."

"Well, that's good news," Madeline said, drifting forward to take her place at the table. "Lydia's renditions on the organ are horrendous enough to banish every evil spirit from Badgers End forever."

"Lydia's musical talent may be somewhat tarnished," Phoebe said with a haughty toss of her head that almost dislodged her hat, "but at least the woman is willing to make an effort. Not like some people who sit around wasting others' valuable time."

"I think the chrysanthemums will be lovely, Madeline," Cecily said loudly. "And the bulrushes will be a nice touch. I'm not sure about the mimosa, though. Isn't that expensive this time of year?"

"It's expensive any time of the year." Madeline shook her long black locks back from her face. "Fortunately I know someone who can supply me with enough for what I need at a very modest price."

"Most likely confiscated from the back of a cart," Phoebe muttered.

Madeline straightened her back. "I beg your pardon? Are you accusing me of stealing?"

Phoebe smiled. "Of course not, my dear. But you have to admit that some of the company you keep does lead one to doubt their integrity."

"My acquaintances may not be above reproach," Madeline said quietly, "but they are infinitely preferable to the insufferable snobs who think they own the earth and everyone on it."

Cecily cleared her throat. "Ladies—"

"It's too bad the privileged class doesn't own the earth," Phoebe said, glaring across the table at Madeline. "Then, perhaps, we could be rid of the thieves, vagabonds, and murderers who make this world such a dangerous place to live nowadays."

Madeline leaned across the table, her fingers curled, her eyes flashing fire. "Well, Phoebe dear, let me warn you. There is much more to fear from the unearthly beings than the human ones. May I remind you it is almost All Hallows' Eve, when the witches are free to roam the earth and wreak their havoc on those who dare to confront them. Be careful of the words you speak, or you might well regret opening your mouth so wide."

Phoebe's face turned white beneath the wide brim of her hat. Her mouth opened, then shut again, and she began rapidly fanning her face with her lace-edged handkerchief, while the other hand patted her heaving bosom.

Apparently satisfied, Madeline rose gracefully to her feet.

"If there is no more to discuss on the flower arrangements, Cecily, I shall leave. Unlike some people, I have important things to see to this afternoon."

Cecily nodded her head. Her attention was on Phoebe, who appeared to be struggling for breath. "Please let me know the estimated cost of the flowers," she said, "and we will discuss how many we can afford."

"I'll inform you just as soon as I get a firm price." Madeline floated to the door, paused long enough to give a casual flip of her hand, then disappeared, closing the door with a heavy thud behind her.

"Are you not feeling well?" Cecily asked, leaning forward to pat her friend's arm.

Phoebe made a gasping noise in her throat, but her color seemed to be returning, bringing a spot of bright red to her cheeks. "That . . . woman is insufferable," she spluttered. "And quite demented, if you want my opinion. All that drivel about spirits and witches—really! I do believe the ridiculous woman actually believes all that nonsense." Having recovered her senses, Phoebe sat up straighter in her chair and settled her hat more firmly on her head. "Of course, what can one expect from someone who is thought to be descended from the gypsies?"

"That is merely rumor, as you well know," Cecily said, feeling compelled to come to the defense of her friend.

"Rumors often have some truth in them. The woman doesn't even wear a corset in public, for heaven's sake. Utterly scandalous, if you want my opinion. Of course people are going to think the worst."

Phoebe rose from her chair and gathered up her black satin purse. Slipping the silk cord over the long sleeve of her glove she added a trifle pompously, "In any case, rumor or not, if I were Madeline, I would take great care to whom I spoke in that heathen manner. She might well be mistaken for a gypsy, and considering what happened to that poor thing up there on Putney Downs, it could prove hazardous to be regarded as one of their tribe."

"I'm sure Madeline knows how to take care of herself," Cecily said, beginning to lose her hold on her patience.

Grasping her parasol, Phoebe marched to the door. "I certainly hope so. Much as Madeline enjoys taunting me, I would not want anything that dreadful to happen to her." She looked back at Cecily over her shoulder. "Have you given any more thought to the prospect of inviting Ellsworth Galloway to participate in the evening's entertainment?"

Cecily suppressed a shudder. "I do think perhaps that Miss Freidrich might be put out by the competition. Mr. Galloway has a habit of taking over the proceedings, and might well upstage her."

"Oh, goodness. We can't have that." Phoebe opened the door and swept out into the corridor. "In that case, perhaps I shall find someone else to open the evening. I did hear of a very fine juggler. Perhaps I shall look into it."

"Not the one with the chamber pots, I trust," Cecily said, trying not to visualize an outraged opera singer faced with the prospect of following such a tawdry act.

"Oh, heavens no." Phoebe pulled the sleeve of her glove higher up her elbow. "Actually I do believe he juggles food. You know, oranges and eggs, that sort of thing."

Cecily grimaced. She needed a cigar quite badly. "Well, let us trust that he's not a butterfingers," she murmured.

Phoebe's laugh echoed down the corridor. "You worry far too much, Cecily, my dear. I shall return for the final meeting before the ball, after having confirmed the appearance of Wilhelmina Freidrich. In the meantime, leave everything to me. I shall take care of it all, as always."

And that, Cecily thought, as the door closed behind her friend, was exactly the reason she was so concerned.

She sat for several minutes, her eyes on James's portrait, her mind going over the recent conversation. Phoebe's remarks had unsettled her, leaving a little knot of anxiety for some reason.

It was true that many people believed that Madeline carried gypsy blood. Cecily could hardly blame them. Madeline had some strange hobbies and beliefs, and although Cecily was reluctant to admit it even to herself, her friend displayed quite remarkable powers at times.

More than once Cecily had been confounded by the odd incidents involving Madeline. So much so, she had been unwilling to question the event and preferred to let things be.

Sighing, Cecily let her gaze wander around the paneled walls of the library. Rows of dusty tomes lined the shelves that stretched from floor to ceiling, untouched by human hand for more than a decade. Cecily hadn't wasted more than a glance at the dreary titles. Shakespeare or the *Canterbury Tales* did not interest her. She much preferred the stories of the indomitable Sherlock Holmes and his faithful Dr. Watson.

Thinking of Sherlock Holmes and his pipe reminded her of her need of a cigar. Baxter should be in the office still, since it was another hour or two before he conducted his rounds of the dining room. She would have plenty of time to retire to her room and freshen up before seeking him out.

Her spirits racing, Cecily left the library and headed for the staircase, considering the possibility of inviting Baxter to join her for a light meal in the dining room.

Her suite was on the second floor, and she climbed the stairs, trying to remember which items were listed on the menu that day. Whatever it was, she could trust Michel to create a meal fit for a king.

She reached the door of her room and took out her keys

from the pocket of her long, gray skirt. She was thinking about Phoebe and her comment about Madeline not wearing a corset. What would Phoebe say, Cecily wondered as she entered her room, if that good lady knew that Cecily often slipped out of her corset the minute the door of her suite was safely closed?

Trousers, Cecily thought, as she shut the door. That's what women should be wearing. There'd be no more twisted ankles after catching a heel in the hem of a skirt. And no more mud-caked cloth to flap around one's ankles on a wet, windy morning.

Her eye caught something lying on the rich blue carpet at her feet. Frowning, she stooped to pick it up. It appeared to be a note, though it was addressed to no one in particular. The scrawled words covered a sheet of hotel stationery, and were difficult to read.

Carrying the page over to the window to catch the light, Cecily stared at the spidery letters. Whoever owned the hand that had scribbled the message must have been shaking very badly.

The note was short and to the point: *George killed the gypsy girl. He must be stopped. He would kill me also if he knew I had told you.*

Cecily watched the notepaper flutter from her fingers to the floor. Baxter would be most displeased to see this, she thought. It would seem that she would be involved in the murder of the gypsy after all.

"I know you bloody chopped sticks last night," Gertie said, glaring at the belligerent girl standing in front of her. "It's not my bleeding fault madam wants the fires laid in all the rooms."

"Well, I ain't got time to chop another two loads this morning, so there." Doris dashed a wayward lock out of her eyes. In the shadows of the kitchen her hair looked darker, and strands of it kept escaping from the untidy knot on her head. She looked as if she'd dressed in a hurry. Slipping already, Gertie thought in disgust.

"I've got the dishes to do yet, and the glasses to be polished, and the serviettes washed—"

"I know everything what you have to do," Gertie interrupted. "Blimey, I did it long enough meself, I should know. All right, chop one load this morning and the other tonight, after you've done the rest of the work."

"Like throwing your orders around, don't you?" Doris said, tossing her head. "I'll do as much as I can. I'm only human, I can only do so much."

Gertie's jaw dropped as she watched the girl flounce across the kitchen floor and out of the door, her skirts swishing around her skinny ankles. Must have got out the bleeding wrong side of the bed, she thought as the door slammed shut, hurting her ears.

Who would have thought that meek little mouse who'd bawled her eyes out yesterday had such a temper? Just went to show, one never knew what people were really like inside.

Shaking her head, Gertie turned back to the silverware drawer and began counting out the forks. She had far too much to worry about, never mind Doris's changing moods. Like Michel's mood for one, if he came in and found her still messing about in the kitchen instead of laying tables in the dining room. He'd have her guts for garters, that he would.

Making a determined effort to put Doris Hoggins out of her mind, she started counting.

Doris Hoggins was very much on someone else's mind that morning. Samuel hadn't thought about much else since his encounter with the new housemaid the night before. He was whistling as he crossed the yard, already imagining what he would say to the shy young girl when he saw her next.

Although he wouldn't admit it, he had taken the longer way around to the stables in the hopes of catching a glimpse of her shapely ankle and trim waist.

He had reached the corner of the kitchen wall when he heard the rhythmic thud of an axe slicing through wood. Frowning, he remembered Doris saying she wouldn't be chopping wood until the next day. Someone else must have taken over the task.

Rounding the corner, he stopped short, his mouth dropping open in amazement. Doris was there all right. And she was wielding the axe as if it weighed no more than a sack of feathers. Up and over, then crashing down on the log, sending sticks flying in all directions.

It didn't seem possible that she could swing that heavy axe so easily. The longer he watched her, the stranger he felt. It had taken all his strength to keep up the steady rhythm last night. His shoulders had ached for an hour afterward.

Slowly Samuel advanced on the unsuspecting girl. She had her back to him and was far too engrossed in her task to notice him. Maybe she was just tired last night, he told himself. A good night's sleep could work wonders for building stamina. He knew that well.

He waited until she paused to take a breath before saying brightly, "Top of the morning to you, Doris. I can see you have found a whole new wealth of strength today. Mind sharing your secret? I could do with some extra stamina myself, that I could."

He saw her back go stiff and straight, but she didn't turn around. The funny feeling in his stomach told him that something was wrong. Carefully he circled around Doris until he could see her face.

Her gaze met his, and his heart sank when he saw her fierce scowl. Now that the sun lit up the yard, he could see her eyes were green. Last night they had looked dark and brown. She had such a pretty face to be twisting it into a grimace like that, he thought, and gave her a tentative smile.

"I reckon you'll not be needing lessons from me after all," he said, gesturing at the axe she held in her slim hands. "That's a fine pile of sticks if I ever saw one."

"I need no lessons from the likes of you," Doris said, her voice sharp and biting. "I am quite capable of doing things for myself, thank you very much."

Taken aback, Samuel could only stare at her. She seemed not at all like the shy young thing he had aided the night before. Where had all that sweetness and light gone?

"Well, be on your way," Doris said, raising the axe once more. "I have work to do and can't be standing around here all day arguing with a stable lad."

"I happen to be the stable manager," Samuel said, feeling a shaft of pain that took away his breath. "Not that it matters, I can see that. Never fear, I'll give you a wide berth from now on."

Touching his cap with his forefinger, he turned sharply on his heel and marched across the yard to the stable gate. Behind him, the steady thud of the axe resumed.

The answer came to him as he reached the stable doors. The shy young girl act was put on entirely for his benefit last night. Doris had seen him approaching and had pretended a weakness, hoping that he would take pity on her and offer his help.

Samuel slapped his hand on the rump of the chestnut in the first stall. That had to be it. He was well versed in the wily ways of women, having read about the subject often enough in the magazines he found in the dustbin after Gertie had finished with them.

It was a shame she'd thought it necessary to deceive him that way. He would have been glad to help her even if she could wield an axe like a seasoned huntsman.

Whistling softly, Samuel moved down the stalls, patting each of the horses in turn. He should be flattered that a pretty young girl like Doris should desire his attention.

As for the show of bad temper, why, that must have been embarrassment. After pretending to be such a weak, helpless female, Doris must have been extremely ashamed to be caught out by him in such a manner.

Perhaps it was just as well he'd found this out quickly, before his heart had been taken by her gentle manner. When Samuel Rawlins gave his heart to a lover, it would be to the kind of sweet, amiable girl he'd first thought Doris to be.

Having been bullied and beaten by the heavy-handed, loudmouthed woman who'd borne him, he knew whom and what to avoid. From now on, he told himself as the faint thud of the axe still echoed across the yard, he would stay out of the way of the unpredictable Doris Hoggins.

CHAPTER

❖ 5 ❖

Baxter was not in his office when Cecily peered in there later that morning. Having more on her mind than merely the desire for a cigar, she set out to track him down. Her first stop was the kitchen, where Mrs. Chubb stood in front of the stove stirring a huge cauldron of fragrant soup.

"That smells absolutely wonderful," Cecily exclaimed, earning a rare smile from Michel.

"Thank you, madame. It ees indeed my pleasure to serve such a perceptive palate. You would enjoy a bowl of my mulligatawny soup, *non?*"

"Thank you, Michel, perhaps later. I'm looking for Baxter at the moment. Has anyone seen him, by any chance?"

Mrs. Chubb stepped back and fanned her scarlet face with the skirt of her apron. "Mercy, that fire gets hot. I do believe Mr. Baxter is on the third floor, mum. Gertie spoke to him when she was laying one of the fires. I think he's examining the ceilings for water leaks."

Cecily pulled a face. "Well, let us hope and pray he doesn't find any. The rest of the guests are due to arrive soon, and we would have no time for repairs."

She looked around the large kitchen, sending a practiced eye over the scrubbed wooden table and the shiny copper pots and pans hanging from the hooks in the ceiling. Everything was spotless, as always, she noted with satisfaction.

"Where is Gertie?" she asked as Mrs. Chubb stood anxiously waiting for a possible adverse comment. "I haven't seen her in a while. I do hope she's keeping well? Her time is so close now."

Mrs. Chubb nodded, her face displaying relief at the lack of criticism. "Very well, mum. Though you know Gertie, she would have to be half dead to give up her jobs to anyone else, even if she does moan and complain about her aches and pains."

The housekeeper turned back to the stove and grasped the long-handled wooden spoon. Stirring it around in the cauldron, she added, "Gertie's gone to the doctor's office, mum. It's her appointment day. Though heaven knows when she'll be back. That doctor is run off his feet with the ladies and their silly complaints. It's my belief they use that office as an excuse to sit around and gossip all day."

Cecily smiled, thinking of the attractive Dr. Prestwick. "It could be they enjoy visiting with the good doctor."

"That ees more like the reason," Michel declared, slapping a lid onto a saucepan with a crash. "That man ees an 'andsome devil, though he would not stand a chance against a Frenchman, *oui*?"

"Oh, go on with you," Mrs. Chubb muttered. She gave the soup a vigorous stir, creating a whirlpool in the middle of the steaming brew. "All you men are alike. All think you're irresistible, you do. If you ask me, the world would be a better place without men in it."

"Hah!" Michel twirled his mustache with his long fingers. "And where would you be without us, you women, huh? Answer me that!"

"A darn better off, that's what. If this world was run by women, we wouldn't have half the mess we're in now, I can tell you."

Silently seconding that notion, Cecily left the kitchen to the tune of crashing saucepans as Michel defended his gender.

After climbing three flights of stairs, she wished she had taken Michel up on his offer of the soup. Her stomach had begun to make noises of protest at her neglect.

She had almost reached the third landing when she saw the stout figure of Colonel Fortescue charging toward her with his clumsy gait.

There was no way to avoid him, and she prepared to make the best of the situation. Greeting him with a smile, she hoped fervently she could escape from him without too much trouble.

"Oh, there you are, madam. I've been wondering where you were hiding yourself. Trying to avoid that nasty chap, Galloway, what? What?"

"Not at all, Colonel," Cecily said, pressing herself against the banister to allow him to pass. "I have been quite busy, actually, making preparations for the Guy Fawkes Ball."

The colonel paused on the step ahead of her, apparently in no hurry to descend. "Oh, jolly good show, madam. Are we to enjoy the dancing girls again? Haven't seen them since the dancing at the maypole, I do believe."

"I'm sorry, Colonel, but Mrs. Carter-Holmes has arranged for an opera singer this time. The concert should be quite entertaining, I should think."

Colonel Fortescue's face dropped. "Great Scott, madam, you are not telling me that pompous oaf, Galloway, is going to sing, are you? I heard him the other day in the water closet. Dashed awful, it was. Sounded like the mating call of a blasted elephant."

Cecily grasped the banister and put one foot on the stair above her in an effort to bring the conversation to a close. "No, Colonel," she said, "I can assure you Mr. Galloway will not be singing. The lady's name is Wilhelmina Freidrich, and I believe she is quite well known in the fashionable circles of London. You should enjoy her performance."

The colonel made a slight movement to the center of the stair, effectively blocking her progress. "Thank the Lord for that. Can't stand the bloke, you know. Even made me feel sorry for that idiot what's-his-name . . ." The colonel lifted his chin and stared shortsightedly at the ceiling, his eyelids blinking up and down in his effort to think.

"Cyril Plunkett?" Below her, Cecily heard the Westminster clock chime the hour of eleven. Perhaps Baxter would appear to rescue her, she thought, thinking of all the tasks she had to accomplish that day.

"That's the chappie. Meek little bugger, what? Looks as if he could be knocked over by a feather. Dashed surprising that was, when he stood up to that ignorant bastard."

Giving her an abashed glance, the colonel coughed loudly. "Sorry, old bean. Got carried away there."

"Quite all right, Colonel. Now if you'll excuse me?"

"Mind you, he seems deathly afraid of that Lady Belleville. Can't say as I blame him. Quite daffy, you know. Poor thing thinks she's got blasted birds sitting on her shoulders. Be jolly messy if she did, what? What?"

"Very," Cecily murmured. "I'm afraid—"

"Saw them all the time, you know," the colonel said, patting the pocket of his jacket as if he were looking for something.

Cecily frowned. "Birds?"

The colonel blinked his bloodshot eyes at her. "What? What birds is that, then?"

"You were saying about Lady Belleville . . ."

"Oh, her! No, no, old bean. Mating elephants. Saw them in Africa, during the Boer War. They used them, you know."

"Used them?"

"Yes, those little blighters with the bows and arrows. Used the elephant to hide behind while the animals were . . . er . . . occupied, if you know what I mean. Damn clever, what?"

Cecily was very much afraid she did know what he meant. "Yes, very interesting, I'm sure. Now I really must—"

"Wouldn't think those huge beasts could manage it standing up, would you? By Jove, they could—"

"Madam? You were looking for me?"

Cecily looked up into Baxter's face with a rush of relief. He stood at the top of the stairs, and his stony expression told her he'd heard the gist of the conversation.

The hard glint in his eyes made her feel sorry for the colonel, and she said quickly, "I was just telling Colonel Fortescue that I was on my way to see you."

"What? Oh, yes, yes, of course, old bean. Wouldn't want to hold you up. Oh, no, that would never do. Never do." Obviously flustered, the portly gentleman blundered down the stairs, almost knocking Cecily off her feet.

Baxter took a step forward, his hand outstretched, but she

managed to right herself. Behind her the colonel muttered, "Time I was off, anyhow. Got to partake of the daily swig of the old mother's ruin, you know. Got to keep the old pecker up somehow."

Baxter said something under his breath that Cecily couldn't catch. She had the distinct impression it was just as well. Marching briskly up the rest of the stairs, she gave Baxter a wide smile. "Thank you for rescuing me. I do believe I was about to receive a lecture on the mating habits of the African elephant."

Baxter rolled his eyes up at the ceiling. "Good Lord. The man should be shot."

"He very nearly was," Cecily said as she led the way down the corridor. "That's why he behaves that way. We do have to make allowances, Baxter. The poor man was fighting for queen and country, you know."

"Spoken like a true military wife," Baxter said dryly. "Might I be so bold as to ask, madam, just where are you leading me?"

She grinned at him over her shoulder. "Somewhere where we can have some peace and quiet. Somewhere where I can enjoy one of your delectable little cigars."

Ignoring his groan of protest, she opened the door of the vacant suite and walked in. Shivering, she crossed her arms and hugged her body. "I should have worn my wrap," she said, glancing at the empty fireplace. "These rooms get so cold in the winter when they are unoccupied."

"Shall I fetch the wrap for you, madam?"

She looked back at Baxter, who stood in the open doorway. "A generous gesture, Baxter, and one I appreciate. But I shan't stay long in here, and besides, the cigar will give me some warmth, will it not?"

His gray eyes studied her intently. After a moment he

reached into his top pocket and took out the slim package. Without a word he handed her a cigar and lit it for her.

Drawing in the aromatic taste of tobacco, she closed her eyes and imagined her tension drifting from her lips with the smoke. "My thanks to Sir Walter Raleigh," she murmured. "What would we have done without him?"

"We would no doubt be a great deal healthier had he not introduced such a barbaric habit," Baxter said, sounding a trifle harassed.

Cecily opened one eye and looked at him. "Do come in, Baxter. You don't have to close the door if you are concerned about my reputation, but I refuse to hold a conversation with you standing out in the hallway."

He frowned at that, but stepped inside the room, closing the door halfway.

"May I remind you," Cecily added, "that you also indulge in this barbaric habit."

"Gentlemen can handle smoking. Cigars were never meant for women, and I'm quite sure Sir Walter Raleigh would turn in his grave if he could see the consequences of his actions. Not to mention your late husband."

"I see." She took another long draw on the cigar and puffed the smoke in his face. "Barbaric for women but not for men, is that it? I seem to have had this argument with you before, Baxter."

"On more than one occasion," he admitted, looking unhappy. "But that is not what you wanted to discuss with me, I presume?"

Remembering why she was there, Cecily felt a pang of apprehension. "No, Baxter, it's not." She reached into her pocket and drew out the note she'd found earlier. "Perhaps you should read this."

He took the sheet of paper from her, his gaze quickly scanning the scrawled words. Then he handed the note back to her, murmuring, "To quote our beloved late queen, we are not amused."

"Amused? Hardly. It is disconcerting, to say the least, to discover that the murderer could be someone among us."

He gave her a sharp look. "You are not taking this seriously, madam?"

"I most certainly am. Whoever George might be, he is known to someone in this hotel."

Baxter took the note back, stared down at it for a few moments, then handed it back to her. "In my opinion, madam, I would say that this note is most likely a macabre joke played on you."

Cecily looked up at him in surprise. "A joke? Someone is making fun of the murder of a young woman?"

"If I might remind you, some of our guests are not exactly in full possession of their wits. I would say that few of them display a modicum of good taste. At least a couple of them are on the border of insanity."

"Even so—"

"Pardon me for interrupting, madam, but are you acquainted with a man named George?"

Cecily thought for a moment, then shook her head. "Not as I can recall."

"Exactly."

"But what does that have to do with anything? George could be anyone outside the hotel. It is obvious the person who wrote the note is the person who knows George. And that could be someone in the hotel, since the note was written on hotel stationery."

"I feel almost certain it must be a joke," Baxter said stubbornly. "Otherwise, why should he tell you about it, if George is likely to kill the author of the note when he found out about it?"

"How would George find out about it, unless I told him?

And since I don't know who George is . . ." Cecily let her
words trail off. It was true, the whole incident sounded so
lame when faced with Baxter's logic.

"I do trust, madam, that you are not considering involving
yourself in this murder? I don't have to remind you of the
grave risks you run."

"Yes, yes, I know." Cecily puffed on the cigar again. One
part of her felt obliged to agree with Baxter's opinion. Yet
her instincts warned her not to take the note too lightly.

There was always the possibility that Baxter's conviction
could be colored by his concern that she would become
involved in yet another murder case and run afoul of the
law, in the person of Inspector Cranshaw, no less. That
particular gentleman was not someone with whom she cared
to lock horns.

Nevertheless, at the moment there was little she could do
but wait and see what the constabulary made of the murder.
Meanwhile, Baxter had little to worry about. Unless the
hotel or its staff were directly involved, she reminded
herself, she would not interfere in the investigation.

Even so, the memory of those scrawled words continued
to disturb her for the rest of the day.

Dr. Prestwick's office had to be the most popular place in
town, Gertie thought, as she fought her way past a row of
fashionably shod feet to get to the one empty chair in the
corner.

She hated coming to the doctor's. Especially on a wet
autumn day. This waiting area was a small room, heated
by a small coal furnace in the corner. With women of all
sizes and ages packed into the tiny space like sardines, the
air was too stuffy to breathe.

The smell sickened her stomach. Body sweat, damp
wool, and the putrid stink of chemicals clogged her nose and

made her feel like fainting. Except there was nowhere to fall without getting stabbed by a parasol.

She just hoped she wouldn't have to come anymore after his time. She couldn't wait to have the flipping baby and be done with it. In fact, it seemed to have sunk lower in her stomach, as if it was anxious to get out and take a look at the world.

Gertie smiled. She was sort of looking forward to seeing the little bugger, too. This would be her very own baby. And no one would be able to take it away from her, including Ian and that wife of his. This baby belonged to her, and she was going to make bloody sure nobody ever got a hand on

As if in answer, the baby stirred inside her and gave her gentle prod. She laid a hand on her swollen belly, feeling fierce surge of tenderness. She would protect this child of ers with her very life if need be. Gertie Brown might be a nobody, but she was going to be the best bleeding mother a baby ever saw.

Preoccupied with her thoughts, she hardly noticed the woman next to her getting up, and another taking her place. Then a soft voice said, "Gertie? I hardly recognized you. When is the baby due, then?"

Looking up, Gertie saw the pleasant, rosy-cheeked face f Nora Northcott, the constable's wife. Gertie had spent a great deal of time with the motherly woman when she'd first arrived in Badgers End.

At fourteen she'd been in constant trouble with the law, and Nora Northcott had taken her under her wing, giving her understanding, sympathy, and advice. It had been the constable's wife who had found her the job at the Pennyfoot, and had reluctantly handed over her rebellious young charge o Mrs. Chubb, who had then licked the young girl into shape.

It had been almost two years since Gertie had seen Nora, but she had often remembered the kindness the woman had given to her. She smiled at the familiar face now, saying, "If the doctor is right, I'll be having the baby right about the time the bloody bonfires are lit on Guy Fawkes Night."

"Oh, my." Nora clutched her throat. "I do hope the fireworks won't scare the poor thing."

"Not half as much as they'll bleeding scare me." Gertie patted her stomach. "He'll have nothing to worry about, though, 'cause I'm going to take care of him."

"You want a boy?" Nora laughed. "Why do mothers always want a boy and fathers always want a girl?" Her face changed. "I'm sorry, Gertie. I heard about Ian Rossiter. That was an awful way to treat you."

Gertie shrugged. "Aw, well, it wasn't bleeding meant to be, was it."

"Someday you'll meet a nice man," Nora said, although the way that she said it, Gertie knew she didn't hold out much hope. Who would want a woman saddled with someone else's nipper? No one, that's who.

Deciding she wanted to change the subject, Gertie said, "What're you doing here, then? Hope it's nothing too bad."

Nora shook her head. "Just me back. Been giving me a lot of trouble lately. Getting old, that's what."

More likely having to put up with P. C. Northcott, Gertie thought, but kept her mouth shut.

"As for Stan, he's the one who should be down here. Got a wicked cold, he has, and won't take nothing for it. I told him to come down with me, but he says the place is always full of nattering women, and he's not going to sit there with all those eyes on him."

Gertie laughed. "The only man these women want to blinking look at is Dr. Prestwick. That's what half of them come for, I reckon."

Nora nudged Gertie's arm with an elbow. "Go on! He is good-looking, though, don't you think?"

"He's all right. Mind you, I'm off bleeding men right now, so nobody looks good to me."

"Well, I just hope Stan takes care of that cold. I don't want him catching pneumonia."

Gertie yawned and moved restlessly on the chair. "Must have caught cold walking about in the woods, I suppose, looking at dead bodies."

Nora sent a quick glance around the room. "You know I can't talk about them things," she whispered. "Stan would have me head."

"It's all right." Gertie shifted again to ease her back. "It were a strange murder, though. Fancy going to all that trouble to cut off her head and hide it. The guy must be bonkers, if you ask me."

"He didn't want anyone to know who she was, from what I can make out." Nora looked around again to make sure no one was listening. "In any case, the inspector won't spend too much time on the case. Stan says it was only a gypsy girl who was killed, and the gypsies take care of their own. And if you ask me, it's better that way."

"Miss Brown!"

Gertie looked up to see Dr. Prestwick standing in the doorway, beckoning her, amidst a chorus of twitters and fluttering of fans.

Saying goodbye to Nora Northcott, Gertie crossed the room, conscious of eyes on her bulging body. They all must know about the way Ian dumped her. She reached the door and set a fierce glare around the room, making each woman drop her gaze.

Feeling better, she stepped into the doctor's surgery, though she couldn't help wondering whether the inspector would have treated her the same way if it had been her up on the Downs instead of the gypsy girl.

CHAPTER

❊ 6 ❊

The rain had stopped by the time the kitchen staff began preparing the evening meal. The kitchen was a warm haven from the chill, damp air outside, and the tempting aroma of steak-and-kidney pie made Gertie's tummy rumble. At least, she hoped it was hunger and not the baby getting ready to be born. She had too much to do to drop everything now.

"Hurry up with that silverware," she yelled at Doris, who stood by the sideboard examining each piece as if she had all day.

Doris looked up with a start. "Mrs. Chubb said as how I should look them over for spots."

"Well, they was all bleeding polished this afternoon. I did them meself, so there's no blinking spots on them. Flipping heck, you're not going to buy the bleeding stuff. Get a move on, or we won't get the tables laid in time."

Doris picked up the heavy tray and scuttled across the kitchen, reaching the door just as Mrs. Chubb barged through it. The crash that followed stung Gertie's ears.

Doris's wail was answered by a string of oaths from Michel, who added to the noise by crashing a few lids about on the stove.

"Quiet!" Mrs. Chubb demanded as Doris's wail grew louder. Michel swore again, and another saucepan hit the ground.

The housekeeper marched across the floor until she was nose to nose with the chef. "I said quiet!" she yelled.

"I hear what you say," Michel roared back, his tall white hat bobbing as he brandished his ladle. "*Mon Dieu* everyone in the whole village can hear what you say. What is this I am working in, a loony bin, *non*?"

Mrs. Chubb's jaw worked silently for a moment, then she swung around. "Doris, stop that sniveling and pick up that silverware. Gertie will have to polish them all over again before they can be used."

"Yes, Mrs. Chubb," Doris said tearfully, then dropped to her knees and began scooping up the knives and forks, throwing them onto the tray with a loud clatter.

"Cor blimey," Gertie muttered, "why is it me what always gets the rotten jobs? Why can't Doris wipe the silverware? She bleeding dropped it."

"Because she has to get outside and finish chopping the sticks. We still have eight more fires to lay, and they all have to be done by tomorrow night."

Grumbling under her breath, Gertie opened the sideboard drawer and took out the silver cloth. She'd be late again tonight, she thought, picking up a fork to attack it. All that twit Doris's fault.

She sent the girl a glare of resentment as Doris handed her the rest of the silverware. "You'd better get out of here before I put in my tuppence worth," she said, wishing she could give the silly bugger a piece of her mind.

"Yes, Miss Brown." Doris gave her a nervous smile then rushed out of the kitchen, letting the door swing to behind her.

Gertie stared after her, taken aback by the girl's subdued attitude. Whatever had got Doris Hoggins in such a state that morning certainly hadn't lasted. She was back to being the meek little mouse again.

"Gertie, stop daydreaming and get on with that polishing," Mrs. Chubb said, beginning to roll up her sleeves. "I still have the pastry to make for the pies, and it's almost six o'clock. I don't have time to do your jobs as well as mine, so get on with it."

"All right, don't get your knickers in a twist." Gertie began rubbing faster with the cloth.

"Oo la la, our housemaids are getting impotent," Michel muttered, bending over to open the oven door to peer inside.

"I think you mean impudent," Mrs. Chubb said, frowning at Gertie. "And you are right. Just watch your tongue, my girl, before I box your ears."

Gertie opened her mouth to answer, but shut it again when the door flew open, letting in a draft of cool air.

"My, that was quick." Mrs. Chubb swung around to look at Doris standing in the doorway.

"I ain't chopped any sticks yet," Doris said, her hands twisting knots in her white apron. "I can't find the axe."

"Whatcha mean you can't find the axe?" Gertie demanded, transferring her frustration onto the worried-looking girl. "You had it this morning when you chopped the wood, didn't you?"

Doris looked around the kitchen as if expecting to find the axe lurking in some dark corner.

"Well," Mrs. Chubb said more kindly, "what did you do with it after you used it this morning, Doris?"

Doris shook her head helplessly, lifting her hands, and dropped them again. "I don't know," she whispered.

"Strewth!" Gertie swept several strands of hair out of her eyes with an impatient hand. "I'll go and see if I can find it." She thrust the silver cloth at Doris. "Here. I want every blinking piece polished by the time I get back."

"Yes, Miss Brown," Doris said, and immediately began vigorously buffing a fork.

Grumbling to herself, Gertie stepped out into the dark night air. She rubbed her upper arms with her hands as she marched across the yard to the coal shed, clicking her tongue in disgust when she saw the door standing open. The twit couldn't even close a door behind her properly. At least she wouldn't have to struggle to open it, she told herself as she peered into the shed.

Doris was right. The axe wasn't hanging on the nail where it had hung ever since Gertie could remember. Nor was it anywhere in the shed, as far as she could see by the light from the kitchen windows.

She reached for the oil lamp and matches, cursing under her breath when it took several attempts to light the wick. Holding the lamp above her head, she stood for a moment looking around the dark shapes inside the shed. Someone must have taken the bloody axe. And she didn't want to think where it might be.

"No one seems to know where it could be," Mrs. Chubb said, standing in the middle of Cecily's drawing room. "Doris was using it this morning to chop sticks, but when she went out tonight to finish the rest of them, the axe had completely disappeared."

Cecily leaned back in her velvet-padded chair and smiled at the housekeeper. "Perhaps Doris simply mislaid it in the dark. Did she light the lamp?"

"No, mum, usually the light from the windows is enough. But Gertie went out there, too, and she couldn't find it. We think someone must have taken it."

"But who—" Cecily stopped short, remembering the colonel's words. *Sharp as the devil, those blades are. One slice and right through the neck as clean as a whistle.* "Oh, my Lord," she said softly.

Mrs. Chubb looked a trifle pale. "What do you think we should do, mum?"

Cecily collected her thoughts. There was no sense in letting her imagination run away with her. After all, the axe had been there in the shed after the body of the gypsy had been found. It was simply a grisly coincidence, that was all.

"Send Samuel out to purchase another axe, if you will, Mrs. Chubb. It's too late tonight, of course, but first thing in the morning. Tell him to ask the assistant at Whites's Hardware to put the charge on our account. I'll inform Baxter of the purchase."

"Yes, mum." Mrs. Chubb bobbed a slight curtsy and backed out of the door.

Left alone, Cecily stared for a long time at the pattern on the carpet. Her gaze traced the intricate design of green vines swirling around huge pink and cream roses. She saw in her mind's eye a sheet of paper lying on that carpet. *George killed the gypsy girl. He must be stopped.*

But "George" couldn't have taken the axe. The poor girl had died before the axe had disappeared. Yet a small niggling doubt remained in Cecily's mind. Coincidence, as she had discovered, very often turned out to be something quite different. She could only hope that in this case the missing axe was just that. Coincidence.

Samuel had finished his chores for the day and was looking forward to spending an hour down the George and Dragon before turning in for the night. He wanted to practice his darts game. Now that Ian Rossiter had left town, the team was looking for a replacement, and Samuel wanted desperately to step in.

He was about to leave, dressed warmly for the long walk to the pub, when Doris confronted him at the gate. A thick fog had rolled in from the sea, and he could barely see the outline of the kitchen wall as he listened to the housemaid's soft voice.

"Mrs. Chubb sent me to tell you that the axe is missing from the shed."

He looked at her in surprise. The gas lamps in front of the hotel cast a strange orange glow across the yard, their posts shrouded by the wreathing mists that swirled across the Esplanade.

"It was there this morning. You were using it, remember?" He also remembered the way she'd treated him, as if he wasn't good enough to speak to her. The memory hardened his resolve to keep his distance.

"Tell Mrs. Chubb I'll look for it in the morning," he said, closing the gate firmly and latching it. "It's too late to look for it tonight."

"Gertie looked for it and couldn't find it. Mrs. Chubb said to tell you that madam wants you to buy a new one."

Pulling his cap down on his head, Samuel sighed. "Not tonight, I hope?"

Doris shook her head, her eyes downcast, her gaze directed at his boots. "No, Mrs. Chubb said that madam said to go first thing in the morning."

He studied her for a moment, a strange feeling creeping over him. This didn't seem like the same person he'd confronted that morning. This was more like the shy young girl he'd first encountered the night before.

She stood shivering in the moist night air, her thin shawl barely covering her shoulders. In the dim light he could see the sad look on her face, as if she'd just lost something that meant a lot to her. The mist left tiny droplets of moisture clinging to the soft curls peeking out from under her cap.

Her clothes looked too big for her slight body. The long black skirt draped over the top of her shoes, threatening to trip her up if she didn't take care to hold up the hem as she walked.

"I'm sorry," she said, so quietly he almost lost the words in the echoes of the ocean pounding the beach. A storm coming, his mind registered, while his gaze remained on the forlorn girl standing in front of him.

She looked like a child, lost and a little afraid, and determined not to show it. His heart warmed, and, forgetting his convictions of a moment ago, he touched her lightly on the arm.

"Cheer up," he said brightly, "it's only an axe. It's not your fault if someone takes a fancy to it and walks off with it. It's not the first time it's happened, and I don't suppose it'll be the last."

She lifted her chin, though she kept her gaze fixed on his feet. "Mrs. Chubb says to ask them to put it on the hotel account."

"Right." He pulled in a breath, conscious of the smell of seaweed and sand that always seemed stronger on a foggy night. The breeze had stiffened, sending clouds of mist billowing across the yard. He could now see the outline of the kitchen wall.

In the corner of the kitchen door he thought he saw a

shadow move. Narrowing his eyes, he took his gaze off Doris and concentrated on the space between the kitchen and the steps that led up to the hotel lobby. If someone was there, he would have to cross the yard in the light of the lamps.

He stared intently at the shifting shadows, but could see nothing but the branches of the sycamore tree bouncing gently in the brisk breeze.

"I had better be going in," Doris said, taking a step away from him.

"No, wait!"

She paused, looking up at him with a surprised expression on her dainty features.

He hesitated, not certain what he was afraid of. It was just a trick of the light, no more. Yet something had made him uneasy. She looked so fragile, as though a puff of wind could blow her off her feet. Maybe it was the gossip about the gypsy girl found in the woods. He kept imagining how that body must have looked without a head.

A shiver traveled down his body, and, making up his mind, he took a firm hold of her arm. "I'll walk you back to the door."

"That's awfully nice of you, Samuel," she said softly. He liked the way she gazed up at him with her shy smile. When she said his name, it sounded different somehow.

"No, it's not really," he said, pretending to look all around him in horror. "I'm afraid of the dark, I am. I don't want to cross over there all by myself. I need you to protect me."

She laughed, a delightful sound that seemed to dance on the wind. It made him feel wonderful to make her laugh. A part of his mind warned him this could be another game she was playing, like last night. Perhaps tomorrow she would give him the drop-dead treatment again.

But right now he liked the feel of her slender arm beneath

his fingers, and the warm feeling it gave him to look down into those big brown eyes and see her pleasure reflected in them. And he felt very glad indeed that Doris Hoggins had come to work at the Pennyfoot Hotel.

"The axe is missing?" Baxter said, rolling his eyes to the ceiling. "Pray don't tell me that Mrs. Chubb is convinced our axe murderer is prowling the hotel just waiting for the opportunity to pounce on her and chop off her head."

"It is not a laughing matter, Baxter." Cecily puffed out a stream of smoke from her cigar a little more forcefully than she'd intended.

Baxter coughed, though the gray cloud had dissipated long before it reached him. He stood at the end of the long table in the library with his back to James's portrait.

Cecily's gaze strayed to the image of her late husband. It saddened her at times that the pain she had once felt at his passing no longer troubled her. In the early days she had been certain she would never recover from the loss. The demands of the hotel, however, had kept her mind and her hands busy, so much so that the months and even years had slipped by almost without her noticing.

Then there had been Baxter, of course. Shifting her gaze back to him now, she gazed thoughtfully at his face. He was her trusted friend, her confidant, her loyal and dependable right hand in the myriad business matters that were part of running a busy hotel.

Yet during the past months she had become gradually aware of more personal feelings for the man who had given James his solemn promise to take care of his good friend's grieving widow.

At first she had thought it to be merely a sense of loss for the companionship and close intimacy she had shared with her dead husband. But now she knew it was more than that.

She had become extremely fond of Baxter, and her greatest regret was that he found it impossible to return her affections.

On a rare occasion she had glimpsed an expression, caught an odd phrase, suggesting that perhaps he might have cared for her if things had been different—had she not been the owner of the Pennyfoot Hotel and he the employed manager.

At times the longing became quite acute, though she could never allow him to know of her anguish. That would embarrass them both.

With a sharp movement she stubbed out the cigar in the silver ashtray, producing an acrid smell of burned tobacco. Much as she adored the hotel and the busy life she led, there were times when she cursed the chains that James had so tightly bound about her. Her promise to keep the Pennyfoot in the family had cost her a great deal.

"Madam?"

She looked up, meeting Baxter's steady gray gaze with a sudden skip of her heart.

"You are displeased with me, madam?"

Aware that she was scowling at him, she straightened her features. "I'm sorry, Baxter. I was deep in thought."

"Might I enquire as to the nature of your thoughts?"

For a moment his gaze seemed to hold her captive. She heard the clock on the mantelpiece ticking far more loudly than usual. An almost irresistible urge to say what was in her heart rendered her breathless as the words trembled on her lips.

For just an instant she saw an answering light leap in his eyes, then he said quietly, "Forgive me, madam, for intruding on your private thoughts. If you wish to be alone . . ."

Realizing he had assumed she was thinking about James,

she hurried to set him straight. "Oh, no, it's quite all right. As a matter of fact, I was thinking about the missing axe and where it could be. You must agree it is a strange coincidence, considering the recent murder on the Downs."

Baxter shrugged and stretched his neck as if he found his stiff white collar too tight. "Coincidence, yes, madam. I would agree with that. After all, if you are considering the possibility of the utensil being used as a murder weapon, I should remind you that the murder was committed before the loss of the axe."

Watching him, Cecily felt a momentary sadness. He seemed relieved that the moment of tension had passed. She gathered her thoughts, saying, "I am aware of that. If it were not for the note, I would think no more about it. I can't help feeling uneasy, however. I do wish I knew who had played such a cruel joke, if indeed it was a joke."

"It is entirely possible that the same prankster is the culprit who ran off with the axe."

She sat up straighter, staring at him in dismay. "That's not a comforting thought. Who would stoop to such thoughtless tricks? Surely not one of our staff?"

"It is simply a suggestion, madam. I can think of no other reason why someone should want to take off with an axe."

"And I can think of no one who would do such a thing."

"I can bring to mind at least two people who are sufficiently disturbed to act without rhyme or reason."

Cecily shook her head. "If you are referring to Colonel Fortescue, I agree he can be somewhat unstable at times, but he is certainly harmless."

"Perhaps. And Lady Belleville?"

"Somehow the thought of Lady Belleville creeping around with an axe in her hand just doesn't seem feasible."

"Perhaps her canaries flew off with it."

Cecily grinned. "That is definitely a consideration."

She leaned back, feeling better in spite of her worries. "You know, Bax, all in all the hotel business is quite an interesting vocation, don't you agree?"

His rare smile warmed her heart. "I wouldn't wish to be in any other occupation, madam. Or in any place other than here at the Pennyfoot."

And that, Cecily thought ruefully, would have to satisfy her. For now.

CHAPTER

❈ 7 ❈

The fog lifted sometime during the night, leaving the air smelling clean and sweet as the sun climbed out of the sea the next morning. The breeze was fresh, however, and Cecily drew her shawl tighter about her shoulders as she stood in the roof garden overlooking the Esplanade.

She didn't visit the tiny rose garden very often in the winter. James had created the little sanctuary after the first summer season at the hotel. During the busy months the gardens offered no respite from the ever constant questions and comments from the guests, and James had felt the need of a private place where he and his wife could be alone to exchange thoughts and ideas without fear of interruption.

After he had passed away, Cecily opened the roof garden

to the guests, so that they, too, might find a moment's peace from the busy activities of the hotel. Somehow she knew that James would have preferred that. He would not have wanted her to mourn for him alone, using the garden as a private shrine.

At first it had been painful to stand at the wall without him. It had been even more difficult to allow strange people to intrude in the place where she and James had shared so many happy times together. But now the memories had grown dim, and the ache of loss had almost disappeared, leaving only an occasional pang of nostalgia.

Now she enjoyed the moments she managed to steal from her busy schedule. The view from the garden was quite spectacular. She could easily see the wide sweep of the bay with its bobbing fishing boats nestling at the foot of the majestic cliffs.

Above the golden sands, the sloping meadows of Putney Downs flowed down to the village of Badgers End on one side, while the wooded hills on the other formed the border of Lord Withersgill's estate.

Thinking of the woods, Cecily felt a chill deep in her bones. The mysterious note found under her door still played heavily on her mind. In spite of Baxter's assurance of the opposite, Cecily couldn't help feeling that whoever had gone to the trouble of writing her that message was not a prankster.

A flash of color at the end of the Esplanade caught her eye. Long before she could discern the features, Cecily knew the identity of the woman trotting briskly along the railings that bordered the sands.

Her enormous hat was a magnificent concoction of ribbons and ostrich plumes in brilliant shades of purple and pink, and her tightly laced body was encased in pale gray wool trimmed with white ermine. Phoebe Carter-Holmes had arrived for the final committee meeting before the November Fifth Ball.

Wondering if Madeline could be far behind, Cecily took a last look at the shimmering ocean, then left the roof to go down and greet her visitors.

She found Phoebe already seated in the library, while Madeline hovered near the French windows, staring silently into the gardens that lay behind the hotel. She must have entered through the back door of the kitchen, Cecily decided, since she hadn't seen her arrive.

She started to cross the room and was startled when Madeline strode over to the table and threw a large envelope down. It hit the polished surface and slid rapidly across, landing neatly in Phoebe's lap.

"Well, really!" Phoebe picked up the offending package with the tips of two fingers, as if afraid it would bite her.

Madeline appeared not to notice. She seemed to be quite upset by something, and Cecily took her place at the table with the fervent hope that the two women were not in the middle of a battle royal.

"I cannot believe that the constabulary of this town can be so prejudiced and narrow-minded," Madeline declared, her dark eyes smoldering with indignation.

Relieved that Phoebe was not the root of Madeline's anger, Cecily used her most soothing tone. "Sit down, Madeline, and tell us what has happened to upset you so drastically."

"Yes, poor dear," Phoebe murmured. "You are not about to be arrested for dispensing fertility brews to the young men of the village, I trust?"

Madeline directed her stormy glare directly at Phoebe. "Does she have to be here?" She lashed the air with her hand, almost knocking over a huge vase of yellow chrysanthemums. "I really don't think I can put up with her nasty, snide remarks right now."

Cecily sent Phoebe a warning look. "Phoebe will behave, won't you, dear?"

Phoebe sniffed loudly and straightened the brim of her hat with a sharp tug. She kept her mouth tightly closed, her lips pressed together in resentment.

"I happened to see Mrs. Chubb as I was passing through the kitchen," Madeline said, shaking her hair back from her face with a highly dramatic gesture. "She told me that Gertie had met Mrs. Northcott in the doctor's office yesterday afternoon."

"Oh, that's right." Cecily nodded, trying not to notice Phoebe fidgeting in her chair and tapping her parasol against the table leg. "I remember Mrs. Chubb saying that Gertie would be down there."

"I really can't see what all those silly women find so fascinating about Dr. Prestwick," Phoebe said, smoothing down the lacy frills at her throat. "I find the man quite vulgar at times. All that smiling and winking. Quite uncouth, if you ask my opinion."

"No one did," Madeline said curtly.

Phoebe bristled. "There's no need to be rude, Madeline. I was merely passing a comment."

"And managing to interrupt me at the same time. You must have the limelight at all times, mustn't you?"

"Perhaps if you had something of interest to say—"

"Perhaps if we let Madeline finish what she wanted to say, it might be of interest," Cecily said firmly.

"I seriously doubt that, but please do proceed." Phoebe sat back with an air of someone exercising great patience.

Ignoring her, Madeline concentrated her attention on Cecily. "As I was saying, before Phoebe rudely intruded, Gertie spoke with Mrs. Northcott. Apparently she told

Gertie that the police will not be pursuing the murder on the Downs with any real interest."

"Did she say why?" Cecily asked as Phoebe uttered a bored and conspicuously loud sigh.

"She most certainly did, and that's what has me so outraged. The constabulary has the audacity to claim that because the victim is merely a gypsy, there is no need to pursue the case since the gypsies will take care of matters for them."

Madeline flung herself away from the table and threw her hands in the air. "Can you imagine such biased incompetence? They simply consider the death of a gypsy too insignificant to matter. Now, if it had been one of the gentry, they would have had the dogs combing the woods by now."

"Oh, do calm down, dearie," Phoebe muttered. "It's not the end of the world, for heaven's sake. No doubt the constables are right and the gypsies will discover the murderer and punish him according to their rules. After all, they do live by a far different creed than do we gentlefolk. I am quite sure they will mete out a far harsher punishment than anything the constabulary can manage, being the heathens that they are."

"And what do you presume to know about it?" Madeline demanded, coming back to the table. Placing her hands flat on the surface of it, she leaned across, bringing her face close to Phoebe's.

"Take care what you say about the gypsies, Phoebe Carter-Holmes. They see all and know all. They may be lacking in the social graces that you and your kind deem so important, but they deserve the same justice as is afforded the highest lord or lady in the land."

"Perhaps if they weren't so ready to steal what they want from honest folk, instead of working for it——"

"Ladies!" Cecily rapped on the table with her knuckles. "I

really don't have time to sit and listen to you squabbling all day. Can we please get on with the proceedings here?"

To her immense satisfaction, both women clamped their mouths closed. Madeline threw herself down on her chair, sprawling in a way designed to annoy Phoebe.

Phoebe chose to ignore her. Instead she turned to Cecily and said brightly, "Well, I had an interesting encounter with Mr. Galloway this morning. He really is quite charming. Are you certain you don't want to invite him to join Miss Freidrich at the concert?"

"Quite sure." Cecily looked at Madeline, who was studying Phoebe with an odd expression on her face. "You have the prices for the flowers, Madeline?"

The other woman nodded and reached for the envelope. "In here. I've worked out what it would cost to do the large arrangements on the stage, as well as a small one for each table."

Cecily opened the envelope and withdrew the sheet of paper.

While she studied it, Madeline said softly, "Phoebe, a word of warning is in order here."

"Oh?" Phoebe's tone clearly stated that she was not interested in anything Madeline had to say.

"Yes, it's about Ellsworth Galloway." Madeline paused, and Cecily looked up, feeling a little prick of uneasiness.

"What about him?" Phoebe demanded, glaring at Madeline across the table.

"If I were in your shoes, I would avoid the man at all costs." Madeline leaned forward and fixed Phoebe with an intent stare. "The man is evil, Phoebe. We may have our differences, but I would not want something bad to happen to you. Ellsworth Galloway has an evil aura. I have seen it."

Phoebe uttered a short laugh that didn't sound altogether convincing. "What utter nonsense you talk, Madeline. The man is renowned in all the best circles, a famous opera singer, and a most charming and intelligent man. All this mumbo jumbo of yours is becoming most tiresome, I must say."

Madeline leaned back in her chair and stretched her arms lazily above her head. "Very well, Phoebe, but don't say I didn't warn you."

"These prices appear to be quite fair, Madeline," Cecily said, thrusting the pages back into the envelope. "I'll show them to Baxter, but I'm quite sure he will agree with me."

"Very well." Madeline pushed back her chair and rose in a graceful movement that completely belied her previous inelegance. "I will proceed with the purchase, then?"

"Yes, please do." Cecily looked at Phoebe, who still appeared to be disgruntled by Madeline's remarks. "Did you manage to secure the services of the juggler, Phoebe?"

Phoebe shook her head, sending shivers up the ostrich plumes. "No, I'm afraid he was otherwise engaged for that evening. I heard about a young man who was quite clever at balancing plates on the end of poles, however. He twirls them around and then catches them before they fall off."

Madeline uttered a derisive laugh. "Well, Cecily, there goes your china." She drifted to the door without seeming to touch the floor. "Give my regards to Ellsworth Galloway the next time he charms you, Phoebe. Unless he spirits you away to the underworld, I will see you at the ball." With another laugh and a wave of her hand, she was gone.

Phoebe clicked her tongue in disgust. "The young man brings his own plates, so I'm told," she said, frowning at the closed door. "I really do wish Madeline wouldn't be so vindictive. I don't criticize her flower arrangements, even if they are a little primitive to be considered artistic."

"Madeline means no harm," Cecily said, laying the

envelope to one side. "Now, about this entertainer. Will he be able to give us a good performance?"

"I should think so." Phoebe shook herself like a bird ruffling its feathers. "If not, there is always Albert Brewster and that strange dummy of his. I wonder if all ventriloquists believe their dummies are alive."

Cecily smiled. "I shouldn't wonder. In any case, it appears that you have everything well in hand, Phoebe, so I shan't worry about it any further." Gathering up the envelope, she rose from her chair. "I shall see you on Thursday night, then?"

"Yes, of course." Phoebe stood, fussily rearranging the folds of her skirt. "I have no doubt the entertainment will please everyone, as always."

Cecily refrained from reminding her friend that invariably some disaster or other occurred at these functions. "I am sure it will be a wonderful evening, Phoebe. And thank you so much for all your hard work."

"Not at all. It is indeed my pleasure." Flushed with pride, Phoebe pranced across the room, pausing in the doorway to send a coy look over her shoulder. "No matter what Madeline might think," she said, "I happen to admire Ellsworth Galloway."

Cecily almost expected her to kick up her ankle behind her as she left.

She couldn't help remembering Madeline's words about Galloway, however, when she met that gentleman in the hallway a few minutes later.

"I am happy I have run into you," Ellsworth Galloway said as he blocked her way with his ungainly bulk. He stood with his legs braced apart and his hands clasped behind his back, rocking back and forth on his feet. He reminded Cecily of a giant balloon tethered to the ground.

"What can I do for you, Mr. Galloway?"

His eyes looked like two slits beneath the fuzzy brows. "I wish to complain."

Where was Baxter when she needed him? Cecily thought grimly. She arranged a polite smile on her face. "I'm sorry to hear that. What exactly is the problem?"

"It's that maid of yours, Gertie. The one with the filthy mouth. I have never heard anything so vulgar in my entire life."

Cecily winced. Gertie must have been extremely put out. Usually she managed to contain her more colorful phrases when encountering the guests at the hotel.

"I'm sorry, Mr. Galloway, I apologize for anything she might have said. Rest assured, she will be severely reprimanded."

"Reprimanded?" Galloway unclasped his hands and shook a finger in Cecily's face. "Madam, I insist that the little slut be dismissed. It is bad enough that a gentleman be forced to look at a woman's body in that state, but to hear her utter such filthy language is too much."

Cecily controlled her temper with difficulty. "Mr. Galloway, perhaps you would care to repeat whatever it was she said to you."

"Oh, she didn't say anything to me. I overheard her screaming at that pitiful little thing who works in the kitchen. Doris, I think her name is."

Cecily longed to tell the pompous idiot what she thought of him. Instead she said evenly, "I am sorry if you overheard the kitchen staff, and I shall remind them to keep their voices down. Since the words were not directed at you, however, I see no reason to take such drastic steps as to dismiss Gertie. Now if you will excuse me?"

"She should darn well be dismissed, madam. No woman should be seen in public looking like that. Certainly not in a place of business catering to members of Society. Utterly disgusting, I call it. Really, madam, the entire atmosphere of the place is becoming tawdry. I think I shall have to find alternative accommodations."

"If that is your wish," Cecily murmured, hoping fervently that he meant it. "Now, if you will please excuse me, I have important matters that demand my attention." *Far more important than your petty complaints*, her tone implied.

For a moment Galloway looked at her as if he would argue the point, then with a grunt he stood aside and allowed her to pass.

As she hurried down the hallway to Baxter's office, Cecily couldn't help agreeing with Madeline's assessment of Ellsworth Galloway. The man was positively ignorant. If not evil.

"Where is that bleeding Doris?" Gertie demanded, glaring at Michel as if it were his fault the housemaid had disappeared.

"How in the world should I know?" Michel said, cracking eggs expertly with one hand on the side of the bowl.

Gertie watched the yellow yolks slide into the bowl, leaving the whites behind in the shell. She could never figure out how Michel did that. Every time she tried, she either got the whole mess dumped in the bowl together, or worse, on the floor.

"I sent her up to start laying the fires," Mrs. Chubb said, appearing in the doorway of the scullery. A slab of bacon swung from her hand as she crossed the kitchen to the stove.

"I thought we didn't have enough sticks," Gertie said, wishing Mrs. Chubb would tell her when she sent Doris on an errand. It was hard enough getting the jobs done without having to guess where her helper was supposed to be.

"We had enough to start with." The housekeeper threw the bacon into a pot of boiling water and clamped a lid down on it. "There you are, Michel, that should be enough for the midday meal."

"Well, I suppose I'd better get on and lay them bloody tables, then," Gertie said, moving to the door. "They won't get blinking done by themselves, that's for sure."

She stopped short as the door flew open, almost catching her in the belly. "Strewth! Bleeding watch it, will you? You almost hit the baby then."

"Sorry," Doris muttered, brushing past her with her head down. "I didn't know you was there, did I."

"What's that you've got in your hand, Doris?" Mrs. Chubb asked, reaching for the heavy sack the housemaid carried.

"It's more sticks for the fireplace." Doris dumped the sack on the floor. "I ran out of them so I've just been out there and chopped some more."

Gertie swung around to stare at her. "What with?"

"With the axe, of course, what else?"

Blimey, Gertie thought, Miss Uppity was at it again. She'd never seen anyone change moods like that in all her born days.

"Where did you get it?" Mrs. Chubb opened the sack and peered inside as if she didn't believe what the girl had told her. "Did you find the one that was missing? Or did Samuel get back already with a new one? If so, he was pretty darn sharp about it."

Gertie watched Doris lift her face and stare at Mrs. Chubb as if she'd gone completely bonkers. "Whatcha talking about?"

Mrs. Chubb dropped the sack and folded her arms across her chest. "The axe, that's what I was talking about. Didn't you wash your ears out this morning, young lady? And I'll thank you to use some proper respect when speaking to your elders, if you please."

About bleeding time she got her comeuppance, Gertie thought with smug satisfaction. She was beginning to think the bloody girl could do no wrong. But being saucy to Mrs. Chubb was going to get her nowhere. Gertie knew that only too well.

"I used the axe I always use," Doris said, her face turning a bright red. "The one what hangs on the nail in the shed. What other one would I use? I didn't even know there was another one."

"There isn't. I mean there wasn't." Mrs. Chubb shook her head as if trying to clear it. "Any rate, it doesn't matter as long as you have the sticks. Just get up them stairs and finish laying the fires. Gertie, you'll have to fold the serviettes before you lay the tables. And polish the wineglasses. Doris can help you when she's finished with the fires."

"Bloody heck, how am I going to do all that and get me tables done?"

"Do the best you can." Mrs. Chubb turned to Michel, who seemed engrossed in the gooseberry fool he was creating. "Funny that. I would have sworn Samuel wouldn't have had time to bring back a new axe before midday. He must have left at the crack of dawn."

"I can assure you, he did not." Michel stuck a finger into the green mixture and tasted it. "I saw him leaving about an hour ago." He closed his eyes and smacked his lips. "Perfect, even if I say so myself. I am a great chef, am I not?"

"The best." Mrs. Chubb shook her head, obviously struggling with her thoughts. "Doesn't make sense, that it don't. Unless he met a gypsy on the road and bought an axe from him."

Michel threw back his head and groaned. "The axe is more important than my gooseberry pudding, *oui*? Who cares where Doris get the axe? As long as she still has her head it really does not matter, *n'est-ce pas*?"

Mrs. Chubb shuddered. "For God's sake, Michel, don't even joke about it. It's no laughing matter."

Something about the way she said it gave Gertie the shivers.

She tried not to think about it as she tramped to the dining room. She tried not to think about anyone losing their head. Not even that blinking Doris.

CHAPTER

❖ 8 ❖

"I do wish, madam, that you would send a message for me to come to you, instead of coming all the way to my office like an inferior subordinate."

Cecily smiled at Baxter as she settled herself in the large leather armchair. "In the first place, I prefer your furniture. This chair is so comfortable."

"Thank you, madam." Baxter finished buttoning his coat before he looked at her. "It was a present from your late husband."

"Yes, I know. You almost didn't get it. I tried my utmost to persuade James that I needed it more than you did."

"If you would like it, madam, I'll be happy to—"

"No, no, I wouldn't dream of it." Cecily laid the envelope

on his desk. "These are the costs for the flower arrangements for the ball next Thursday. Perhaps you should look them over."

"I take it you have already given Miss Pengrath permission to purchase?" Baxter said, as he drew the pages out of the envelope and scanned them.

"Well, yes, I did say I thought you would approve, but if you have an objection, it will be a simple matter to change the order."

He sighed, slipping the pages back inside the envelope. "I have no objection, as I am quite sure you anticipated. I would, however, prefer to be consulted before these decisions are made. It would allow me to feel more useful to the running of this establishment."

Cecily pulled a face. "I'm sorry, Baxter. Things were becoming somewhat heated between Madeline and Phoebe, and I wanted the matter settled as soon as possible."

"Very well, madam. But in future, perhaps?"

"Next time, Baxter, I promise. After all, no one knows better than I how lost I would be without you." Cecily frowned, remembering her confrontation with the belligerent baritone.

"I really do wish that Ellsworth Galloway would make good on his threat and find somewhere else to stay. The man makes me feel most uncomfortable."

"He has said something else to upset you?" Baxter looked down at her, a quizzical expression on his face.

"Yes, he did. He complained about Gertie's condition. As if expecting the birth of a child was obscene, for heaven's sake. How in the world does he suppose he arrived on this earth, I'd like to know?"

Baxter cleared his throat. "Yes, madam. I trust Miss Brown is keeping well?"

"Very well, thank you, Baxter. The baby is due just abou
any day now."

"No doubt the arrival will cause quite a stir in the
Pennyfoot. This must be the first time a baby has been bor
here."

Cecily smiled. "At least since it has been a hotel. I'n
quite sure babies must have been born here when i
belonged to the Earl of Saltchester. After all, it was hi
ancestral home."

"I do wonder what became of the family. It must be so
distressing to lose one's home because of an ill-advised
investment."

"It must indeed." She paused, remembering the early
days when she and James had worked so hard to transform
the decaying mansion. "I do hope the earl would be pleased
with the renovations."

"Undoubtedly, madam. How could he not? The place wa
deteriorating rapidly until James took it in hand." Baxter
stared up at the ceiling, apparently lost in thought.

Cecily waited for several moments before saying, "I:
anything wrong?"

He dropped his chin, looking a little abashed. "I was
thinking about the day the Pennyfoot opened for the firs
time. If I remember, the day was quite a nerve-racking
experience."

"Ah, yes." Cecily threw back her head and laughed
"Poor Mrs. Chubb was so nervous she dropped everything
she touched. As I recall, Michel was so angry with her he
waved his hands about and managed to sweep an entire
cauldron of soup onto the floor. Luckily it was no longer ho
so no one was hurt, but oh, my, the mess it made."

"And Gertie had forgotten to open the dampers on the
fireplaces, causing smoke to pour into the rooms."

"And we were up all night cleaning the rooms in time fo

the guests the next day." She looked up to find him watching her, a strange expression on his face. "What is it, Baxter?"

He continued to stare at her, as if making up his mind about something, then he gave a slight shake of his head. "No matter, madam. Just memories."

She wished very much that he had spoken the words he found so hard to say. Whatever they might be. "Well, I'm happy to say that things have improved tremendously since those uncertain beginnings. I'm sure James would be most happy that we have been able to carry on in the tradition that he set for us."

"He would indeed, madam. You have every reason to be proud of your achievements. He couldn't have left the hotel in better hands."

Cecily looked up at him and said sincerely, "Your hands, too, Baxter. As I have said many times, I couldn't have managed all this without you."

"Nor I without you, madam."

The silence grew between them, while neither seemed to know quite what to say next. Finally Cecily said with reluctance, "I had better go down to the kitchen. I want to make sure those fires are laid as soon as possible. The rooms felt quite damp when I last visited them."

"Let us hope that Gertie remembers dampers this time."

"I think Doris will be the one to lay the fires." Cecily rose from her chair with a frown. "I must have Mrs. Chubb inspect them before they are lit. By all accounts Doris is no better than Gertie when she first started. Of course, she is very young."

Baxter grunted. "I'm afraid it is more difficult to find competent help nowadays. The young people are leaving the countryside for the cities, where they can earn bigger salaries for less work. The future of farming looks very bleak."

"We can hardly blame the youngsters. They want something better out of life than the long hours and harsh conditions of working the land."

"But if they all leave the countryside, what will become of the farms and the villages? They will gradually disappear, as they are beginning to do already."

Cecily leaned across the desk and patted his arm. "It's called progress, Baxter. That word you hate so much."

He looked at her with such a serious expression she felt a pang of apprehension. "My greatest fear, madam, is that the Pennyfoot will no longer be able to offer the services to which our guests have become accustomed. I should hate to see the hotel forced to close down."

Cecily straightened, looking him directly in the eye. "As long as I am on my two feet, Baxter, this hotel will not close down—even if I had to do the entire work myself."

He matched her stare for a moment, then nodded. "Yes, madam."

She left him standing at his desk, and the concerned look on his face stayed with her all the way to the kitchen.

She found Mrs. Chubb and Gertie engaged in one of their wordy battles when she pushed the kitchen door open. The smell of pork roasting in the oven made her mouth water, and she sniffed appreciatively as she entered the warm room.

"I told you not to put that milk jug on the windowsill," Mrs. Chubb said, glaring at Gertie, who stood with her arms defiantly crossed in front of her. "You know the cats jump into that window. That's the second jug of milk to go over today."

"I didn't bleeding put it up there. Doris must have gone

and done it. Flipping heck, why do you always go and blame me for every bloody thing?"

Neither of them had noticed Cecily standing there, and she coughed loudly.

Mrs. Chubb swung around, her eyes sparkling with anger in her flushed face. "Oh, pardon me, mum, I didn't hear you come in. Gertie was making such a racket—"

"*I* was? It was you what was making all the blinking noise."

"Gertie!" Mrs. Chubb silenced the girl with a glare. Turning back to Cecily, she said more quietly, "What can I do for you, mum? Is there something wrong? Doris hasn't done something, has she?"

Gertie growled in the back of her throat, then stomped over to the pantry when Mrs. Chubb gave her another sharp look. "Not as far as I know," Cecily said, "but I do think it might be wise to inspect the fireplaces when she is finished. Just to make sure the dampers are open and the fires are laid properly."

"Yes, mum. I've already planned to do that. We don't want another fiasco with smoke in the rooms."

Cecily smiled. "Baxter and I were just talking about that this morning. It doesn't seem possible it was so long ago."

"That it doesn't, mum." The housekeeper looked over her shoulder to see if Gertie had left the room. "I don't want you to think I'm complaining, mum, but I'm a little worried about Doris."

"She has been giving you trouble?"

"Not exactly, mum. More like she has the trouble. She seems to have a problem with her memory. Can't remember things, so to speak. I don't know if it's just because she's confused with all the jobs she has, or if she's ill in some way. In her mind, I mean."

Shocked, Cecily shook her head. "Oh, I don't think so,

Mrs. Chubb. After all, the child is very young, and she has come from a very unfortunate background. I'm sure she will settle down after a few weeks. Just try to be patient with her, would you, please?"

Mrs. Chubb vigorously nodded her head. "Oh, of course, mum, you know I will. I wouldn't have said nothing, only that business with the axe—" She broke off, then added quickly, "I'm sure it's just my imagination. All that gossip about the murder and then the axe missing." She drew in her breath sharply. "Oh, that reminds me, mum, I wanted to thank you for getting the axe replaced so promptly. Samuel must have flown on wings to get back with it so quickly."

Cecily stared at her in amazement. "He's back already? But he didn't leave until after breakfast, I'm quite sure. He must have found the original one after all."

Mrs. Chubb nodded, looking skeptical. "That's what I thought, mum. I didn't think he—"

She was interrupted by the door flying open. Samuel stood in the doorway, an axe in his hand, his eyes alight with excitement. "You'll never guess what—"

"Samuel," Mrs. Chubb said sharply. "Where are your manners? Take off your cap when you're in the house. And use some respect in front of madam, if you please, young man."

With a sheepish expression, Samuel pulled off his cap and shoved it in his pocket. "Pardon me, mum. I wasn't thinking. I heard—"

"That's enough, Samuel. Whatever you have to say can be said later."

"No," Cecily said, her gaze shifting to the axe in Samuel's hand. "I'd like to hear what Samuel has to say. Where did you get the axe, Samuel?"

He looked at her, his brow creasing. "I just bought it from

Harry Whites, like you said. I told him to put it on the hotel account and—"

"You just bought it?" Mrs. Chubb interrupted. "You just got back now?"

Samuel looked even more confused. "Yes, I did, Mrs. Chubb. I hurried as fast as I could, but I had to wait for him to sharpen it and I thought I'd better unharness the trap before I came in with the news."

"What news is that?" Cecily said, beginning to feel a familiar chill up her arms.

"Another murder!" Samuel looked as if he would burst in his anxiety to get the words out. "Up in the woods again. Another gypsy, they say. Killed yesterday. Her head was missing, just like the last one. It was chopped off with an axe."

The silence in the kitchen seemed to hang thick and still as both women lowered their gazes to the axe swinging in Samuel's hand.

"Oh, my good Lord," Mrs. Chubb whispered.

News traveled fast in an establishment as intimate as the Pennyfoot Hotel. By the time the midday meal was served, everyone, it seemed, had heard about the second murder.

When Cecily left the dining room to return to her suite, Lady Belleville was holding an earnest conversation with Ellsworth Galloway in the hallway.

"No doubt about it, my dear lady," Galloway said as Cecily approached them with great reluctance, "the murderer is a gypsy. Just the sort of heathen thing one of them would do. I mean, all that business about taking the head. Downright satanic, I call it. The work of a devil. No Christian man would dream of doing such a thing."

"No Christian man would kill another person, I should think," Cecily said, unable to hold back the retort.

Lady Belleville uttered a twittering laugh. "Oh, my dear, how droll. Of course she is right, Mr. Galloway. But I must say I agree with you. Most likely a jealous lover, I would say. These gypsies are such passionate people, so I've heard."

"Yes, that is most likely the case." Galloway turned his beady eyes toward Cecily. "I understand Wilhelmina Freidrich will be singing at the ball on Thursday."

Cecily nodded. "Mrs. Carter-Holmes, who arranges all our entertainment, assures me she is an excellent soprano."

"Quite so, quite so." Galloway stroked his beard, preening himself like a questing peacock. "I did wonder why I wasn't approached. Not that I would have accepted, of course. A man does have to be most particular as to where he lends his presence. Reputations have to be protected, don't you know."

Cecily thinned her mouth. "Precisely," she said, "which is why we hesitated to invite you."

Galloway's face turned dark as he eyed her suspiciously. "I was referring to *my* reputation."

"Well, of course," Cecily said sweetly. Without giving him a chance to answer, she turned to Lady Belleville. "I do hope your meal was satisfactory."

The plumes on the dowager's hat dipped and swayed. "Oh, absolutely divine, my dear. The boiled bacon was delicious, and the roast pork and applesauce simply melted in my mouth. Please give my compliments to the chef."

"I'll be happy to do that, Lady Belleville. I'm sure Michel will be most gratified by your compliment."

"Not at all. He deserves the praise." She looked over her shoulder, down the long hallway. "I don't suppose you have seen a stray canary, have you? One of them is missing. I can't seem to find it anywhere."

Galloway pointedly cleared his throat. "I must be on my

way, if you will excuse me, ladies. I have another engagement."

Cecily gave him a curt nod, while Lady Belleville appeared not to have heard him. "He was there," she went on, fluttering a tiny fan in front of her face, "sitting on my shoulder this morning, listening to the other birds singing in the trees outside. I explained to him that it would be most dangerous for him to join the other birds in the gardens. I do hope he didn't wander off."

"I'm sure he is somewhere in your suite, Lady Belleville," Cecily said soothingly.

"I searched the boudoir, of course, but he wasn't in there. I wonder if he might have flown on top of the canopy above the bed. I can't get up there to see, you see."

Cecily heard the grandfather clock chime in the foyer and took her cue. "Well, if you don't find him, I'll have Baxter climb up there to have a look. Now, I'm afraid I must be off to complete my duties."

"Oh, of course." Lady Belleville smiled and nodded. "Thank you so much, my dear. So comforting to know someone sympathizes with an old lady. Most people think I'm senile, you know."

"Oh, I'm sure they don't." Cecily backed away, still exchanging comments, until she reached the foyer, then with a sigh of relief she headed for the stairs.

Trying not to think what Baxter would say when asked to climb on Lady Belleville's bed in order to find one of her "birds," Cecily quickly climbed the stairs to the second floor.

She hadn't as yet told Baxter about the reappearance of the axe. Her common sense told her that someone had merely borrowed the thing and brought it back. Maybe John Thimble, the gardener. Though she couldn't imagine why he would need it, unless to chop off a broken branch. And he wouldn't have needed to keep it all day.

Still puzzling over the problem, she reached her door and unlocked it. She saw the note the minute the door swung open. It lay on the carpet, silently challenging her to pick it up.

She closed the door first, then stooped, reaching for it with unsteady fingers. It was folded in half, a sheet of hotel stationery as the other note had been.

The message had been scrawled in the same untidy hand, and the words were every bit as direct. It read: *You must stop George from killing the gypsies. Don't let him know I told you.*

Cecily stared at the words, no longer able to deny her growing conviction. She saw again the axe swinging in Samuel's hand, with his voice raised in excitement.

Not only did it appear that someone in the hotel knew the identity of the murderer, it would also seem that the murder weapon had in fact been borrowed from the Pennyfoot Hotel, and then returned.

In which case, Cecily thought with grim resignation, once more she was indeed involved in the grisly business of murder.

CHAPTER

❈ 9 ❈

"I am afraid I was wrong in my estimation," Baxter said when Cecily tracked him down in the conservatory to show him the second note. "In view of the second murder, it would appear that someone in this hotel has knowledge of the murderer after all. Knowledge, I might add, that should be given to the police."

"I agree." Cecily reached for a dead leaf on a large aspidistra and snipped it off the branch. "Since we do not as yet know the name of that person, however, I see no reason to involve the police at this point."

She avoided looking at him, but she knew quite well that he stared at her with disapproval. She knew he was thinking about all the times she had risked both their lives in order to see justice done.

She also knew that he would do his best to dissuade her from following her usual course of action, knowing all the while how futile his efforts would be.

Hardening her heart, she added deliberately, "Also, the axe has been returned."

"The axe that was missing yesterday?"

"Yes. Samuel purchased a new one, but Doris had already chopped the sticks, apparently with the axe that had been returned. Of course, someone could have borrowed it."

"Someone such as the murderer, perhaps?" Baxter suggested, sounding more than a little desperate.

"I was thinking it could have been John Thimble."

He shook his head. "John has not been at work since last Friday. He is recovering from a sore back."

"I see." She hadn't really been convinced that the gardener had taken the axe, but to have it confirmed so decisively was disturbing, to say the least.

"Madam," Baxter said quietly, "I sympathize with your concerns, but nevertheless someone by the name of George is running around willy-nilly, chopping off the heads of young girls. The note is correct about one thing. The murderer must be stopped."

"We can't be sure the murderer's name is George," Cecily said. "Perhaps someone is writing these notes to confuse us and put us off the track of the real culprit."

"All the more reason to inform the police." Baxter held out his hands in appeal. "I beg you, madam, do not involve yourself again. Hand these notes over to Inspector Cranshaw and allow him to do his work on the case without interference. I am so afraid he will lose patience with you and do something drastic."

"Inspector Cranshaw is not interested in pursuing the

case." Cecily paced across the polished parquet floor of the conservatory, hearing again Madeline's outraged protest.

"The victims are gypsies, and according to the inspector, so is their killer. In which case, again according to our astute inspector, the gypsies will take care of their own affairs, happily with neatness and a modicum of fuss, thus saving the constabulary the trouble and expense of doing the job themselves."

"The inspector told you that?" Baxter asked, sounding incredulous.

"Not exactly," Cecily had to admit. "Madeline told me."

"And the inspector told her."

"Well, no, Mrs. Chubb told her."

"And she got it from . . . ?"

Cecily sighed. "Gertie."

"Who got it from . . . ?"

Cecily stopped pacing and came to a halt in front of him. Tossing her head, she said tartly, "There are times, Baxter, when you can be most infuriating. I can assure you the news came from a most reliable source."

"Who was . . . ?" Baxter prompted without batting an eyelid.

"Mrs. Northcott, who happens to be the wife of Police Constable Northcott, in case you might have forgotten."

Baxter nodded sagely. "Aha! That does explain things quite a bit."

"Baxter—"

"And if I might add, madam, there is no need to be snippy."

"Snippy?" Cecily faced up to him like a cockerel ready to do battle.

"Most definitely snippy, if you'll pardon me for saying so."

Aware that he was actually enjoying himself, she made an

effort to curb her temper. "Nevertheless, I'm quite sure the sentiment was accurate. You must be aware of the attitude of our local constabulary where the gypsies are concerned."

"That's as may be, but I am quite sure that if the inspector saw these notes, he would understand that someone here in this hotel could very well know the identity of the murderer. That could place the guests and the staff in danger. Or perhaps you have not considered that fact?"

"I've considered it, of course. There are just too many questions to be answered yet. I refuse to involve this hotel with the police again, unless I have positive proof that one of our guests is guilty of murder." She turned to go, then looked back at him. "I think I will pay Dr. Prestwick a visit. I have a small problem with headaches lately. Perhaps he can suggest something that will help."

He looked as if the hotel were about to fall down around him at any moment. "I do hope it is nothing serious, madam."

"I really don't think so, Baxter. Please don't worry. You worry about me entirely too much."

"It is my responsibility to look after you, madam. I gave my word."

She grimaced, wishing that just once he would say he worried about her for his own personal reasons rather than constantly reminding her of his duty to James. "Well, you may rest assured," she said, her voice sharpening just a little, "I am perfectly capable of taking care of myself."

Looking affronted at her tone, he said quietly, "I am not totally convinced of that. For good reason. Since I will be wasting my breath attempting to persuade you to let well enough alone, I can only hope that you will not directly involve yourself, or myself, in any more dangerous escapades. I am getting far too old to indulge in such behavior."

In an effort to make up for her irritation, Cecily grinned

at him as she headed for the door. "You, Bax? Never. We are only as old as we perceive ourselves to be. And people such as you and me will always be young at heart."

He mumbled an answer she couldn't hear as she swept through the door and down the hallway. Perhaps, she told herself as she once more climbed the stairs to her suite, it was just as well.

Normally Cecily would have sent her calling card to the doctor's house before paying him a visit. Since she didn't want to waste any time, however, she ordered Samuel to take her there in the trap after surgery hours, hoping that she would find the doctor at home.

Dr. Prestwick was, in fact, raking leaves in his garden when the chestnut came to a halt in front of the white picket fence that bordered the house. Looking up at the sound of the trap, he paused in his work, his handsome face wreathed in a smile.

"Why, Cecily, what a truly pleasant surprise. To what do I owe this unexpected pleasure?"

She returned his smile with a gracious wave of her hand, then allowed Samuel to assist her down from the trap. "I shan't be long," she told the footman, "so you may wait for me here."

"Yes, mum." Samuel touched his cap then climbed back onto his seat, settling himself down for the wait.

Dr. Kevin Prestwick sprang for the gate and dragged it open as Cecily reached it. "My dear, you are looking younger and more beautiful than ever. It warms my heart to see you." He reached for her gloved hand and brought it to his lips, warming her skin through the fabric with the touch of his mouth.

No matter how much she told herself that he acted the same way toward every woman with whom he came in contact, she could not prevent the flutter of her heart at his flattery. Kevin Prestwick was a master of the art, which was why his surgery was filled to capacity each and every morning.

"Good afternoon, Dr. Prestwick," she said a trifle breathlessly. "It's a pleasure to see you also."

"It would please me far more if you would use my Christian name, as do most of my patients. I have to remind you of that each time I see you."

He drew her into the garden and began walking up the path. "Now, tell me what brings you to my humble abode at this hour?" He stopped suddenly and turned her to face him, looking deep into her eyes. "You are not ill, I hope? Could it be that I have been so struck by your beauty that I have missed noticing a malady of some sort?"

Cecily smiled up at him, conscious as always of the warm admiration in his dark brown eyes. "I am perfectly well, Doctor, thank you."

"Kevin, if you please. I am so relieved. Then this is a visit entirely for pleasure, I take it?"

"Not exactly." Aware that they were heading for the front door of his cottage, which stood ajar, she paused. While she was the first to fly in the face of convention, she had no wish to endanger the good doctor's reputation. No further than it was already, at any rate.

"I came to ask you about the murders on the Downs," she said, turning her back on the door. "I assume you were called in to examine the bodies, as usual?"

The doctor grimaced. "You disappoint me, Cecily. I had hoped you had come to enjoy my company." He laid a hand on his chest in a dramatic gesture. "My heart is sorely wounded. It may never recover."

His expression was so comical, Cecily burst out laughing.

"Really, Dr. Prestwick, you should know that the heart cannot be damaged by disappointment."

To her surprise, he grew serious. "Do not be too sure of that, my dear. Many a man, or woman for that matter, has died of a broken heart. When one loses the will to live, the body loses the power to fight."

Remembering that the doctor had lost his wife a few years earlier, Cecily couldn't help wondering if Mrs. Prestwick had died of a broken heart. Perhaps it had been too painful to watch her husband dallying with all the ladies.

Though Cecily was quite sure Kevin Prestwick meant nothing by his flattery, nevertheless it must have been difficult for his wife to witness his flirtatious manner, particularly considering the nature of his profession.

"I have to remind you, dear lady," the doctor continued, "that I am not in a position to discuss the details of the murder. I can assure you, you would not want to hear them in any case."

For a moment Cecily considered giving him a demure smile and fluttering her eyelashes, the way Phoebe always did when she wanted something. Then her conscience caught up with her. She simply could not stoop to such tricks.

Instead she looked him straight in the eye and said firmly, "Dr. Prestwick—"

"Kevin, please."

"Very well, Kevin. I'm fully aware that you can't reveal the important details of the case. But I understand from a reliable source that the investigation is not being pursued with any real enthusiasm by the constabulary. In which case, perhaps it would not matter quite so much if I ask a question or two?"

Dr. Prestwick frowned. "Who informed you that the case is not being investigated?"

"I'm not at liberty to divulge that," Cecily said primly.

Prestwick nodded. "Well fielded."

She smiled, having rather enjoyed turning the tables on him. "Perhaps if I were to ask what I want to know, then you could decide if you were able to answer or not."

He looked at her for a long time, while she tried very hard not to let his scrutiny unsettle her.

"Cecily," he said quietly, "it is my very great regret that you do not share my admiration. You are, indeed, a remarkable woman."

"Thank you, Doctor."

He shook his head in reproof, and she added hastily, "I beg your pardon . . . Kevin. Perhaps you could tell me about when the murders took place?"

He thought for a moment, a troubled expression on his face. "Perhaps I can. If you will tell me something."

"If I can."

"Why are you so interested in these gruesome events? I can assure you, it was not a pretty sight. Even I, who have been witness to many a hideous sight, have seldom seen anything this horrific. I tell you, Cecily, this is the work of a madman. I would hope most sincerely that you do not intend to involve yourself in these heinous crimes, as you have been wont to do in the past."

Cecily wrinkled her nose at him. "You are beginning to sound like my manager, Kevin. I am merely satisfying my curiosity, nothing more. If you are not able to tell me—"

"Oh, very well, I will tell you. I cannot see what harm there is in that." He drew a hand through his thick brown hair, as if frustrated with the conversation. "The first murder, as far as I can tell, was committed sometime during the morning hours. My closest estimation would be about eleven o'clock."

Cecily nodded. "And the second?"

He raised his eyebrows at her, apparently struck by a thought. "When did you hear of the second murder?"

"This morning. My stable manager heard the news in the village."

He shook his head, wry amusement flitting across his face. "News does indeed travel fast in these parts."

"In a small village, Doctor, people have little else to do other than gossip."

"Is that why you refuse to enter my house with me?" He gave her an impish smile. "I am a doctor, you know. I treat patients every day in my house."

"During surgery hours, yes. With many other people present."

"You do not trust me, Cecily." Again he struck a dismal pose. "Oh, how I am wronged."

"I do not trust the jealous old biddies who will say anything to malign both you and me out of sheer spite." She drew her gloves higher up her arms in a small gesture of defiance.

His levity vanished as he studied her. "You are quite right, my dear. I would not wish to sully your impeccable reputation. You mean far too much to me." Before she could recover from that remark, he added lightly, "Now, what was it you wanted to ask me?"

She had to gather her thoughts together before answering him. "The second murder. Can you give me an estimate of the time it was committed?"

"Yes, I can. The body was discovered shortly after the horrible deed. I would say the unfortunate woman was killed as dusk was approaching. Late afternoon, after four o'clock, I would say."

"And you are certain the murder weapon was an axe?"

"As sure as I can be."

"It couldn't have been a sword, perhaps?"

The doctor's shrewd gaze studied her face. "Do you, perhaps, know something I should know?"

Cecily shook her head, summoning a quick smile. "Just settling questions in my mind, Kevin, I assure you."

Narrowing his eyes, he murmured, "Something tells me I shall regret holding this conversation with you. I have the distinct impression that you are not being as forthright with me as I am with you."

"Your imagination, Doctor. Now, the murder weapon. Could it have been a sword?"

After a long pause, Kevin Prestwick shook his head. "No, I do not believe so. The blade that was used caused a jagged edge to the neck. A sword would have sliced through far more cleanly. I would say it took several blows before the head was actually severed from the body."

Cecily felt bile rise in her throat and fought to maintain her composure. "In both cases?"

Her discomfort had not escaped the doctor. He peered closely at her face with a frown of concern. "I am sorry, my dear, I did warn you. Yes, I would say the same weapon had been used both times. Now, I really cannot tell you any more than that. I'm afraid I may have already told you far too much."

"I won't keep you any longer, Doctor." Cecily swallowed hard as she held out her hand. "Thank you so much for satisfying my curiosity."

Kevin Prestwick took her hand and bowed low over it as he touched her gloved fingers with his lips. He looked up, his head still bowed over her hand. "Please, my dear, promise me you will not involve yourself in this case. It is brutal, and seemingly without reason. One would be foolish indeed to attempt to deal with a madman such as this. When faced with a crazed killer, one can only destroy, before he himself is destroyed."

"I trust I shall never be forced to make such a decision," Cecily said with feeling. "Good day to you, Doctor."

"Kevin."

She smiled down at him. "Kevin."

Letting go of her hand, he straightened. "I trust it will not be so long before I see your lovely face again. Not in my surgery, that is."

Before she could stop to think, the words popped out. "Perhaps you would care to come to the Guy Fawkes Ball on Thursday? You are quite welcome to bring a guest, if you would like."

"Thank you, my dear. I would like that very much." He paused at the gate and pulled it open for her.

Passing through, she reflected that Baxter would be most displeased when he learned of the doctor's presence at the ball. Baxter thoroughly disliked Kevin Prestwick, though Cecily had yet to learn the reason why.

She could only assume that Baxter highly disapproved of the doctor's manner, not understanding that it was simply a way of relaxing his patients. She had heard it referred to as a good bedside manner. Dr. Kevin Prestwick had the very best bedside manner she had ever encountered.

She thanked him as he gave her his arm to assist her into the trap. "It was good to see you again," she said, settling herself on the creaking leather seat.

"The pleasure was entirely mine." He inclined his head in a slight bow. "I shall look forward with great anticipation to the ball. Perhaps you will allow me one dance?"

She felt like a young girl again as she gave him a smile, murmuring, "Perhaps." She basked in the memory of the admiration in his eyes on her return to the hotel.

The sea looked gray as the trap sped along the Esplanade. With an anxious eye Cecily surveyed the white flecks in the waves surging toward the beach. The morning sun had disappeared behind dark clouds, and the wind whipped sand across the empty road, sending little whirls of dust into the shop doorways.

A large brown and white dog loped along the sands, no doubt hurrying for shelter from the coming storm. Cecily shivered as the chill settled about her shoulders. She was quite anxious herself now to return to the warmth and comfort of the Pennyfoot. The images that Dr. Kevin Prestwick's words had left in her mind were too horrible to contemplate.

To her surprise, Baxter stood at the top of the steps as the trap halted in front of the hotel. Before Samuel could spring from his seat, the harried-looking manager ran down the steps and offered his hand to Cecily.

"I was becoming concerned, madam," he said as he put her gloved hand in his. "There is a storm coming, and I worried that you might be caught in it."

Eyeing him, she wondered if that was all he was worried about. Stepping down from the trap, she gave him a wide smile. "I have been caught in storms before, Baxter, and I have survived."

"Yes, madam. Nevertheless, I am relieved you have returned before the deluge. I should not want you to become ill, with all the festivities of the weekend approaching."

A large drop of rain spattered on the pavement at her feet, followed quickly by another, then another. In the distance a low rumble warned of the incoming storm.

"I'm sorry if I worried you, Baxter, but it would seem that I arrived back in the nick of time." Cecily lifted her skirt and quickly mounted the steps as Samuel urged the chestnut into a trot.

As the clatter of hooves disappeared around the side of the hotel, Baxter said behind her, "For which I am truly thankful. I can only hope that will always be the case."

Cecily wondered if the uneasiness she felt was due to the approaching storm or Baxter's unwarranted concern. Or perhaps it was due to the image of a young girl's body, lying decapitated in the dark woods on Putney Downs.

CHAPTER

❖10❖

Having warmed herself by the leaping fire in the library Cecily began to feel more comfortable, though Baxter still hovered anxiously at the end of the table.

"I have ordered a cup of tea from the kitchen," he said running a hand over his ruffled hair. "I suggested a spoonful of brandy in it. I think it might be of some help to keep out the chill."

His gesture reminded Cecily of Dr. Prestwick, and she smiled. "Thank you, Baxter. That was very thoughtful. Though I'm quite sure all of this nurturing is unnecessary."

"I sincerely hope so, madam."

Her smile faded as she studied him. "Baxter, is something wrong? Has something else happened?"

"Not that I'm aware of, madam."

"You seem upset about something. I do hope you're not keeping anything from me."

"Would that I could, madam."

"Then what is it?"

He coughed, fidgeted with the button on his jacket, then looked down at his feet. "I have been concerned about your health. You mentioned a problem with headaches. I was wondering if Dr. Prestwick has been able to diagnose the problem."

Cecily's face cleared. "Is that all? Oh, think no more about it, Baxter. I'm afraid that was simply an excuse to see the doctor. I thought you might give me an argument if I told you I was going to see Dr. Prestwick in order to ask him about the murders."

Baxter looked up, his eyes glinting like the frozen surface of Deep Willow Pond. "Then I have been worrying unnecessarily, madam. I trust the good doctor was forthcoming with the information?"

Feeling guilty, she nodded. "I'm sorry, Baxter. I didn't mean to worry you. Dr. Prestwick was helpful, yes, inasmuch as he could tell me."

"I'm happy that your journey was not wasted. Now, if you will please excuse me, I have urgent matters that need my attention."

Cecily looked at him, distressed by his reaction. "Don't you want to know what he told me?"

"Unless he insisted that you go immediately to the police, I can only assume that whatever he told you only served to strengthen your inimitable resolve to involve yourself in affairs that could very well prove to be your undoing." He reached the door and looked back at her. "As you very well know, madam, I would prefer not to be drawn into any more of your misadventures."

Hurt by his stubbornness, she said quietly, "I should miss your help, Baxter."

She didn't care for the look he gave her, or for the way he muttered, "For what it is worth, madam."

He closed the door quietly after him, and she stared at it for a long moment, then let out her breath in an explosive sigh. She had no idea what had nettled him so, but she didn't have time to worry about it.

Someone in the hotel had been writing notes to her about a man called George, who could be a crazed murderer. It was imperative she find the author of those notes and get at the truth. It was entirely possible that he had witnessed the actual murders.

Cecily's gaze drifted to the portrait of her late husband. "What do you think, James?" she murmured. "Perhaps I should talk to our guests and try to discover where they were yesterday afternoon when the murder took place."

She waited a moment, her gaze on the painted eyes of James Sinclair. Then she said softly, "Yes, I thought you would agree with me. And please don't worry about Baxter. He'll eventually see things my way."

Even so, she felt a nasty little ache in her midriff when she spoke the words. She could never be quite sure what went on in Baxter's mind. She could only hope that he hadn't meant those words he'd spoken to her, or lost patience with her entirely.

It was at times like this, when all was not well between them, that she realized how very much she depended on him, how lost she would be without his stalwart presence and loyalty.

Now, if only he could offer her the admiration and affection that Kevin Prestwick was apparently so willing to give, her life would be complete.

Once again her gaze strayed to the portrait. "Forgive me,

James," she said quietly, "but nowadays I'm afraid my thoughts are constantly centered on Baxter. I do hope you're not resentful of your replacement. He is here, and you are not, you see, and once in a while a woman needs a man to care for her. Despite the efforts of women everywhere to establish their independence, I have no doubt that no matter how much we achieve, there will still be room in our hearts for love and support."

Propping her hands on her chin, she smiled at herself. People would think her quite ridiculous for talking out loud to a portrait. But it certainly helped to put things into perspective.

No matter how much she might long for it, Baxter would never be able to give her the kind of love and companionship she sought. Since she was far too old, or unwilling, to search for it elsewhere, it would seem she was destined to spend the rest of her life alone in that respect.

In which case, she told herself as she rose from her chair, she had better become used to the idea and accept it. There were far worse situations in which to be, and at least she still had her head. Not like those poor young women who had lost their lives before they had known what life was really all about.

Firmly putting her spat with Baxter out of her mind, she left the library and headed for the drawing room.

When she entered the room a few moments later, she hoped she would encounter some of the guests enjoying a cocktail or two before dinner.

She might have known Colonel Fortescue would be there, swallowing as many gins as he could consume before staggering into the dining room, where inevitably someone had to guide him to his table.

Cecily really didn't think there would be any point in questioning the colonel, but one never knew what tiny clue could be picked up from even the most inane conversation. And conversations with the colonel were nearly always inane.

She was surprised to see quite a gathering in the drawing room, after all. The storm rumbling outside must have unsettled the guests, for everyone was there.

Lady Belleville sat in the high-backed Queen Anne chair, murmuring to an imaginary bird on her shoulder, as usual. Cyril Plunkett had chosen a chair by the window, where he sat nervously watching the lightning dazzling the sky through the gap in the half-drawn curtains.

The colonel sat slouched in the leather armchair, his head nodding, a glass of gin tilting in his hand, while Ellsworth Galloway paced back and forth across the carpet muttering to himself.

The colonel roused himself when Cecily called out a greeting. "What ho, old bean! Jolly good storm going on outside, what? Listen to that wind howling in the chimney. Makes one dashed glad he's not out on the ocean on a night like this. Why, I remember once—"

A loud clap of thunder interrupted his words, and Lady Belleville uttered a low cry. "Oh, my poor dear birds. How they do despise this dreadful weather. I don't know why I come to the seaside in wintertime. Such awful weather. Awful."

Ellsworth Galloway made a sound of disgust in his throat. "I cannot imagine why any of us bury ourselves in this despicable hole. I could be enjoying the nightlife of London right now. If it wasn't for the ball on Thursday, I would pack my bags and return on the next train."

"Are you certain the ball will be worth your confinement here?" Cecily asked, holding a pleasant smile on her face. "I should not want you to be disappointed."

"I'm only staying to hear Freidrich sing." Galloway

parted his feet and struck a pose with his thumbs hooked
inside his waistcoat. "I will be partnering the lady next
month in a recital and I want to hear her range. It's always
best to be prepared, just in case."

In case of what? Cecily wondered. It sounded like a lame
excuse to her, and she wondered what could be the real
reason Galloway was staying on.

The thunder cracked again, louder this time. Waiting until
the noise had died away, Cecily said casually, "At least this
weather might discourage our murderer from striking again."

"As long as he limits his victims to gypsies," Galloway
said nastily, "I really can't see how he concerns us. As for
the weather, I find it a darn nuisance. I like to spend the
afternoons on the beach, practicing. It's peaceful down there
this time of year without all the rabble that flocks there in
the summer."

"I trust you got your practice in yesterday, then, Mr.
Galloway?" Cecily inquired.

The baritone looked at her as if surprised she had
addressed him. "As a matter of fact, I did, if you must know.
I spent the entire afternoon down there, until it got dark, that
is. That's another thing, it is dark by half past four this time
of year. Damn days are over before you have time to get
started on anything."

Maybe if he got up early in the morning he'd accomplish
more, Cecily thought. But at least he'd answered her
question.

"Well, I'm afraid I must have my afternoon naps," Lady
Belleville said, lifting a finger to her shoulder for one of her
birds. "I just cannot survive through dinner unless I have
slept most of the afternoon."

She peered at her outstretched forefinger and chirped at it.
"Not that I slept very well yesterday afternoon. In fact,

hardly at all." She glared at Cecily as if it were her fault, compelling her to answer.

"I'm sorry you slept badly, Lady Belleville. Perhaps the murder played on your mind?"

The dowager shook her head so violently the veil on her hat dropped down and covered her face. Lifting the netting with her gnarled fingers, Lady Belleville said crossly, "I spend no time mourning the passing of those savages. Things like that happen, I suppose, but it is no concern of mine. After all, it isn't as if they belong in this world, is it?"

Cecily frowned. "I was under the opinion that we all shared the same world, Lady Belleville. We are, after all, human beings."

"I do not consider the gypsies on the same level with decent human beings." The elderly woman looked down her nose as if the very thought repulsed her. "Anyway, I have far more to worry about. One of my birds is missing, as I told you earlier. I just cannot find it anywhere. I want you to ask that manager of yours to search my suite, and if the poor baby isn't found, I must insist on a thorough search of this hotel."

This would not please Baxter in the least, Cecily thought, remembering his frame of mind when she last saw him. Nevertheless, she could hardly refuse one of their more wealthy and consistent guests.

Hoping she wasn't alienating Baxter beyond recall, she said soothingly, "Of course, Lady Belleville. I will ask Baxter to conduct a search as soon as the evening meal is over."

Apparently mollified, Lady Belleville nodded her head. "Thank you. I must ask that all the rooms be searched, of course. I can only hope that the poor little thing hasn't flown through the front door and out into the wicked world. I would simply die if my baby fell into the filthy hands of those terrible gypsies."

"Oh, good Lord," Galloway muttered. "I do not have to sit and listen to this twaddle." He strode purposefully from the room without a backward glance, with Lady Belleville staring after him.

"Well, really! How rude. That man is really quite detestable."

The thunder cracked in answer to her words. At the same time the wind roared down the chimney, sending a puff of smoke into the room.

The colonel, who had lapsed back into his doze, sat up straight in his chair, spilling his gin over the arm. "Rude? I assure you, madam, I had no intention of being rude. If I have offended you, I most heartily apologize. A gentleman is never rude to a lady, not at all. Would never do. No, no, no—"

"Be quiet, you silly man. Between you and the thunder, my birds are becoming quite frightened. I wasn't talking about you, in any case."

The colonel looked confused and stared at Cecily for help. "Did I miss something? Was I rude to the birds?" He looked wildly around the room, spilling more gin. "Where are they, then? Did I frighten them away?"

Cecily winced, making a mental note to have Doris clean the chair later. "It's all right, Colonel," she said, resisting the impulse to go over and dab up the spill. "You did nothing to upset anyone, I assure you."

"Oh, jolly good, jolly good." The colonel blinked his eyelids several times, then erupted in a gigantic sneeze that made Lady Belleville start up from her chair.

"Mercy me," she said, gasping, "I felt quite certain we had been hit by lightning. My poor little babies' hearts are fluttering like butterfly wings."

"Dreadfully sorry, madam. Must be the fire. Dashed smoke makes me sneeze." The colonel sniffed, leaning on one side to search his pocket for a handkerchief.

Finally locating one in his breast pocket, he drew it out and proceeded to blow his nose in a loud trumpet of sound that almost matched the thunder.

"I say," Cyril Plunkett said, starting up from his chair, "that was a wild flash of lightning just then. It lit up the entire Esplanade."

His words were almost drowned out by the crash of thunder that followed.

"Dashed good job it wasn't yesterday evening," the colonel remarked, draining the remains of the gin. "I was on my way home from the George. Would have been caught in this lot. Lost my way coming back here. Seem to do that a lot lately. Must be the old noggin getting old, what? Had a damn good meal down there, though."

Lady Belleville looked horrified. "You *ate* there? You actually ate that inferior food when you could have enjoyed Michel's delectable meals? What were you thinking of, my good man?"

"I say, madam," the colonel said, obviously put out. "I agree the chef here is top-hole and all that, but I happen to enjoy the Cornish pasties and Scotch eggs at the George once in a while. Dashed good stuff if I may say so, what?"

Unable to keep quiet any longer, Cecily said warmly, "I'm glad you enjoyed the meal, Colonel. My son would be happy to know that."

Obviously having forgotten that Cecily's son owned the pub, the colonel looked confused again. "Oh, quite, quite." He said nothing more for a moment, his chin getting lower and lower on his chest.

"I think I will go to the dining room," Cyril Plunkett said in his thin voice. "The thunder might not be so noisy in there. I never could abide storms, and they always seem so much worse at the seaside." As if in answer to his words, thunder once more growled overhead.

The colonel shot up in his chair. "By Jove, that was a close one. Anyone hurt? Get behind the battlements, men, and keep your heads down! Dashed blighters come at you from nowhere—"

"Colonel," Cecily said gently, "it's only thunder."

The colonel blinked at her for a moment, then looked at Cyril. "Oh, there you are. Saw you dashing by in the old bus yesterday, old chap. Nice-looking motorcar that, what? What?"

Cyril looked startled, as if he wasn't sure how to answer the unpredictable man. "I'm afraid I didn't notice you, Colonel. I tend to concentrate on the road. I had three business meetings yesterday, and I was in a hurry to arrive on time."

"Think nothing of it, old chap. No harm done. Carry on." Again the colonel's chin lowered, and he uttered a loud snore.

"Well, it must be time to go to the dining room," Lady Belleville said, getting up with a rustle of skirts. She tapped her shoulder, adding, "Come along, my darlings, it's time for our little stroll. Perhaps we shall find your brother before the night is out."

Looking at Cecily, she said in a plaintive voice, "You won't forget to ask your manager to search for my little one, will you?"

"I promise you, I will see that he takes care of it," Cecily said, praying they wouldn't have to actually search all the rooms to please the eccentric dowager.

Apparently satisfied with that, Lady Belleville left the room, still cooing to her imaginary charges on her shoulder.

"Mrs. Sinclair," Cyril Plunkett said, raising his soft voice in order to be heard above the loud snores of the colonel. "What with this storm and all the talk about murder, I am feeling quite unnerved. I can't help feeling that the isolation of this hotel and its close proximity to the woods can be quite dangerous."

"I assure you, Mr. Plunkett," Cecily said, "you are quite safe within the walls of the Pennyfoot."

The salesman nodded, though he looked unconvinced. His pinched features looked pale and wan, and he kept shooting nervous little glances at the fireplace as the wind rattled down the chimney.

"That's as may be, Mrs. Sinclair, but I have work to do in my room at the end of the day and I find it impossible to concentrate with so many distractions. I feel I would have more peace of mind if I moved to a hotel in Wellercombe for the remainder of the week, whereupon I shall be returning to London."

Dismayed, Cecily could only say pleasantly, "I quite understand. I will have Baxter make up your bill for you in the morning."

Cyril Plunkett nodded, wincing as another crack of thunder exploded outside. Bowing his head, he scuttled from the room, leaving Cecily to wonder how many more of her guests she would lose once they learned that a mad killer was on the loose in Badgers End.

CHAPTER
❋ 11 ❋

Cecily was not looking forward to the task of sending Baxter on a search for an imaginary bird. In the first place, he was at odds with her, and in the second place, any patience he might have had where Lady Belleville was concerned was inclined to evaporate rather quickly.

She waited to talk to him until after the evening meal, when she knew he would be relaxing in his quarters. He wouldn't receive her there, of course. That wouldn't be proper.

Cecily wrinkled her nose as she strolled down the corridor. Baxter and his proprieties could be most frustrating at the best of times, but when he was displeased with her, he could be positively stuffy.

Reaching the door of the office, she tried the handle first, then, finding it locked, smartly rapped on the oak paneling with her knuckles.

Baxter's private quarters led off the office, and he would have to come through there to let her in. She hoped he wouldn't be too exasperated at being disturbed during his off-duty hours. But then, she thought wryly, he should be used to being summoned at all odd hours by now.

The door opened suddenly, before she was fully prepared. Baxter looked as if he'd just woken up from a doze. His hair was ruffled, and he'd removed his wing collar and tie.

One hand quickly smoothed down the errant tuft of hair when he saw his visitor. His expression changed swiftly from embarrassed surprise, no doubt at being discovered out of uniform, to one of alarm. "Madam! Is something wrong?"

Relieved that he seemed to have forgotten their little spat, Cecily gave him a warm smile. "That depends on how you look at it. More of a nuisance, I would say. May I come in?"

He eyed her with suspicion. "Into the office?"

"Of course!" She pretended to look shocked. "You surely don't think I would suggest visiting you in your rooms unescorted, do you?"

His mouth tightened as he gave her his steely look. "Someone has to maintain a sense of decorum, madam." His tone clearly inferred that had he left it up to her, she would lead him into the depths of iniquity.

Sighing, she entered the darkened office and stood patiently while he lit the small oil lamp on his desk. The acrid smell quickly dissipated as the flame sputtered, then settled into a steady glow.

"I do hope you have not taken all this trouble merely to satisfy a craving for a cigar," he said as she took a seat on the armchair.

She looked up at him, watching the lamplight cast shadows across his strong features. "I'm afraid it's a little more bothersome than that, but I do think a cigar is an excellent idea. Perhaps you will join me, now that there is no one about to witness your depravity?"

Aware that she was goading him, though she wasn't quite sure why, she added more softly, "I'm sorry, Baxter. I'm afraid I'm feeling a little testy this evening. I think it must be the storm. Nasty weather always seems to create tension, don't you think?"

"Indubitably, madam. It can make one quite cantankerous at times."

"Well, you didn't have to agree quite so readily." She watched his face, hoping to see some change in his stony expression. Why was it, she wondered unhappily, that they seemed to bicker more often now than at any time since she'd known him?

"I would like that cigar, if you please?" she said demurely. "That's if you have no objection?"

Silently he withdrew the package from his breast pocket and tapped one out for her. He took his time striking the match, then cupped the flame in his hand as he leaned forward to light the cigar.

She drew on it until the end of it glowed, then puffed out the smoke in a little cloud. "It's quite windy tonight," she remarked, settling back on the chair with a long sigh. "It's an east wind, blowing straight in from the ocean. I saw the fire smoking in the drawing room before dinner."

"I will have Samuel adjust the windscreens." Baxter replaced the package in his pocket. "They might have become dislodged."

Cecily nodded, contemplating the tip of her cigar. A narrow band of white ash was beginning to form on the end of it. She wondered how long she could let it grow before gravity had its way and the ash fell to her lap.

Deciding not to wait to find out, she leaned forward and tapped the edge of the cigar on the crystal ashtray on Baxter's neat desk. When she sat back again, she found him watching her, an odd look on his face.

The expression vanished as she met his gaze. "I presume you did not disturb me tonight to discuss the weather?" he said carefully.

"No, I did not." She lifted a hand, then dropped it back in her lap. "I'm sorry, Baxter, but I'm afraid Lady Belleville is being particularly difficult. She insists on a search of her room being made in order to discover the whereabouts of a bird. She believes one is missing."

Baxter's eyes opened wider. "You surely don't expect me to humor her? At this time of night? Heaven knows what she could fabricate if I were to enter her boudoir unchaperoned."

"You won't be unchaperoned, Baxter. I shall be with you. She merely wants you to search the top of the canopy above her bed. I believe she has looked everywhere else."

"And when we don't find it?"

"I think that if we pretend to find one, she might accept it in her imagination as well."

Baxter shook his head, his expression rueful. "I have done many things in the interests of this hotel and the guests, but I have to admit, madam, pretending to hold an imaginary bird in my hand may well test my capabilities."

"If you are not convincing, Baxter, she might very well demand that you search the entire hotel."

"Then I shall politely but firmly refuse."

"And alienate a very important guest? Lady Belleville might be eccentric, but she is well-known in social circles.

I would not want her to embellish her complaints and damage the reputation of the Pennyfoot."

Baxter's mouth twitched, as if he longed to say something, but refrained only with a great effort. "I would suggest that the lady is not merely eccentric. She is downright demented."

"Nevertheless," Cecily said evenly, "she is influential. I'm afraid we must humor her, Baxter."

"Tonight?"

"Tonight." Cecily nodded at the small clock on top of the bureau. "It is not yet ten o'clock. It isn't too late. And I gave her my promise."

Baxter gave a stiff nod. "Very well, madam. If you will wait here until I am properly attired?"

"I will wait here, Baxter. Take your time."

He hesitated, as if not certain what to say next, then with a slight nod disappeared through the door to his rooms and closed it behind him.

Samuel had gone to a great deal of trouble to look his best. His hair was slicked down with a dab of grease, and he'd even used his precious bar of soap to wash himself. He wore his one and only tweed suit, which he usually saved for church, and the bowler that his father had given him, after complaining that it kept slipping down over his bald head.

Samuel intended to make a big impression, and his excitement had him trembling as he carefully opened the kitchen door and peered inside. He'd found out from Gertie that Doris was working late that night, and he intended to steal a few moments alone with her, if at all possible.

To his intense delight, he saw her standing at the kitchen sink, steam wreathing around her head as she clattered dishes around in the soapy water.

Moving silently on the toes of his boots, he hoped they

wouldn't creak as he crept across the floor toward the busy housemaid. Engrossed in her task, she seemed not to hear him, and his heart thudded as he drew closer.

All he could think about was sliding his arms around that tiny waist and giving her a quick hug before she could object. He felt sure she wouldn't chastise him for it; he had recognized that glow on her face and the sparkle in her eye when she'd looked at him the night before.

She liked him. He was as sure of that as he was that cats had kittens. He liked her, too, and he wanted her to know it. He wanted to stake his claim before one of the stable lads fell for her shy smile and big brown eyes. Or were they green? He couldn't remember for sure.

Closer and closer he crept, until he was within reach of her body. Closing his eyes in warm anticipation, he reached out and grasped her about the waist, pulling her back against him for a second or two before letting her go.

He had expected her to squeal. He had even expected her to pretend to be cross with him at first; that was, until he coaxed a smile from those sweet lips.

What he hadn't expected was the loud yelp that sounded like a cry of pain, and the rain of blows that fell about his head, knocking his bowler to the floor.

"Get your filthy hands off me," Doris yelled, bringing the wooden spoon down even harder on his hands, which he'd raised to protect his noggin.

"Strewth, Doris, it's only me. I didn't mean to startle you—"

"Startle me?" Green eyes blazed in her flushed face as she screamed at him. "If you ever touch me again, I'll run a carving knife right through you, so help me I will. Get out of here, you filthy animal. I'm not one of your horses for you to manhandle. I'll tell madam what you did, I swear I will."

"Doris—"

"Don't Doris me! I'll—"

"Mercy! Whatever is this racket going on here?" The sound of Mrs. Chubb's voice cut off Doris's yelling, and Samuel could hear his breath coming hard in the silence.

"I didn't mean no harm, Mrs. Chubb," he said breathlessly, "I just wanted to say hello, that's all."

"He put his filthy hands on me, that he did," Doris said, glaring at him with the spoon raised in her hand. "Crept up behind me when I wasn't looking. I don't want him near me. Tell him to stay out of my way or I'll cut him in half."

"I'm going, I'm going." Samuel stopped to pick up his hat, then backed to the door.

"I think you'd better make yourself scarce, young man," Mrs. Chubb said, casting a wary look at Doris. "And next time you want to come calling, make yourself known first instead of creeping up on a young lady like that."

"I don't want him calling on me ever," Doris said, turning her back on him. "I hate the sight of him, I do."

"Don't you worry, Doris Hoggins," Samuel said stiffly. "I'll not bother you again. Should have known better than to try to be nice to the likes of you."

Slamming the kitchen door, he took a long breath of the chill night air. His face felt hot, and there was a sick feeling in the pit of his stomach. He could have sworn Doris liked him. He knew that women were unpredictable creatures, wont to change their minds in an instant, his father had told him so. But in all his born days he had never met a woman like Doris Hoggins.

Of course, he reminded himself as he trudged down to the gate, Doris wasn't exactly a woman yet. Though she looked like a woman, and she smiled like a woman. And in that brief moment when he'd held her around the waist, she had certainly felt like a woman.

He reached the gate and pulled it open. It was too bad she couldn't act like a woman instead of a frightened child. There weren't too many women left in the village around his age. Certainly none with such a pretty face and beautiful big brown eyes like Doris.

But that temper of hers was as fierce as it was unwarranted, and he just couldn't understand what set her off like that.

Giving up on the puzzle, he jammed his hands into his pockets and set off for the George and Dragon. No sense in wasting his best togs. As long as he was wearing them, he might as well see what was going on down at the pub.

Still, he couldn't feel his usual enthusiasm as he marched briskly down the road, whistling to keep himself company. Somehow he couldn't get the image of Doris's furious face out of his mind. Didn't seem like the same girl, that it didn't. Not the same girl at all.

"Lady Belleville," Cecily called out as she tapped gently on the door. "It's Mrs. Sinclair and Baxter. We've come to search for your bird."

The door opened with a rush, revealing the dowager who wore a tea gown of brown lace embossed with cream velvet roses. A diamond tiara glittered in her hair, matching the drop necklace at her neck. Lady Belleville had obviously dressed for the occasion.

If she was disappointed to see Cecily accompanying Baxter, she made no sign of it as she invited them both into her boudoir. "I think the little rascal may be hiding up there," she said, directing her fluttering gaze on Baxter. "Would you be so terribly kind as to climb up and take a look?"

Baxter gave her one of his stiffest smiles. "I will be happy to, madam. I shall have to stand on one of the chairs, of course, but I am sure I shall be able to see."

"Oh, thank you. So terribly kind of you." Lady Belleville flittered around the room looking like an oversized bird herself. "The others have been so lonely since he left. I keep thinking I can hear him singing, but it could be my ears. I have a ringing sound in them all the time, you see."

"How unfortunate," Baxter said, shooting a desperate glance at Cecily.

"How many birds do you have?" Cecily inquired, in an effort to take the elderly woman's attention away from Baxter.

"Oh, my dear, I lose count. Why, in my day I have had several hundred, I should imagine. Wonderful friends, they are, you know. Such good company, chirping all day long in my ear. I really don't know what I'd do without them."

Baxter grunted something as he hauled a chair across the carpet and stood it by the side of the bed.

"Of course, I have to be careful of the cats, you know—" Cecily's blood froze when Lady Belleville uttered a loud shriek.

Baxter, balanced on the chair, swung around, almost toppling over. "What the—?"

"The cats!" Lady Belleville cried, clutching at Cecily's arm. "Oh, my dear Mrs. Sinclair, what if cats have eaten my little one? Whatever will I do?"

"I'm sure your little bird is much too fast to be caught by any of our strays," Cecily said soothingly. "They all eat so much of Michel's marvelous cooking, they've grown quite fat and lazy. Isn't that so, Baxter?"

"Indubitably, madam." Baxter peered over the top of the canopy, hanging on with one hand to a corner post. "As a matter of fact, I do believe I see the little fellow right here. If I can just reach . . ."

Cecily felt a desperate urge to grin as Baxter thrust out a hand and made an imaginary grab. "Ah, got the little . . . bird."

"Oh, wonderful, wonderful." Lady Belleville clapped her hands. "How perfectly marvelous of you, dear Mr. Baxter. How can I ever repay you?"

Baxter answered her with an explosive sneeze.

"God bless you," Cecily said.

Baxter gave her a frigid look. "Thank you, madam. It's the dust." As if to accentuate his point, he sneezed again.

Lady Belleville screeched once more. "Oh, do be careful! Don't squeeze the poor little thing or you'll break his little bones. They are so fragile, you know."

"It's quite all right," Baxter mumbled as he climbed down from the chair, brushing cobwebs from his sleeve. "The little chap is perfectly fine. Now if I just . . . er . . . sit him on your shoulder here . . ."

Cecily hid a smile behind her hand. In spite of her best efforts, a soft chuckle escaped, and Baxter sent her a glare that promised a lecture later on.

Lady Belleville clasped her hands together, her eyes brimming with tears of gratitude. She stood quite still while Baxter touched her shoulder with his finger and stood back.

"There," he said, doing his best to look sincere. "Home again, safe and sound."

Lady Belleville turned her head, her smile vanishing as she stared at her shoulder. "Where?" she demanded, her voice querulous.

Baxter froze, staring at the dowager as if completely bereft of words.

With a sinking feeling, Cecily pointed to the trembling shoulder. "Right there, Lady Belleville. Look, there it is, preening its feathers. Can't you see it?"

"Of course I can't see it. Do you take me for a fool? What

is this nincompoop trying to do? Make a mockery of me?"

Turning on Baxter, the angry woman shook a finger in his heavily flushed face. "I may be an old woman, my good man, but I can assure you I have all my wits about me. Now I'd appreciate it if you would search this hotel and find that bird for me, instead of wasting my time playing your silly childish tricks."

Turning back to Cecily, she added for good measure, "Really, Mrs. Sinclair, you should have more sense than to associate yourself with someone who has such appalling manners. Most unbecoming for a lady of your station. Now, if you will excuse me, I would very much like to retire for the night."

Mumbling apologies, Baxter rushed for the door and held it open for Cecily to pass through. Barely waiting until he'd closed the door again, he said through gritted teeth, "I cannot for the life of me imagine why I continue to listen to you. Never again will I allow myself to be misled by your idiotic ideas."

Cecily raised her eyebrows. "I beg your pardon?"

Baxter took a deep breath. "Madam," he added as an afterthought.

Cecily could hold back the laugh no longer. "Oh, piffle, Baxter, it was worth a try. I was only attempting to save you the arduous task of searching this hotel."

"And just what leads you to believe I shall be searching the hotel?" Baxter asked, just a little too quietly.

"Well, I did promise . . ."

"So you did." Baxter started down the hallway with his long stride, leaving Cecily struggling to keep up with him. "Since Lady Belleville is no doubt retiring for the night, however, she will be in no position to know whether or not the hotel was searched. I shall merely inform her that I spent the better part of the night looking for her bird, to no avail.

She will just have to accept the disappointment, that's all."

Finally catching up with him at the top of the stairs, Cecily caught his sleeve. "Baxter, has it occurred to you that Lady Belleville might ask the other guests if they saw you search? After all, you are supposed to include their rooms."

"Would madam want me to disturb the other guests at this time of night?"

"Of course not. But it wouldn't hurt to make at least a cursory search. Just in case she takes it into her head to check up on you."

The sound of a rusty voice droning out the words to some unrecognizable tune caught Cecily's attention. Leaning over the balustrade, she saw Colonel Fortescue making his unsteady way up the stairs.

"I have an idea," she said quickly. "Take the colonel with you and search just the landings and the hallway downstairs. Then, if Lady Belleville challenges you in the morning, you will have the colonel's word that you searched the hotel and found nothing."

Baxter looked astounded. "That fool? He's worse than Lady Belleville. He's likely to forget everything by tomorrow and will simply make me out to be a liar."

"He'll remember enough to believe everything you say. He couldn't be a better witness for you."

"I really don't care to have a witness—" Baxter started to say.

Without giving him a chance to finish, Cecily leaned over the balustrade. "Colonel?" she called. "Could we have a word with you?"

"Certainly, my dear. Be with you in a jiff."

She could almost feel the heat of Baxter's temper as the colonel grunted and puffed his way to the top of the stairs. She could only hope that by tomorrow her manager would forgive her for forcing the issue.

After listening to her request, Colonel Fortescue proved to be only too happy to assist in the search, and Cecily left him earnestly discussing the strategy with Baxter, who wore a face of granite.

Feeling a little guilty, she let herself into her room, only to bring herself up short when she saw yet another note lying on the carpet. She snatched it up, scanning it with anxious eyes.

The hastily scrawled lines covered the page. *You are asking too many questions. You must take more care. George is extremely dangerous when angered. Be warned!*

CHAPTER

❊12❊

"I say, old chap, this is jolly good fun, what? What?" The colonel strode along the narrow hallway in front of Baxter, his calves encased in bright yellow and green argyle socks below his tweed knickers. "By George, I do relish a hunt. Though I do prefer larger game, of course. Not much to brag about when bagging a bird, is there, what?"

Baxter mumbled an answer and promised himself he would have it out with Cecily in the morning, without fail. Not only did she force him into a most embarrassing display of idiocy in front of a guest, but he was now conducting an imaginary search for an imaginary bird with a deranged nitwit for an assistant.

The nitwit in question came to an abrupt halt in front of

him, and Baxter narrowly avoided charging straight into the bulky figure.

"Shh!" the colonel hissed. "There it is, by thunder. Lurking in the corner over there. Looks much bigger than I expected."

Baxter frowned, doing his best to peer around the colonel's plump shoulders. "Where is it?" he whispered, peering into the dim shadows beyond the flickering gas lamps. "I can't see anything."

The colonel turned his head, tickling Baxter's jaw with his whiskers. "Over there. In the corner. Perched on that little table. Looks more like a vulture to me. Have to watch their claws, you know. It will take two of us to—"

Baxter straightened. "Colonel—"

"Shh! Don't want to frighten the pesky thing away, now that we've got him. Could do with a net. Oh, well, hands will have to do. I'll grab the wings, you hold onto the—"

"Colonel!" Baxter closed his eyes briefly. "That is not Lady Belleville's canary."

"Canary?" The colonel's eyelids flapped furiously. "Of course it's not a canary, old chap. I can see that. Much too big—"

"It's a pedestal."

"As I said, it's probably a vulture—"

"With a bust of Shakespeare standing on it."

The colonel paused, staring at Baxter with bloodshot eyes. "Shakespeare?"

"Shakespeare. I suggest you take another look."

The colonel turned slowly around as if he expected the thing to jump out at him. "Great Scott! Shakespeare it is. Could have sworn it moved just now. Fancy that! Looked just like a dashed vulture skulking in the corner."

"I think we have indulged in this farce long enough," Baxter said, doing his best to hold back his irritation. "I do thank you for your assistance, sir, but I am afraid the canary appears to have escaped the confines of this hotel. It must have flown out of a window or perhaps the front door when it was ajar."

"Poppycock!" The colonel twirled his mustache with his stubby fingers. "The hunt has only just begun. Can't give up yet. Stiff upper lip and all that, you know. No, by George, we keep on until we find the little blighter. Must be somewhere. We still have all the rooms to search yet."

Baxter sighed. Much as he hated to admit it, Cecily was right. The colonel would lend credence to his story of a thorough search, but only if he could convince the man that they had done so. Though personally, he thought darkly, he seriously doubted that Lady Belleville was worth all the trouble.

"Very well," he said, leading the way once more, "we have three empty suites on this floor. We shall search them one by one, and that will leave only the foyer and the downstairs hallway to be searched."

The colonel blinked at him in confusion. "It will? By Jove, that was quick. Don't remember searching the top floor at all."

"Time passes quickly when one is pleasantly occupied," Baxter said firmly. "Come, let us take a look in here."

"Saw quite a scrimmage with one once, you know," the colonel said as he followed Baxter into the darkened suite.

Leaving the door open, Baxter reached up to light the gas lamps. The flame popped a couple of times, then settled down with a soft fizz.

"Yes," the colonel went on, blithely unaffected by Baxter's pointed silence, "nasty bit of work they are, you know. Claws as sharp as needles. Remember when one swooped down on the major's wife during a parade. She was wearing one of those wig thingammies on her head."

"Really," Baxter murmured, pretending to look carefully around the room.

"By George, that was a sight. That enormous bird rising in the air with a clump of hair dangling from its claws—the major's wife with her hair literally standing on end, shrieking that her diamond pin was stuck in the wig—and the major standing there screaming orders to shoot the thing down."

Baxter nodded and peered behind a blue velvet chaise lounge.

"Young lieutenant got it in one shot. Dropped like a stone. Let go of the wig, of course. The dashed thing dropped onto the head of the color guard. Hair all over his face. Couldn't see a damn thing after that."

"Tricky," Baxter murmured. He pulled the drapes back and peered behind them.

"I'll say it was. He was carrying the Union Jack at the time. Blundered right into the parade stand. Top of the staff almost skewered the major's wife. Missed her by that much."

"Well, the bird doesn't appear to be in here," Baxter announced.

"Bird? What bird? There's no bird in here. I was talking about India, old chap. And that one's dead. Young lieutenant got it in one shot. Dropped like a stone . . ."

Leading the way from the room, Baxter nursed the fond hope that the colonel would drop like a stone and leave him in peace. Tomorrow, he promised himself. Tomorrow he would give Madam Cecily Sinclair a lecture she would not forget.

Pausing at the door of the next suite, he said, "I believe we have already searched this one, Colonel."

"We have?" The colonel peered shortsightedly at the door. "Dashed if I remember now. Don't suppose we'll find the little perisher anyway. Probably flown up on the Downs by now. That's where birds belong, anyway, that's what I always say. Should be flying about in trees, not cooped up in damn cages. Damn cruel, that's what I call it."

For once the old fool had said something Baxter could agree with. With hope rising in his breast, he said cautiously, "What say we give up this hunt for tonight, Colonel? I'm quite sure Lady Belleville will be most appreciative of your efforts to find her canary. I shall certainly tell her that you did your utmost to help."

"Really?" The colonel patted his chest. "Not a bad-looking woman that, you know. Bit batty, of course. Keeps talking to some damn birds that aren't there. She should go up on the Downs if she wants to see birds. Plenty of them up there, what?"

"There certainly are," Baxter said, beginning to move purposefully down the corridor. He was tired, irritable, and hungry. He needed a roast beef sandwich with a dash of horseradish and a hot cup of tea, then blessed peace in the privacy of his room until the morning.

"Saw someone up there yesterday afternoon," the colonel said behind him. "Just remembered that. Don't think the blighter was bird-watching though."

Baxter paused and looked back at him. "What was he doing?"

The colonel thought for a moment, then shrugged his shoulders. "Dashed if I can remember. I'd had a tipple or two at the George, you know. Got lost on the way home." He shook his head. "Seem to do that a lot lately. Must be the old peepers. Have to get some spectacles, I suppose. Hate the damn things. Keep sliding down my nose."

"Who was this person?" Baxter said, trying to sound unconcerned. "Did you know him?"

Colonel Fortescue gave him a vague look. "Not sure that

t was a him, old chap. Could have been a woman, I suppose. 'Fraid I don't remember. Dashed awkward that, what?"

"Did you recognize this person, do you remember?"

The colonel frowned, apparently struggling with his feeble memory. "I think I did. I was going to call out, but the lighter disappeared." He made an attempt to snap his fingers, failed, tried again, then gave up. "Just like that."

"But you would know the person again?" Baxter persisted, his patience beginning to evaporate.

"Don't know, old chap. Had to be someone from this hotel, I should think. Don't know any of the local chappies. If I could just remember who it was . . . Dashed memory never has been the same since those bullets sliced my head during the war." His fingers busily parted his hair. "Still have the scars, you know. Wonder I wasn't killed."

"Quite." Baxter patted the colonel's arm. "Must have been terribly painful. Perhaps a good night's sleep will help."

"What? Oh, yes, I suppose it would."

"Good. Then, if you can remember later who you saw on the Downs yesterday, perhaps you will inform me?"

Colonel Fortescue lifted a hand and brought it down heavily on Baxter's shoulder. "Of course, old chap. Bit curious myself, actually. Whoever it was didn't want to be seen, I can tell you that. I remember that much."

Wincing, Baxter rubbed his shoulder. "Perhaps it might be better if you don't tell anyone else, Colonel. We wouldn't want to unsettle any of our guests, you know."

"No, no, wouldn't do at all. Don't worry, old chap. Mum's the word, what?"

"Precisely." Bidding the colonel good night, Baxter headed back down the corridor. He didn't hold out much hope that the colonel would remember anything useful.

It would appear, however, that someone from the hotel could have been in the vicinity of the second murder about the time it had happened. The author of the note, perhaps? Or the murderer himself?

Whoever it was, Baxter thought bleakly, he would give a great deal to know his identity. Then he could go directly to the police, instead of waiting for madam to hurl them both into the path of danger yet again.

Again Cecily was pleasantly surprised the next morning after breakfast when the expected dispute with Baxter failed to materialize. True, he was a little short when she inquired about the search the night before.

"I do wish, madam," he said, facing her across the library table, "that you would refrain from involving me in your harebrained schemes. I do not appreciate looking foolish in front of guests, nor do I particularly enjoy the company of Colonel Fortescue."

"I'm sorry, Baxter. Was it so terrible?"

Baxter rolled his eyes to the ceiling. "Atrocious. The man is a raving lunatic."

Cecily grinned. "Oh, I don't know. I find him rather disarming at times." She laughed out loud at his incredulous expression, vastly relieved that all apparently was well between them once more.

"I think alarming is a more appropriate word," Baxter said, glancing at the clock on the mantelpiece. "I hope you will inform Lady Belleville that he and I made a thorough search of the hotel and that we regret finding no sign of her canary."

"Don't worry, Baxter, I'll take care of it. I'm sure she will be satisfied, or maybe she's forgotten all about it by now."

"I certainly hope so. I can't rely on Fortescue to vouch for me. He can't remember his name at times. I find it difficult

believe he could see someone on the Downs behaving
suspiciously, and yet fail to remember the very next day
who it was he saw."

Cecily had been only half listening, her mind on the note
she had received the night before. She had been trying to
decide whether or not she should show Baxter the letter,
since he made so much fuss about the last one.

His words, however, gradually registered, and she looked
up, saying sharply, "Colonel Fortescue saw someone?"

Baxter looked a trifle sheepish. "Yes, he did. But he can't
remember who it was. Or what he was doing. If it was a
man, that is. He's not even sure about that."

Cecily covered her eyes with her hand.

"I was going to tell you if he remembered who it was,"
Baxter said, sounding defensive.

"No doubt insisting that we go straight to the police with
the information."

"Once we knew the identity of the murderer, yes."

Cecily looked up at him again. "We can't be sure it was
the murderer. It could have been the person who is writing
the notes, trying to spy on the murderer. And what if our
friend with the notes doesn't really know the identity of the
murderer, but is merely guessing? Or worse, fabricating the
entire thing? We should have a full-scale investigation of
this hotel by the police, and once more our guests will be
subjected to questioning."

"Yes, madam."

She leaned forward to make her point. "I don't like the
guests being questioned, Baxter."

"No, madam."

"So will you please tell me exactly what it was the
colonel said? Maybe we can pick up a clue from his
ramblings."

She listened carefully while Baxter recounted his somewhat bizarre conversation with Colonel Fortescue the night before. "He simply does not remember who it was he saw," Baxter said finally. "Though he did promise to tell me if he did remember. I also took care to warn him not to mention to anyone else that he'd seen this person."

"I'm glad to hear it." Cecily tapped her fingernails on the polished surface of the table. "We don't want the murderer if he is indeed someone at this hotel, learning that he was recognized by the colonel, whether or not he was under the influence of alcohol. It could put his life in danger."

"Mine, too, madam, if the murderer knows the colonel told me about it."

"I had already thought of that," Cecily said soberly. "And as long as we are on this subject, I had better show you something I received last night."

She pulled the folded sheet of paper from her pocket and handed it to him. "I found this on my floor last night."

She watched him read the letter, his face inscrutable as always. Then he slowly folded it and handed it back to her. "You will not reconsider your decision to keep these notes from the police?"

She gave a decisive shake of her head. "I will not reconsider. Not until we have positive proof that the murderer is indeed one of our guests. So far, all we have is conjecture, and most of it a little wild at that."

"In that case, I beg you to be careful, madam. By all accounts this murderer is not one to be reckoned with. He is evil and very dangerous."

She met his gaze, saying quietly, "I'll be careful, Baxter. As you must be, too."

"Yes, madam."

She held his gaze a little longer, then rose, saying briskly, "Well, I must be on my way to inform Lady Belleville of your fruitless search. I hope I can pacify her enough that she will forget the entire episode."

"I shall be in the dining room if you need me, madam."

"Thank you, Baxter." She left him standing at the door, and hurried down the hallway to the stairs. She had almost reached them when a voice hailed her from the foyer.

"Good morning, Mrs. Sinclair. Spiffing morning out there, now that the storm is gone."

Sighing, Cecily turned to face the colonel, who was dressed in a topcoat and a tartan deerstalker cap. "Good morning, Colonel. You are up and about early this morning."

"Couldn't sleep, old bean. Blasted sea gulls woke me up about an hour ago. Thought I'd get a few minutes fresh air and stroll along the Esplanade."

Eyeing his reddened cheeks, Cecily said, "It must be quite chilly out there at this hour."

"It is indeed, madam. Quite invigorating, actually. Does one's lungs good to fill them with fresh sea air."

"Yes, I quite agree." Cecily looked around, but could see no one in the hallways. "Colonel," she said, lowering her voice, "I wonder if I might ask you a question?"

"Fire away, old bean. Anything I can do to help a charming lady like yourself."

"I just wondered if you by any chance happened to remember who it was you saw on the Downs the day before yesterday."

The colonel pulled off his cap. "No, who was it?"

"I don't know, Colonel," Cecily said patiently. "That's why I'm asking you. Now think, can you at least remember if it was a man or a woman?"

The colonel grasped his bearded chin and tilted his head to the ceiling. "I seem to remember . . ." he said slowly.

"Yes?" If only he could remember, Cecily thought with

rising hope, there was a good chance she could track down George, if that really was the murderer's name.

The colonel muttered and murmured for a moment or two, then shook his head. "Sorry, old bean, can't quite get hold of it. But it'll come back to me, never fear."

"You will tell me the minute you remember?"

"Of course, m'dear. Only too happy to oblige, what?"

He was about to turn away when Cecily had another thought. "I wonder, Colonel, have you by any chance met a man by the name of George?"

The colonel's bushy eyebrows quivered. "George? Why, of course!"

"You have?" Cecily glanced around again before leaning forward to whisper, "Someone in this hotel, perhaps?"

The colonel jerked up as if he'd been stung. "Good Lord, I hope not. Man's been dead for donkey's years. Be a bit smelly by now, I should think. Killed by a dragon, I do believe."

Cecily took a deep breath and tried again. "No, Colonel, this George is very much alive and well."

The colonel stared at her for a moment or two, his eyelids working up and down. Then he said loudly, "Oh, you mean *that* George. Why didn't you say so?"

"Shh!" Cecily said, placing a finger over her lips. "Is he staying at this hotel?"

The colonel looked around in a furtive manner. "I don't know. Is he? Won't they miss him?"

"Won't who miss him?"

"The palace, old bean. He is going to be our next king, you know. Just as soon as Edward keels over. He'll be George the Fifth, you know. I remember when—"

Cecily nodded. "Well, thank you, Colonel. I must get on with my chores. I do hope you enjoy your day."

"I'm sure I shall. Won't be long before the ball now,

what? Looking forward to that, by Jove. Should be a topping show, what? What?"

With a feeble wave of his hand, he turned away from her and headed for the stairs. Deciding to wait until he was out of sight before going up to see Lady Belleville, Cecily headed in the opposite direction toward the kitchen stairs.

She was halfway across the foyer when she heard a deafening crash, followed by a hoarse cry. Turning, she saw the colonel standing near the foot of the stairs, clutching his chest and staggering to one side.

At his feet, having apparently missed him by inches, lay the jagged piece of a very large, very heavy flowerpot that had once stood on the very top landing.

CHAPTER

❖13❖

Baxter appeared from nowhere it seemed, just as Cecily reached the colonel's side. "What happened?" he demanded, catching the colonel by the arm. "Are you all right, sir?"

"No, I'm not all right," the colonel muttered. "Damn near shot out of my boots. If that thing had been an inch closer, I'd be pushing up daisies, I can tell you."

"Are you hurt anywhere?" Cecily said anxiously, scanning the colonel's face for cuts or bruises.

"Don't think so, old bean. Dashed pot came hurtling down from the ceiling. What was it doing on the ceiling, I'd like to know?"

Both Cecily and Baxter looked up, to where the landings

tween the curves of the staircase on each floor looked
er the foyer. Then they looked at each other.

"Top floor," Cecily said quietly.

Without a word, Baxter sprang for the stairs and raced up
em with remarkable speed for a man of his age.

Cecily watched him for a moment, then turned back to the
lonel. "Are you quite sure you are all right, Colonel?
rhaps a spot of brandy might help?"

The colonel's eyes lit up. "Topping idea, old bean. Yes,
s. Just what the doctor ordered, what? Don't mind if I do."

"Why don't you go along to the drawing room and rest,
d I'll have one of the housemaids bring you a stiff
andy," Cecily said, anxious to get rid of him before any
ssible altercation on the stairs.

She wished now she had not sent Baxter up there alone.
he had a terrible vision of a madman standing at the top of
e stairs with an axe raised in his hand.

"Jolly good, madam, yes, I think I will toddle off now.
el a bit woozy in the old topknot, if you know what I
ean."

"Quite, Colonel. Your brandy will be right along."

The colonel touched his forehead, turned, then paused a
oment before turning back. "Er . . . madam, could you
ake that cognac, do you think?"

Cecily smiled. "Cognac it is, Colonel."

Muttering his thanks, the colonel wandered off down the
allway.

"Oh, my, whatever happened here?" a light voice in-
uired.

Cecily swung around to confront Madeline, who stood
irectly behind her, her gaze on the shattered vase. Cecily
ad been so engrossed in the colonel's brush with death that
he hadn't noticed her friend enter the hotel.

"It must have fallen from the landing," Cecily said,

wondering how the woman always managed to approa[ch] without any sound.

Madeline lifted her chin and peered up the shado[w] staircase. "Really? How did it get through the banisters?"

"Broken, I should think. Baxter's gone up there now [to] investigate." He should have been back by now, s[he] thought, trying not to become too alarmed by his absenc[e.]

In an effort to distract Madeline's attention, she add[ed] cheerfully, "What brings you here so early in the mornin[g?] I hope there isn't a problem with the flowers?"

Madeline's perceptive gaze rested on her face. "Mimos[a,]" she said briefly. "The hothouses are late with their shi[p]ments, and they can't promise they can get it to me on tim[e.] I was wondering if perhaps baby's breath would be all rig[ht] instead? It won't be as colorful, of course, but I think I c[an] make a nice show of it."

"That will be very nice." Cecily flicked a glance at th[e] stairs. Still no sign of Baxter. Where was he?

"You need to get that aspidistra in water as soon [as] possible," Madeline said, pointing at the mess of dirt a[nd] leaves on the floor. "That's if the poor thing hasn't died [of] shock."

Cecily cast a distracted look at the injured plant. "C[an] you do anything with it? If not, perhaps you can replace [it] for me."

Footsteps sounded on the stairs, and she looked [up] quickly, disappointed to see it was only Cyril Plunke[tt.] Madeline darted forward to kneel by the aspidistra, whi[le] Cecily greeted the salesman.

"Just a small accident," she assured him, as the litt[le] man's curious gaze strayed to the smashed pottery.

"It has made quite a mess," he said, shifting his gaze bac[k] to Cecily.

"I'm afraid so, but we will have it cleaned up in no time[.]"

He turned to go, then looked back at her. "I have decided stay until the weekend, after all," he said in his quiet ice. "Now that the storm is passed I feel better, and it's so uch trouble to change hotels midweek. I'm far too busy th my sales meetings to take the time."

"I'm so glad to hear it," Cecily said with sincerity. erhaps you will attend the ball on Thursday night?"

The salesman shuddered. "Oh, I don't think so. Dancing 't . . . I don't care to . . . I don't dance, you see. esides, I have several business meetings on Friday. I'll ed to get to bed early. Thank you, but I really must be ing now."

Nodding his head, he backed away, then scuttled out of e door as if frightened she would haul him back and mand he stay for the ball.

Madeline rose to her feet, holding the limp plant in her nds, its roots drooping dismally almost to the floor. "I'll e what I can do with it, but I can't promise anything." She oked down at it as if it were a child she held instead of a ump of foliage.

"I say, what a rotten mess," Galloway's voice said behind r.

Madeline raised her eyes to the ceiling as the baritone ushed past her without so much as a glance to acknowl- lge her presence.

"It will be cleaned up as soon as possible," Cecily formed him in a tight voice. "I am just on my way to the tchen to have one of the maids take care of it."

"More incompetence, I suppose. That's what you get for ring a gypsy." Galloway continued on his way across the yer, muttering, "I don't know what this place is coming to. amn hotels aren't what they used to be. I should pack my ags and leave."

The front door slammed behind him as Madeline snorted.

"That man should be tied to a tree and left for the wolves" she said, her dark eyes glittering with anger.

"I'm inclined to agree with you," Cecily said, staring once more up the staircase.

To her immense relief, Baxter's tall figure appeared at the second landing. He looked down at her briefly for a moment, then disappeared around the bend. He appeared to be quite calm and collected, as usual, so she had to assume he had not encountered anyone dangerous.

"I had better leave, too, if I am going to rescue this poor baby." Madeline lifted the leaves to her face. "I will see you on Thursday, Cecily."

Cecily watched her go, then turned to meet Baxter, who was now descending the last few steps.

"Did you see anyone?" she asked, one hand straying to her throat.

"Yes, madam, I saw someone. I literally ran into Lady Belleville on the top landing."

"No one else? Someone must have been there to throw a heavy earthenware pot full of dirt from the top landing."

"Unless Lady Belleville has muscles of steel, whoever it was must have escaped down the back stairs." Baxter paused, staring thoughtfully at the ceiling. "Of course, I have heard of insanity lending superior strength. Perhaps she did manage to lift the pot after all."

Frustrated, Cecily stared at the pile of dirt and shattered pottery. "If she didn't, I would very much like to know who did."

"It could have been anyone, madam. The front door is never locked during the day, and anyone could have walked in."

Full of apprehension, she met his gaze. "George?"

"It is a possibility, madam. I think now is a good time

:ontact the police and tell them what we know. Colonel
Fortescue's life is obviously in danger."

"Someone must have heard me talking to the colonel
about what he saw on the Downs. That was extremely
:areless of me."

"So you will talk to the inspector?"

Cecily struggled with indecision for several moments,
then reluctantly shook her head. "I'm sorry, Baxter. While I
agree that someone apparently tried to silence the colonel,
and that someone could be the murderer, we still have no
idea of his identity."

"If I may remind you, madam, it is the inspector's job to
find that out."

"Granted. But since the police are convinced the murderer is a gypsy, they are not prepared to take this matter too
seriously. They could very well come here and disrupt this
hotel with their questioning, without having any intention of
pursuing the matter."

"Not if they suspect one of our guests to be the murderer."

"But we don't know that, Baxter. All we have are the
notes from someone who thinks he knows who killed those
women."

"And an attempted murder right here in this hotel."

"But, as you so rightly pointed out, that could have been
anyone. Not necessarily a guest."

Baxter stared at her in silence for a moment. "I can see
you will not change your mind," he said at last. "I can only
hope that you are not endangering the lives of other people
with your stubbornness. In any case, the colonel should be
warned."

"I agree." Frustrated, Cecily tossed the problem around in
her mind. Finally she said tentatively, "What do you think
about the possibility of sending the colonel down the
George and Dragon with a note for Michael? I could simply

tell him to keep the colonel there and watch over him for a day or two. Knowing my son, he would do as I ask without too many questions."

"And what would your son tell the colonel in order to prolong his visit?"

Cecily smiled. "I'm quite sure Michael can find a way to confuse the colonel enough that he won't know what is going on."

"By filling him full of gin, I presume. No doubt the ploy will be successful, though I'm not at all sure it is ethical."

Uncomfortable at the thought, Cecily changed the subject. "I hope Lady Belleville accepted your story of the search last night?"

"She accepted the fact that I searched. She did not, however, accept the fact that her ridiculous make-believe bird cannot be found. She is still insisting on a thorough search of the guest rooms. She is now convinced that one of our guests has stolen the canary, and she is demanding that we take immediate action to recover her property."

"I see." In spite of her anxiety over the fallen pot, Cecily could not suppress a smile.

"I fail to share your amusement in this ludicrous situation," Baxter said, pulling his shoulders back in a stiff pose. "It is beyond my understanding why we have to humor such eccentricity, particularly when it interferes with the task of conducting the business matters of this hotel. I really do not have the time to deal with such frivolity."

Or the patience, Cecily added to herself. "Leave Lady Belleville to me," she said aloud. "I will try to the best of my ability to pacify her. We cannot have the guests disturbed by her rantings. If she doesn't behave, I shall have to ask her to leave."

Baxter raised his eyebrows. "Thank you, madam. I am happy you see things my way."

"We can only hope she doesn't spread the word of our shortcomings when she returns to London."

"I am quite sure that anyone who is familiar with the Pennyfoot will not listen to the crazed ravings of a demented old woman, any more than they listen to the unfortunate stories of Colonel Fortescue."

"I sincerely hope you are right." Cecily glanced at the grandfather clock in the foyer. "I had better go down to the kitchen and get this mess cleaned up. I'm surprised Mrs. Chubb hasn't come running to find out what the noise was all about."

"I believe she is visiting her daughter this morning," Baxter said. "I will be happy to go to the kitchen, if you prefer, madam?"

Cecily shook her head. "No, I would like to see how well Doris is learning the kitchen chores. Thank you, Baxter, but I prefer to go myself."

"Very well, madam." He cast a glance up the stairs as if still hoping to catch sight of the culprit, then strode off down the hallway toward his office.

Standing at the sink, Gertie paused in the task of scrubbing a carrot. From the scullery came the sweetest voice she had ever heard, singing a romantic ballad she didn't recognize.

Very slowly Gertie put the carrot back into the water and laid the brush down on the draining board. She'd never heard Doris sing before. She'd never heard anyone sing that good before, not even in the church choir. But then, everyone sounded bloody awful in the church choir.

Creeping across the kitchen to the scullery door, Gertie stood and listened. The notes seemed to rise and fall without effort, making her think of soppy things like punting on the river on a hot summer day, or dancing under the stars on a balmy night, or holding her cheek against the velvet-soft skin of a baby.

She hugged herself, swaying to the music, then her thoughts scattered when the singing was cut off abruptly by a loud sneeze. At the same moment something crashed to the floor, followed by Doris's wail.

"Oh, blimey," Gertie muttered, and rushed into the scullery.

Doris stood by the window, staring at her feet where a large puddle of milk spread rapidly across the floor.

"Flipping heck, Doris, look what you've gone and done now. That was me milk what I was supposed to drink for the baby."

Doris promptly burst into tears. "I'm sorry, Miss Brown, honest I am. It was the cat what made me sneeze. I frightened it, and it knocked the jug down when it went out the window."

"Bleeding cats should all be drowned at birth, that's what I say," Gertie muttered. "You'd better get this bloody mess cleaned up before Mrs. Chubb gets an eyeful of it."

"Yes, miss." Doris flew to the sink and began running the cold water into a bucket.

Gertie waited for her to finish before she could get back to her carrots. "I heard you singing in there," she said as Doris steadied the heavy bucket on the edge of the sink. "You sounded a bit of all right, I must say."

Doris's face turned pink with pleasure. "Thank you, I'm sure. I like to sing."

"So do I, but I don't sound like that. You should have lessons. You could be on the stage one day."

Doris turned sparkling eyes on her. "Oh, do you really think so? I want that so much. I want to sing in all the big Variety halls in London."

"Variety?" Gertie caught hold of the handle as Doris tried

to lug the heavy bucket off the sink. "Here, I'll give you a hand."

"Thank you, Miss Brown. That's very kind of you, I'm sure."

"S'all right." Gertie helped her carry the bucket across to the pantry. Watching the girl fall on her knees to swab the creamy puddle, she waited a minute, then said, "Whatcha want to go and do that for?"

Doris looked up with a startled expression. "Do what, miss?"

"Sing in Variety. I mean, that's a bit common, isn't it? Why don't you do something posh like opera? There's an opera singer going to be at the ball on Thursday. Perhaps madam will let you go and listen to her."

"I don't want to sing opera," Doris said, wringing out the heavy cloth. A stream of muddy white water swirled into the bucket, clouding the contents. "I want to sing Variety."

"But why?" Gertie itched to take the cloth from the housemaid's feeble fingers, but held herself back. She couldn't be behind the twit all the time.

"Because it's more fun." Doris looked up with a shy smile. "And because I want to meet a toff," she added, a flush creeping over her cheeks. "They admire the singers on the Variety stage. I heard they line up at the stage door to meet them, and they take them out and buy them fancy gifts and take them to fancy restaurants for dinner. Some of them even get married."

"You've been reading too many of them women's magazines," Gertie said scornfully. "Cor blimey, Doris, wake up. Toffs don't marry the likes of us. They might want to take the singers out for a cheap thrill, but they don't marry them. Toffs only marry toffs, you mark my words."

"Yes, miss." Doris went on mopping up the floor, but Gertie had the distinct feeling that the housemaid wasn't listening. The little twerp had made up her mind she was going to meet a toff, and no one was going to tell her otherwise.

She'll learn, Gertie thought, as she went back to scrubbing carrots. She could almost feel sorry for the poor kid. She had a lot to learn, and none of it was going to be that bloody marvelous.

Cecily wasn't entirely surprised to discover another note lying on her carpet that evening. In fact, she would have been quite disappointed had it not been there. Eagerly opening the folded sheet, she carried it closer to the lamp for a better look. Maybe this time, she thought hopefully, there would be a clue as to the author.

As always, the writing scrambled across the page in an untidy scrawl. *George hates gypsies. Tell the one who came today not to come back. If she does, George will kill her.*

Cecily stared down at the page, her enthusiasm swiftly fading. The note had to be referring to Madeline. That meant whoever dropped the flowerpot that morning had waited around long enough to see her.

If it had been anyone other than a guest, he would surely have been noticed, since Baxter must have reached the top landing before Madeline had arrived.

Pacing the thick carpet, Cecily concentrated on the events that morning. Three people could have seen Madeline enter or leave the hotel. Lady Belleville would have had a clear view of the lobby from the top landing. Cyril Plunkett had passed by Madeline on his way out of the hotel, as had Ellsworth Galloway.

It would seem, Cecily thought dismally, that one of her guests could very well be a murderer after all.

CHAPTER

❧ 14 ❧

Gertie could not get the sound of Doris's voice out of her head. She woke up with the melody running through her mind the next morning, and even found herself humming the tune as she poured cold water into the washbowl from the jug.

Shivering, she stripped off her flannel nightgown. She couldn't wait until she could go into the kitchen and warm her bum in front of the stove.

Splashing cold water on her face, she thought again about Doris. The girl was bleeding marvelous with that voice. Wouldn't it be something if she, Gertie Brown, discovered her? Then, when Doris was rich and famous, she'd remember the poor sod who'd helped her. Perhaps she'd even make her manager or something.

Carried away by her fantasies, Gertie finished her wash, then got into her clothes as fast as her bulky stomach would allow.

The kitchen felt no warmer than her room when she carried the oil lamp in there a few minutes later. Still humming Doris's tune, she lit the gas lamps, then laid newspaper in the grate and the sticks crisscrossed on top. After picking out small lumps of coal, she carefully balanced them on top of the sticks, then reached up for the matches on the mantelpiece.

A loud sneeze behind her scared her half out of her wits. Dropping the matches, she swung around to face Doris, who stood wiping her nose on her sleeve. "Bloody hell, Doris, why do you always have to creep up on me like that? Scared me half to death, you did."

"Next time I'll scream at the top of me lungs," Doris said in the surly tone that warned Gertie she was in one of her bad moods.

"Awright, Miss Smartmouth, you don't have to give me any bleeding cheek. Pick them matches up for me, please. I can't get down there to get them."

Doris looked for a moment as if she would refuse then, apparently having second thoughts, stooped to pick up the matches. "I'm going out to chop the sticks," she said, handing the box over. Before Gertie could answer her, she'd marched out of the back door and into the yard.

Gertie stared after her in mute resentment. The girl didn't deserve her help. Still, she did have a beautiful voice, and something ought to be done about it. Maybe Ellsworth Galloway could do something to help her.

Making up her mind to talk to him about it at the first opportunity, Gertie reached down to light the fire. She was lifting a tub of water onto the stove when Doris came back from the yard, a sack of firewood in her hands.

"There's an axe missing again," she said shortly as she dumped the sack on the floor.

Gertie turned to face her, wincing as a sharp pain caught her low in the belly. "I thought there was two of them out there."

Doris answered her with a loud sneeze, then wiped her nose on her sleeve again. "There was." She opened the sack and started emptying the sticks into the wood bin. "But someone must have taken one of them again. 'Cause now there's only one."

"The message is obviously referring to Madeline," Cecily said, having handed the latest note to Baxter in his office. "Which means that the murderer has to be one of three people."

Quickly she explained her reasoning, while Baxter stood at his desk slowly nodding his head. When she was finished, he looked down at her, his brow creased in concern.

"I do hope, madam, that you will now take my advice and give this information to the police."

"Not yet, Baxter." She saw the frown darken his face and added hurriedly, "I have a plan."

His look of despair made her feel quite sorry for him. "A plan," he repeated in a voice of doom.

"Yes, Baxter, a plan. Since we have now narrowed the field down to three people, it should be quite a simple matter to search their rooms while they are at breakfast."

Baxter propped his hands on his desk and closed his eyes. "Search their rooms. I seem to remember having done this before."

"Yes, Baxter. Several times, in fact. That should make us quite expert at the task by now, wouldn't you say?"

"Expert criminals, yes, madam."

Cecily let out a gusty sigh. "Piffle, Baxter. We are simply saving the constabulary a job and protecting our guests at the same time."

"And what if someone should return to the room while we are in the process of searching it?"

Cecily smiled in triumph. "We have the perfect excuse, of course."

Baxter raised an eyebrow. "We do?"

"We most certainly do."

"Perhaps you'd care to share it with me?"

"You are the one who created it."

His mouth tightened. "I would appreciate it, madam, if you would stop playing games and explain what you mean."

Taking pity on him, she gave him a broad smile. "Did you or did you not, Baxter, tell Lady Belleville that you would search the guests' rooms for her canary?"

For a long moment his narrowed gaze rested on her face. Then he said quietly, "Madam, you are quite devious."

"Thank you, Baxter."

"And quite clever, I might add."

"For a woman?"

He wouldn't be drawn into that familiar argument. Instead he said soberly, "You are aware, I hope, that you could be wrong in your assumption. There could have been a fourth person on the stairs who simply managed to escape my observance."

"It is possible, I agree, but unlikely. Besides, whoever wrote the notes must be fully aware of the murderer's movements. That would indicate that it is someone in this hotel, would it not?"

"I'm afraid I must agree. Which brings us back to Colonel Fortescue. Has he left the hotel yet?"

"Yesterday afternoon," Cecily assured him, trying to

ignore the stab of guilt. "I told Michael in the note to keep the colonel there as long as possible, at least until I let him know it's safe for him to come back."

"I don't know why we just didn't send him back to London," Baxter muttered. "He would have been a great deal safer."

"And it would have been far more difficult to persuade him to go. You know how much he's looking forward to the fireworks display."

"And what if we haven't learned the identity of our murderer by then?"

Cecily raised her chin. "We shall just have to hope that we do so before the fifth. We'll have a house full of guests, all at the mercy of a killer, if indeed he is in the hotel."

Baxter sighed heavily. "Have you considered the possibility that if we do uncover the murderer during this search, he might attempt to silence us if he discovers us in his suite?"

"Well, naturally, we shall do everything we can to avoid being caught. I am merely saying that should we be interrupted, we do at least have an excuse why we are there."

"And what if we discover that one of our guests is indeed the murderer?"

"Then I suppose we shall have to do what we usually do. Find a way to incriminate him."

"I see." His tone suggested she had just stated the impossible.

Cecily smiled and rose to her feet. "Come now, Baxter. Where is your spirit of adventure? Your trust?"

"It is my spirit of adventure and trust that allows you to lead me into perilous situations, madam. One of which, I fear, will someday be the death of us."

Cecily quietened the little stab of apprehension his words

produced. "We have always managed admirably in the past, Baxter. No doubt we shall do so again. Now, let us go to the foyer so that we can be sure all three guests are in the dining room for breakfast. The gong should sound anytime now."

Even as she spoke the metallic boom of the gong echoed throughout the hotel.

"The voice of judgment," Baxter remarked dryly, as he followed her out of the office. "I sincerely hope this won't prove to be our undoing."

Cecily silently echoed that sentiment as she led the way to the foyer.

"Go on, sing for them," Gertie said as Doris stood in front of the kitchen door with her lips clamped tightly together.

"Maybe she does not care to sing," Michel said as he threw a handful of herbs into the oxtail soup. "One can only sing with the mouth when the heart sings, also."

"She loves singing, she told me." Gertie looked at the rebellious housemaid. "Tell them what you told me."

"I can't sing," Doris said flatly.

"Yes, you can. I heard you yesterday."

"Never mind, Gertie," Mrs. Chubb said, lightly patting Doris's shoulder. "Maybe she'll sing for us later, when she feels better."

"I tell you I can't sing. I never could. It's—" She broke off, and Gertie uttered a loud sniff.

"She's bleeding lying. I heard her singing. She told me she wants to go on the stage, she did." Her voice rose in frustration. "I flipping heard you. Why are you making me out to be a bloody liar?"

Michel banged a lid down on the saucepan. "I do not care to hear her sing. So just let her be."

"I want her to sing so I can prove I'm not lying."

"All right," Doris said, glaring at Gertie. "If you want me

sing, I'll sing. But I've got a cold in me nose, so I'll sound terrible."

Gertie folded her arms in triumph. "Go on, then. Sing that one what you sang yesterday. It was really pretty."

Doris frowned. "I don't remember what I was singing yesterday."

Beginning to lose her patience altogether, Gertie said, "You know, that one what goes . . ." She hummed a few bars of the melody that had haunted her all night.

"Mercy," Michel said, throwing up his hands. "I certainly hope she can sing better than that."

"Put a sock in it, Michel," Gertie said rudely. "Wait until you hear her."

"There's no need to be insolent, my girl," Mrs. Chubb said as Michel banged another lid down. "Now, Doris, why don't you let us hear you sing? It sounds like such a nice song."

Gertie nodded in satisfaction. "Yeah, go on, sing it." Looking at Mrs. Chubb, she added, "She's really good, she is."

"All right, but don't say I didn't warn you." Standing in the middle of the kitchen floor, Doris opened her mouth and bellowed out the first few notes of the song.

"*Sacre bleu!*" Michel cried, covering his ears with his hands. "What is that?"

Doris stopped the awful noise and tossed her head. "It's me singing," she said. "I told you I couldn't sing and I can't. So there." With that, she flounced to the door and disappeared.

Gertie stared after her, speechless for once.

"The girl is right," Michel muttered. "She sounds like a cat with its tail caught in the door."

"She certainly doesn't seem to have much chance of

being on the stage, that's for sure," Mrs. Chubb said, hurrying over to the sink.

Gertie finally found her voice. "I don't bloody believe it, I don't. You should have heard her yesterday. Sounded like a bleeding nightingale, she did. Now she sounds like a sick cow."

"Maybe she is just having a bad day," Michel said, tasting the soup on the end of his ladle. "She says she has the cold. No one can sing with the cold. Not even Michel, the greatest chef in the world."

"Sez who?" Gertie muttered.

"Come now, Gertie," Mrs. Chubb said in her stern voice, "we have work to do. We can't stand around chattering all day. Those serviettes have to be ironed and folded. Madam is expecting a large crowd for the ball this weekend."

"She bleeding did it on purpose," Gertie announced, reaching into the corner cupboard for the irons. "I know she did. She wanted to make a fool of me, that's what. I'll bloody get her for that, I will."

She stomped across the tiled floor and dropped the iron stands on top of the stove, then stood the irons on them. "Ungrateful little bugger. To think I was going to help her become rich and famous. See if I do anything for her again. I was going to ask Mr. Galloway to listen to her. She can go to—"

Michel snorted in amusement while Mrs. Chubb snapped, "Gertie, that's enough."

Gertie dragged the basket containing the laundered serviettes across the floor. She longed to say more but decided she'd better keep her mouth shut. She didn't know why Mrs. Chubb was standing up for Doris, but she knew better than to argue with that tone of voice.

For several minutes no one spoke as they went about their chores. Gertie managed to relieve some of her frustration by

amming the iron down extra hard onto the thick linen
rviettes.

The housekeeper finished sorting out the silverware, then
me over to start counting the neatly ironed serviettes
owing in a pile on the table.

Gertie kept her head down, still smarting from the
justice handed to her.

Finally Mrs. Chubb must have realized how upset she
as, for she said quietly, "We have to make allowances for
e girl, Gertie. She has had a rough upbringing, the poor
ar."

"None of us has exactly been raised in bleeding luxury."
ertie lifted an iron from the stove and spat on it, producing
loud sizzle. "What makes her so special?"

"She was badly beaten by her aunt, so madam tells me,"
rs. Chubb said, laying the serviettes on a large silver tray.
Madam says the child has got terrible scars all over her
dy. She still has a burn on her back where the woman hit
r with a smoldering hot poker. Haven't you ever noticed
at she never leans back in a chair? That's because her back
ill hurts her."

Gertie felt a stirring of pity for the young girl. "Gawd,
w bloody awful," she said, attacking the next serviette.
No wonder she's so flipping moody."

"Yes, well, I know it can be irritating." Mrs. Chubb
cked up the tray in both hands. "Perhaps if we are all extra
ce to her, she'll come out of those bad moods. Sometimes
e can be very sweet, you know."

"Yeah, I know." Gertie stood the iron back on its stand.
t's not like the same person at all, at times. It's bloody hard
know how to treat someone like that."

"Treat her with kindness," Michel said, "and sooner or
ter she will . . . how you say . . . recapitate."

"What?" Gertie stared at him. "I thought that meant cho someone's head off."

"That's *de*capitate." Mrs. Chubb carried the tray to th door and paused. "I think Michel meant reciprocate."

"No matter," Michel said, turning back to his soup.

"You know," Gertie said thoughtfully, "wouldn't it b something if Doris was the one what was chopping people heads off? Per'aps she's trying to get back at her aunt f beating her up."

"Mercy me," Mrs. Chubb said, hooking the door ope with her foot, "what nonsense you do come up wit sometimes. However could you think that child coul possibly be going around murdering people? Whatev next."

Gertie tossed her head in defiance. "It might sound lik bleeding nonsense to you, but who is it what keeps losir the flipping axe? You answer me that."

Cecily waited impatiently as Baxter fitted his master ke into the lock on Lady Belleville's door.

"There is something slightly amiss with your reckoning he said, as the door slid quietly open. "Lady Belleville aske me to inspect the other guests' rooms. Not her own. I woul assume she has already performed a meticulous search her own environment."

"No doubt," Cecily said. "That is why I suggeste starting with her suite. It will be some time before anyor will be finished with breakfast, so we are in little danger being interrupted by Lady Belleville, at least."

"It is those words, 'at least,' that I find most trouble some," Baxter muttered as he entered the dowager's draw ing room.

Cecily followed him in and closed the door behind he "The boudoir first, I think. I'll look in the chest of drawe while you search the wardrobe." She hurried through the door to the boudoir and crossed the room to where the ornate chest stood in the corner.

"Perhaps madam would be so kind as to inform me what exactly we are looking for?" Baxter inquired from the doorway.

"Clothes, Baxter. Bloodstains. I doubt very much if murders as messy as these ones could be carried out without a great deal of blood."

"Without question. But I would expect someone as treacherous as the murderer would also be astute enough to discard the clothing."

Cecily pulled open a drawer and peered inside. "That's entirely possible, of course. But he or she might have missed something, such as shoes, gloves, a handkerchief, perhaps."

"Very well." Baxter opened the door of the wardrobe with a loud squeak. "But I must tell you, madam, I find the task of going through a woman's personal clothing most distasteful."

"Then it's just as well you have never married, Baxter," Cecily said lightly.

Baxter loudly cleared his throat, but refrained from answering her.

Cecily worked in silence for several minutes, carefully sorting through the neat piles of underwear in a way that would leave them apparently undisturbed.

Having gone through the entire contents without finding anything unusual, she then decided to peer under the bed. Baxter, it seemed, was still engrossed in the wardrobe.

It was necessary to lie facedown on the carpet and wriggle under the bed in order to have a clear view. Spread-eagled on her stomach, Cecily eased herself under the springs until she could see the entire area.

A pair of gray kid shoes lay just beyond reach, apparentl[y] having been kicked there by an impatient foot. Wriggling i[n] further, Cecily touched one of them with the tips of he[r] fingers and managed to draw it toward her.

It was unlikely that anyone would wear shoes such as thi[s] to commit a murder, she thought, but she never liked t[o] leave a stone unturned.

Finding the shoe unmarked, she wriggled further unde[r] the bed and drew the second one toward her. She coul[d] make out a dark smudge on that one, though it was difficu[lt] to tell in the dark shadows beneath the bed.

Deciding to pull the shoes out to take a better look, Cecil[y] started wriggling backward from beneath the bed. Almos[t] immediately she jerked to a stop when her bun caught in on[e] of the springs, holding her fast.

No matter how she tried, she could not get her hand int[o] a position to unsnag herself.

Finally she had to admit defeat. In a small voice she said[,] "Baxter? I need some assistance here."

His voice sounded muffled as he answered. "Madam?"

Realizing he must still have his head inside the wardrobe[,] she spoke a little louder. "I said, I need your assistance, i[f] you please."

This time his answer came quite clearly. "Right away[,] madam."

She could see his black shoes on the other side of the bed[.] They crossed the carpet and disappeared. He must hav[e] thought she was in the drawing room.

Waiting impatiently, she saw his feet come back into th[e] boudoir. "Madam? Are you in here?"

"Yes, I'm in here, Baxter. I'm under the bed."

The shoes hesitated for a moment, then walked carefull[y] around the bed. "Goodness, gracious!" Baxter said. "Wha[t] in heaven's name are you doing down there?"

"Counting the orchids in the carpet," Cecily said, losing
her patience. "What do you think I'm doing, Baxter? I'm
searching under the bed, of course."

"Yes, madam. I assumed that. I was merely wondering in
what way I can assist you?"

"You can unhook my hair from the springs. It's caught up
somewhere, and I can't move."

Baxter's knees cracked sharply as he crouched down
beside her. "You are not able to free youself, madam?"

"No, Baxter, I am not. Now, will you please reach in and
unhook me? I think a hairpin must have caught in one of the
springs. I can't get free without pulling out a large clump of
hair, which would be painful to say the least."

"Very well, madam, but I can't promise not to hurt you."

Cecily sighed. "That's quite all right, Baxter. You can't
hurt me any more than I'm hurting right now. But, please,
do try not to leave the major part of my hair hanging on the
bedsprings."

"Yes, madam." There was a slight pause, then a cough.
"Madam?"

Cecily closed her eyes. Any movement was painful, and
she preferred not to crane her neck to look at him. "Yes,
Baxter?"

"I shall have to . . . er . . . lie down in order to reach
your head."

"Baxter, just do whatever you have to do, but please
hurry. I should really hate it if Lady Belleville were to return
and find me in this position."

"Yes, madam."

It really felt most peculiar to be lying there on the floor
with Baxter wriggling alongside of her. She could hear his
breath. He sounded as if he'd been running uphill. Then she
couldn't hear him breathe at all as he slid his fingers over
the top of her head.

"Ouch," she said as a sharp prick of pain stabbed throug her scalp.

"I do beg your pardon, madam, but I have almost got If you would just hold still . . ."

"I am holding still," Cecily said crossly. "I cannot much else while I'm held fast like this."

The door opened without warning, allowing whoever ha entered to hear the latter part of the conversation. Besid her, she felt Baxter go rigid, as a shocked gasp erupted fro the doorway. Then a soft voice said breathlessly, "Plea excuse me. I'll come back later."

The door closed with a firm thud.

CHAPTER

❈15❈

ho do you suppose it was?" Baxter whispered urgently.
Cecily eased her head sideways to look at him. His face
s quite close to hers, and she could see his look of
guish. "One of the maids, I presume," she whispered
k. "Most likely here to clean the room."

"I'm aware of that, madam. But which one? Good Lord,
t was Gertie—"

"I don't think it was Gertie. It sounded like Doris."

"Do you think she recognized us?"

Cecily couldn't answer, except to give a slight shake of
head. The resulting tug on her hair brought tears to her
s.

"Madam? You are trembling. Are you all right?"

She struggled valiantly for several moments, then co
hold it in no longer. Her laugh exploded, spilling the te
on her cheeks.

After a long pause, in which she did her best to con
her mirth, Baxter said in a strange voice, "This really is
laughing matter, madam. Heaven knows what the child v
say to spread gossip around the staff."

"Maybe so, Baxter, but you have to admit it must h
been quite a sight to see the two of us sprawled beneath
bed."

"I would hazard a guess that your words served
confuse the issue even more."

"If taken out of context. I have to agree with you the
"Yes, madam."

He made an odd sound, and she peered at him, trying
see his expression more clearly. "Did you say somethi
Baxter?"

He shook his head, his lips pressed together.

"That wasn't a laugh I heard, was it?"

To her great delight, he answered her with a soft chuck

"There you are," she said, feeling very pleased w
herself. "It does one good to laugh once in a while, do
you agree?"

"Perhaps. I do feel somewhat concerned, however, ab
the possible repercussions. I should release you from yo
bondage before someone else discovers us in this m
compromising position."

She lay still while he worked at her hair, and breathe
sigh of relief when he finally released the painful hold. S
waited a moment or two while he slid out from the bed, th
followed him out.

Dusting herself down, she felt a little self-conscio
"Thank you, Baxter. I don't know how I should ha

naged without you. I would have had to wait until
neone came to rescue me."

"We can only hope that our reputations are not sullied
ond salvation," Baxter said soberly.

'I doubt if our intruder recognized us in that position."

Baxter shuddered. "I sincerely hope not, madam. I loathe
dwell on the tale that could evolve from this incident,
ce embellished by gossiping tongues."

"Probably no more than any other time." She gave him a
cked grin. "This isn't the first time we have been
covered in a compromising position. Though I must
nit, this was the most painful."

Baxter's morose expression changed swiftly. "I do hope I
n't hurt you, madam? Your hair was in quite a tangle."

"You were very gentle, Baxter. Thank you."

"Yes, madam."

His gaze warmed, and she raised a hand to her head,
are that she must look quite frightful. "I think I had better
something about this," she said, moving over to Lady
lleville's dressing table. "If someone sees me like this,
ere will be more fuel for the gossip."

She peered into the mirror, doing her best to repair the
mage done by the bedsprings. After securing the bun once
ore, she tucked all loose strands inside and pinned them.
nally satisfied, she patted her handiwork, saying, "This is
e best I can do, but it will have to suffice for now."

"If I might be permitted to say so, madam, you look
peccable, as always."

Meeting his gaze in the mirror, she felt her cheeks warm.
Vhy, thank you, Baxter. That's one of the nicest things
u've ever said to me."

"Yes, madam." He fidgeted for a moment, then cleared
s throat. "I think it might be prudent to leave this suite,
fore Doris returns."

"Yes, you are right, of course." Giving herself one l[ast] glance in the mirror, she headed across the room to the do[or]. "Well, at least we shan't be disturbed in the other t[wo] rooms. The maids have finished cleaning that floor by no[w]."

"Yes, madam."

He sounded unhappy, and she knew he was concern[ed] about the risks they were taking. Poor Baxter, she thought [as] they trudged up the stairs, he really did have to put up w[ith] a lot from her. She should take more care to av[oid] embarrassing him in front of the staff.

Even so, it was his chuckle that stayed with her throu[gh]out the rest of the day, and the intimate moments they h[ad] shared lying together beneath the bed in Lady Bellevill[e's] boudoir.

"Are you sure the axe is gone again?" Mrs. Chubb aske[d] staring at Gertie in dismay.

"That's what Doris says." Gertie rolled up her sleeves [in] order to attack the dishes. "She says there was the two [of] them there, and now there's only one again."

"Mercy me." Mrs. Chubb dropped the tray on the tab[le] and clutched her throat. "Makes me go cold again, it do[es]. What if it's the murderer who's taking it to kill those po[or] women? What if he decides to turn on us here at the hote[l]? We could have a mad killer lurking about waiting to ch[op] off our heads."

"That would certainly help to make things quieter arou[nd] here," Michel muttered, slamming a pot down on the stov[e].

"Don't be daft," Gertie said as she plunged her hands in[to] the soapy water. "He only kills bleeding gypsies, don't h[e]. And what makes you think it's our axe he's using? It wou[ld] be all bloodied, wouldn't it?"

"Not if he washed it all off, it wouldn't."

"Well, then, why would he go to all that trouble to put [it]

ack, if he's going to use it again? Seems to me he'd be
linking stupid to take the chance of being caught. Why
oesn't he just keep it? Don't make bloody sense, does it?"

"I don't know." Mrs. Chubb opened a cupboard door and
rought out a tub of flour. "All I know is it gives me the
reeps, what with the murders and all, and our axe coming
nd going like it has legs. It must be someone in the hotel
king it, or else we would see someone strange walking
round."

Gertie sniffed and rubbed her nose with the back of her
and. "Well, if you ask me, I don't think the blinking axe is
iissing at all. I think it's that bleeding Doris what's playing
ames. She's bleeding barmy, that girl."

"I told you why she's like that," Mrs. Chubb said,
anging the flour bin down on the table. "Sometimes I think
'm talking out the back of my head. You don't hear half of
vhat I say, you girls. Where is Doris anyway?"

"She's cleaning the rooms. She started late this morning.
aid she had a cold and didn't feel well." Again Gertie
niffed. "Bleeding gave it to me, an' all, I shouldn't wonder.
feel bloody horrible today."

Mrs. Chubb gave her a quick look of concern. "You all
ight, duck? You do look a bit peaky. Not having any pains,
re you?"

Gertie shrugged. "I'm all right," she said gruffly. "Just
ired of lugging all this weight around on me stomach, that's
ll."

Mrs. Chubb started to answer, but just then the door
pened, and Doris walked in, a sullen look on her face.

"All finished, are we, then?" the housekeeper said, busily
neasuring flour into a large earthenware bowl.

"No, I didn't do Lady Belleville. Someone was in the
oom with her when I got there so I said as how I'd go back
ater."

Mrs. Chubb stopped measuring and stared at her. "Some one was in the room? Who was it, then?"

"Dunno. All I saw was their feet."

Gertie put down the soapy plate she was holding. "Their feet? That old hag had someone in bed with her? Coblimey, what's she say when you went in?"

"Nuffing. And they wasn't in the bed. They were under it."

Doris crossed the kitchen and went into the scullery to put away the brooms and brushes.

Mrs. Chubb and Gertie exchanged a long glance. "See? I told you she was blooming barmy," Gertie whispered.

Mrs. Chubb shook her head, as if trying to make sense of everything. "Well, you'd better go in there and tell her she has to go back and clean that room before noon. The guests will be arriving tomorrow for the weekend, and we have to keep those fires going. It will take her all afternoon to keep an eye on them, that it will."

Gertie sighed and dragged her arms out of the water. Drying them on her apron, she trudged across the floor to the scullery.

When she reached the door she saw Doris standing by the shelves, holding a large black cat in her arms. She was speaking to it in a low soft voice, her fingers gently stroking its ears.

"Here!" Gertie said sharply. "Whatcha doing with that cat? That's a bleeding stray, that is. You know we're not supposed to make a fuss of them or we'll never be bleeding rid of them. Mrs. Chubb'll have your blinking head."

The cat sprang from Doris's arms at the sound of Gertie's voice and vanished through the door. "I was just comforting it," Doris muttered. "I tripped over it and I thought it might be hurt."

"You can't hurt them bleeding cats. Any rate, serves them

eeding right for coming scrounging in here, bringing their
ipping fleas with them."

Remembering why she was there, Gertie added belliger-
atly, "And Mrs. Chubb says you got to clean Lady
elleville's room before noon, 'cause you have to watch the
res this afternoon."

Without a word, Doris gathered up the brooms again and
ished past Gertie, who stood scowling after her. She never
ould understand that girl, she thought as she went back to
ie sink to finish the dishes.

Mrs. Chubb looked up from the table as she passed.
Doris go to clean that room, then?"

"Yeah." Gertie swished her hands in the water and came
p with a stack of saucers. "She's in one of her bleeding
ioods again." She paused as a thought struck her. "You
now what, it's a bleeding funny thing, but Doris never
ould get near a cat without sneezing. Now all of a sudden
ie's in there cuddling one and not sneezing at all."

"Maybe it was just her cold coming on before," Mrs.
'hubb said. "Anyhow, we can't stand here gossiping about
ie poor child all day. Get on with those dishes or you'll still
e standing there when Michel gets back."

Bleeding heck, Gertie thought, wiping her nose on the
ack of her hand. She couldn't do nothing right, and that
leeding Doris couldn't do nothing wrong.

One by one she stacked the saucers onto the draining
oard, her mind still on the vision of Doris holding the cat
ractically under her nose without so much as a sniffle.

Nothing," Cecily said in disgust as she and Baxter left
llsworth Galloway's room. "I thought we should find at
east some small spot of blood somewhere to give us the
dentity of the murderer."

"I believe we have learned something, at least," Baxter said as he followed her down the stairs.

"What's that?" Cecily had only half her mind on the conversation. She was still thinking about Baxter's chuck as he lay beside her on the floor. She had heard him laug so rarely. If only he would shed that reserve that restricte him, and allow himself to relax and enjoy life.

He could be such wonderful company. He was s dependable, loyal, and completely trustworthy. How sh adored his dry sense of humor and the intelligence th enabled him to give her a good argument now and agai She could enjoy life so much with a man like that, sl thought wistfully.

"I would venture to say," Baxter said from behind he "that the lack of evidence would indicate that none of tl three persons whose rooms we have searched are guilty these murders."

Dragging her mind back to the discussion, Cecily sighe "It would appear that way. I can't imagine how anyo could commit such a gruesome crime without leaving son trace of blood on their belongings. Particularly if they a staying in the hotel."

"There is one more possibility, of course," Baxter said they reached the foot of the stairs. "It is one that I have th utmost regret in considering, of course."

"Yes." Cecily looked at him, knowing exactly how h felt. "I have also come to that conclusion. There is th possibility that the murderer could be one of our staff her at the Pennyfoot."

"Yes, madam. Either that, or the person writing th notes."

"I have a theory about those notes, Baxter. Perhaps w can go to your office, where I'll explain without fear being overheard."

Baxter looked up the stairwell, as if expecting to see flowerpot come hurtling down on them. "Of course, adam."

He led the way down the hallway, while Cecily followed, eling subdued now that her manager was back to his rmer controlled self.

The delightful times when he allowed himself a brief spite from his dutiful attitude toward her were all too frequent. And as always, his retreat to normal left her with feeling of frustration and disappointment.

She shook off her melancholy when she sat down at his :sk a few moments later. "I think this is the perfect time to ijoy one of your cigars, Baxter," she said, giving him her ide smile. "If you would be so kind as to offer me one of em?"

"If I may say so, madam, I think you are smoking entirely o much lately," Baxter said, giving her a stern look. "It is ost harmful to your health."

"Smoking is not beneficial to your health either, but you ontinue to enjoy the habit," Cecily reminded him. "Be-des, anything that can relax me as well as a cigar does, in't be that hazardous for my well-being."

"I have a very strong sense of guilt every time I light up ne of the pesky things for you. It just isn't proper for a lady) smoke. I can't help feeling that had James not died—"

"Had James not died," Cecily cut in before he could nish, "a great many things would be different."

Seeing his hurt expression, she changed her tone. "As I m constantly pointing out, Baxter, we are living in a nanging world, where women are doing all sorts of things ey wouldn't have dreamed of a few years ago."

"That doesn't mean it's fitting, or even beneficial. I fear iat one day women will achieve the independence they rave, only to find themselves no longer cherished and

protected by the men they have scorned. What will they (
then?"

"Live their lives the way they see fit, instead of bei
governed by tyrants and bullies who believe that women a
merely chattel."

"Not all men consider women as such," Baxter sa
stiffly. "Much as this might surprise you, madam, there a
many men who treasure their wives and appreciate t
companionship and care a good woman can give to h
husband. Did not James value your contribution to yo
marriage?"

"I hope he did." Cecily thought about it for a mome
"Even so, there were certain things he expected of m
certain rigid rules that he expected me to adhere to, whi
were not necessarily to my liking. He treated me well, a
I adored him, but since his death I have come to value n
freedom from the tight reins he held on my life."

The troubled look on Baxter's face deepened. "M
apologies, madam. I had no right to pry into your person
affairs."

She smiled up at him, aware that she had distressed hir
"Not at all, Baxter. In whom can I confide, if not to you, n
most trusted friend?"

"Thank you, madam."

"James and I had a very good marriage," she went o
"and I was devastated to lose him. But I must admit it
refreshing indeed to be treated as a responsible, intellige
person of authority, instead of merely someone's wife."

To her utmost dismay, a shutter seemed to close over h
face. "I will do my very best to bear that in mind," he sa
quietly.

She wished desperately that she could take back thos
words. Although she wasn't quite sure why she wanted to (

, except perhaps, to change that look of rejection in his yes.

"I am no different from thousands of women, in England nd elsewhere," she said a trifle defensively. "All we really ant is to be considered intelligent human beings, with a ght to live our lives the way we choose. The same rights fforded men. Women are not allowed to vote for their hoice of who shall govern them. Why not? Are we so upid, or uninformed, that we cannot make a rational ecision?"

Baxter lifted his hands, then dropped them again. "Not at ll. But the vast majority of men do not care to be married o a woman who is intent on pursuing her own life."

"In that case, women will just have to accept that fact if ley are determined to be independent."

"How do you suppose women would support themselves left to their own devices? They can't all inherit hotels."

Stung by his tone, Cecily retorted, "They are quite apable of earning a living. Many women are employed as ypists, nurses, shop assistants, factory workers, seam-tresses, or even hotel managers."

"But are they receiving a livable wage for that work?" He hook his head, staring off into space as if trying to escape rom the hole he'd dug. "I seriously doubt it."

"Which is exactly why we must have equal pay. That is ll women want, Baxter. We don't want to eradicate all men rom the earth, we just want to live side by side with our ounterparts in harmony and independence, sharing their ves, as partners."

Baxter shifted his gaze back to her face. "While I admire nd respect your views, madam, I would venture to say that ou are an exception among women. I have yet to come cross a woman with your courage and resolve in the face of dversity."

Consoled immeasurably by his words, she smiled at him. "Thank you, Baxter, I greatly appreciate your comments. I must tell you, however, there are many, many women far more courageous than I, and the prisons are full of them."

"Which does not exactly give me peace of mind," Baxter said dryly.

Her smile widened. "Have no fear. I have no intention of chaining myself to fences or setting fire to men's club rooms. I have far more to worry about right here. Which reminds me, may I please enjoy a cigar while I explain to you my theory about the notes?"

He looked at her for a long moment, then pulled the package from his pocket. "I have the distinct impression, madam, that you have already made great strides in your personal quest for independence. No matter how much I protest, I invariably comply with your requests, whether or not they are within the realm of duty. Your every wish is my command, it would seem."

Cecily took the cigar and waited for him to light it. "No, Baxter," she said quietly. "Not always."

He gave her a curious glance, but refrained from questioning her remark. She was rather glad, for she had no idea what she would tell him. She could not tell him what she felt in her heart, even if it were her place to do so.

He would never accept any kind of personal bond between them. Even if he cared for her, she was quite sure he would never allow his feelings to surface. The very strength and resolve she so admired in him was, at the same time, her enemy.

And that, she thought with deep regret, was the saddest thing of all.

CHAPTER
✠16✠

"Madam?"

Cecily looked up to find Baxter eyeing her quizzically. "I'm sorry, Baxter, I was deep in thought."

"I assumed that, madam. This business of murder is troubling you a great deal, I know. At the risk of sounding tiresome, I implore you to seek the help of the police, before the situation escalates beyond our control."

"I will, Baxter, just as soon as I have pinned down the identity of the murderer and can be sure he will be arrested."

Baxter sighed, then apparently discarded the attempt. Instead, in a voice of resignation, he asked, "You say you have a theory about the notes?"

"Yes, I do." Cecily puffed on the cigar, without finding

her usual solace in the aromatic smoke. "I believe the notes were written by the murderer himself. I believe it's his way of drawing attention to himself."

"Why would he do that? Surely the purpose of a man who kills is to divert attention from himself, in order not to be apprehended."

"One would think so. But I read somewhere—I think it might have been in one of my Sherlock Holmes books— that sometimes a man who kills, particularly one who kills more than once, needs the recognition for the murders in order to be fulfilled. I think the murderer is calling himself George in order to escape detection, but is nevertheless informing us of the deed in order to get that recognition."

Baxter looked a trifle pale as he stared down at her. "There are some very sick people in this world," he said slowly. "It worries me a great deal to think it could be someone we know, right inside these walls."

"It worries me, too," Cecily said with feeling. "All our weekend guests will be arriving tomorrow. I'm afraid that many more people will be exposed to the danger."

"Then surely it is now time to discuss the situation with Inspector Cranshaw."

She tapped his desk with her fingernails for a moment, then slowly nodded her head. "Much as I hate to admit defeat, Baxter, this time I'm afraid I might have to do so. If I haven't learned the identity of the murderer by tomorrow night, I will inform the police and allow them to conduct their investigation."

"While I sympathize with your concerns, I would feel a great deal easier if the situation were in their hands," Baxter said.

Cecily shrugged. "I wish I could share your conviction. I still have doubts that the constabulary will take anything I tell them too seriously. The inspector considers me a meddling fool with a wild imagination, who can't keep her nose out of trouble."

Baxter didn't say he agreed with the inspector, but his expression implied it.

Ignoring him, Cecily added, "The inspector is convinced the murders remain the business of the gypsies and should be left to them to deal with, and you know how stubborn and obtuse the inspector can be in such matters."

"Not to mention P.C. Northcott," Baxter added darkly. "Though I have to sympathize with the police in this case. Too often the gypsies have gone to great lengths in order to prevent the constabulary from interfering in their affairs."

"Nevertheless, I must try to find this man. He is a deranged killer and a dangerous menace to society. He must be tracked down and stopped."

"For once," Baxter answered reluctantly, "I must admit I agree with you."

Cecily awoke with a start the next morning, disturbed from her sleep by a persistent tapping on the door. With a feeling of dread she donned her dressing gown and hurried through the drawing room to open the door. She could only hope that her visitor wasn't the bearer of bad news.

To her relief, when she opened the door she saw Doris standing in the hallway holding a steaming jug of hot water in her hands.

"Good morning, mum," the housemaid said shyly. "Gertie's not feeling well, so I brought you your wash water."

Concerned again, Cecily opened the door wider. "It's nice to see you, Doris. There's nothing seriously wrong with Gertie, I hope?"

Doris shook her head and carefully carried the jug to the washbasin. "No, mum, she's just tired, that's all. Mrs.

Chubb thought she shouldn't be climbing the stairs today, so I came instead."

"Well, please tell Gertie that I hope she feels better soon. I'm afraid, though, she will be tired now until the baby is born."

"Yes, mum." Doris poured the water into the basin and stood the jug on its stand.

Cecily watched her for a moment, then said quietly, "Doris, you don't have to stand at the door when you bring water in the morning. Gertie usually brings it in and stands it on the dresser. That way I can have a few moments to wake up, instead of falling out of bed as I am wont to do when woken abruptly."

Doris nodded and bobbed a shaky curtsy. "Yes, mum."

Cecily frowned and tried again to put the girl at ease. "Do you like working here at the Pennyfoot, Doris? Are you happy here with us?"

The thin face broke out in a smile, making her look almost pretty. "Oh, yes, mum. I love it here, I really do. Everyone is so nice to me, and no one hits me, and I have a nice room to sleep in. I just wish—"

She broke off, closing her mouth tight.

Cecily peered closer at the girl. She seemed much too thin, and her color wasn't good. She had a sickly kind of pallor that indicated poor health. The black dress hung on her shoulders and only served to emphasize her ashen complexion.

"Are you not feeling well?" Cecily asked, wishing she had been a little more observant toward her newest servant. "I hope you would tell Mrs. Chubb if you are ill. No one in this hotel has to work if she is not well."

Doris looked a little startled. "No, mum, I am feeling quite well, thank you. I think I might be catching . . ." She hesitated, looking more frightened than ever for a reason

Cecily couldn't fathom. ". . . a cold," she finally finished.

Immediately contrite, Cecily said kindly, "Oh, dear. I'm afraid this damp cold weather causes a lot of ills. Perhaps you would feel better if you had a good rest? Tell Mrs. Chubb I told you to lie down for a while and that she can bring you a nice hot toddy. That will soon perk you up."

Doris looked even more frightened at that. "Oh, no, mum, I couldn't really. I'll be all right, I promise. I had best be getting back to the kitchen now, mum. Thank you."

She bobbed another quick curtsy, then scurried out of the room as if she had a herd of elephants stampeding behind her.

Cecily sat on the edge of the bed, staring thoughtfully at the water jug. Perhaps the work was too hard for the frail child. She had not yet recovered from her dreadful ordeal at the hands of her aunt. Sometimes it was difficult to remember that she wasn't at all like Gertie, who was as strong as a horse.

One did tend to take the servants for granted, she thought a little guiltily. She must make more time to assure herself that all was well belowstairs. Perhaps some lighter tasks could be arranged for Doris, until she had time to fill out and grow stronger.

Sighing, she got up from the bed, remembering her promise to Baxter. She had this one day to discover who was committing these ghastly murders, and it didn't seem at all likely that she would be successful. Apart from the notes, she had no real evidence to go on.

Some unknown person had dropped a flowerpot on Colonel Fortescue. Some unknown person who might have seen Madeline in the lobby that morning. Baxter was right, it could have been anyone. And the lack of evidence in any of the suspects' rooms would suggest that they were all innocent of the crimes.

Cecily dropped her face flannel into the water, then wrung it out. This would be the first time she'd had to admit defeat. She didn't like it one bit.

To make matters worse, she had a niggling feeling—an odd, yet familiar instinct that she had experienced more than once before. Somewhere in the back of her mind, she already knew the answer to the puzzle. If only she could put a finger on it. That was the most frustrating element of the entire predicament.

"Are you sure you don't want to lie down?" Mrs. Chubb said, watching Gertie anxiously as she sat folding serviettes at the table. "I don't want anything to happen to you now that you're so close to having that little one. Perhaps you should put your feet up and have a rest."

"I'm all right," Gertie said, a stubborn look on her face. "I'm just tired, that's all. It's bleeding hard trying to sleep with a flipping lump on your belly. Keeps kicking me, it does."

"It's just anxious to get out in the world now." Mrs. Chubb went back to the stove and lifted the lid off a large pot of porridge. Giving the gluey mixture a brisk stir with the wooden spoon, she added, "The sound of them fireworks going off tomorrow night will probably set you off. It would be something if it was born on the Fifth of November, wouldn't it?"

"At least I wouldn't forget his bleeding birthday," Gertie muttered. "Knowing what a bloody awful memory I have, it would be a blessing, it would. I'd have to call him Guy Fawkes, then, wouldn't I?"

"Mercy me, I hope you do no such thing." Mrs. Chubb peered into the tea caddy to make sure there was enough tea. Finding it almost empty, she opened the cupboard door and reached in for a bag of Indian assam.

"How do you know it's going to be a boy, anyway?" she said as she poured a stream of dusty black tea leaves into the caddy.

"I know it's a boy. No bloody girl has a kick like that." Gertie pushed her chair back and got slowly to her feet. "Where is that flipping Doris? I hope she hasn't dropped the bloody water or something. I've never seen anyone what blinking drops things the way she does."

"It has a lot to do with her nerves." Mrs. Chubb took down the silver teapots from the shelf and began lining them up alongside the stove. "She jumps at anything, that girl."

Gertie groaned, stretching her back. "I never saw anyone as blinking moody as her, either. One day she's all sweet and smiling, the next she's snarling like a bloody hungry lion."

"Not really." The housekeeper measured the tea into the pots with an expert hand. "Have you noticed that she's always grumpy in the mornings, but by the afternoon she's back to her shy pleasant self again? I reckon she has nightmares or something about the way she was beaten, and it takes her all morning to get over it."

Gertie stared at her. "I never thought about that. Now you come to mention it, she is bleeding grumpy in the mornings. Per'aps she's pregnant?"

Mrs. Chubb gave her a reproving glance. "Bite your tongue, young lady."

Gertie shrugged. "Well, roll on the afternoons, then, that's all I can say. At least her bleeding back must be getting better. I saw her yesterday leaning her back against her chair."

"Well, let's hope that'll improve her temper somewhat. Must have been terrible for the poor lamb, having to work with a back like that."

The door opened at that moment, revealing the very person they'd been talking about. Mrs. Chubb felt guilty as she looked at the girl. She had no right to be gossiping about the staff behind their backs. Poor kid had enough troubles on her plate, that she did.

"Was madam awake when you took her water up?" she asked Doris, who seemed startled by the question.

"Yes, she was." Doris hesitated for a moment, then added, "She was so nice to me. She asked if I was feeling all right and everything." She shot a glance at Gertie, who sat watching her with suspicious eyes. "Oh, and Gertie, madam told me to tell you she hopes you will feel better soon."

"Thank you, I'm sure," Gertie said, feeling a mite sheepish.

Doris glanced up at the clock on the mantelpiece. "I had better get on with the tables, Mrs. Chubb. I know Michel doesn't like it if they're not done by the time he gets here."

"Here," Gertie said, pushing the tray of serviettes across the table. "These are all done. You won't need all of 'em, but there'll be a lot more for lunch with the weekend lot coming in."

Doris nodded and picked up the tray. "Will we be able to watch the fireworks? I do love fireworks, and I've never seen any up close."

"We all watch them," Mrs. Chubb said. "Now get along and get those tables done, or none of us will have the time to watch anything."

"Yes, Mrs. Chubb." With her shy smile, Doris headed across the kitchen, watched in silence by the other two women. She had almost reached the door when it flew open.

Samuel stopped short when he saw Doris standing right in front of him. He and the housemaid stared at each other in silence for a moment, then Samuel gave her a brief nod.

He made to brush past her, but paused when she said in a demure voice, "Good morning, Samuel. It's a fine morning out there, isn't it?"

He looked at her suspiciously. "It might be, once the sun comes up."

She gave him a sweet smile. "As long as it doesn't rain for the fireworks tomorrow. I'm looking forward to watching the display."

Samuel shifted on his feet and glanced at Mrs. Chubb, who stood unashamedly watching him. "If you like, Doris," he said casually, "I'll show you the best place to see them tomorrow night."

Doris's face lit up with excitement. "You will? Oh, Samuel, that would be so wonderful. Thank you." Still smiling happily, she brushed past him and went out the door.

After a short silence, Gertie said gruffly, "Well, that clobbers that idea, doesn't it?"

"Yes," Mrs. Chubb murmured, staring at the door as if she expected it to open again. "I imagine it does."

"What idea?" Samuel said, crossing the floor to the stove.

"Oh, we was just talking about Doris and her moods," Gertie said, smothering a yawn. "Mrs. Chubb says she's always grumpy in the mornings, but she seems flipping happy enough this morning, doesn't she?"

Samuel nodded, a puzzled expression on his face. "Don't understand it meself, I don't. One day she wants to talk to me, the next she acts as if I was dirt."

"That's just what I was bleeding saying, wasn't I, Mrs. Chubb?"

"Well," the housekeeper said briskly, "we don't have time to stand around and talk about Doris all day. We have work to do."

She looked pointedly at Samuel, who stood warming his back at the stove.

"Oh, right," he said, "I almost forgot what I came to tell you. Guess what? There's been another murder."

"Go on!" Gertie hugged herself as if she were cold. "Who is it, then?"

Samuel shrugged. "Dunno. It was another gypsy girl from what I heard. The milkman just told me. Found her dead last night, they did."

"And was her head gorn again?" Gertie asked, her eyes widening.

"Yeah. Just like the last two." Samuel straightened and pulled his cap from his pocket. "All I can say is, I'm glad I'm not a gypsy. Though mind you, I wouldn't want to be walking around those woods alone on me own, either. Never know who you could bump into, right?"

He went out the door with a wave of his hand, leaving Mrs. Chubb staring after him.

"Fancy that," Gertie said, sounding a little nervous. "Another one of them gypsies gorn. There won't be any left at this rate. That'll make someone happy, I reckon. It must be someone what hates gypsies to keep knocking them off like that."

"There are lot of people who hate gypsies," Mrs. Chubb said slowly, "but they don't go around chopping off their heads. The thing that worries me the most about it is that every time we lose an axe there's another murder."

"Bloody hell," Gertie said in a hushed voice. "I'd forgotten about that."

"Well, I hadn't." Mrs. Chubb dusted her hands on her apron and headed for the door. "I think I had better have a word with madam. I'm beginning to believe we are harboring a murderer in the Pennyfoot. And I don't want to be the next one to lose my head."

"Another murder," Baxter said gloomily. "I find it hard to believe the constabulary are not taking this situation seriously. Surely three murders in a row would be enough to galvanize them into taking some action?"

"Perhaps they are," Cecily said, leaning back in her chair. She let her gaze wander over the library shelves. "I feel I should warn Madeline about the last note I received. Particularly since the axe is missing again. I'm afraid that does rather confirm our suspicion that the culprit is staying in the hotel, and Madeline will be here in the ballroom in the morning, working on the flower arrangements for the ball tomorrow night. In view of the note, she could be taking an enormous risk."

"I agree." Baxter gave her a stern look. "You haven't forgotten your promise to talk to the police today?"

Cecily shook her head. "No, I haven't forgotten. I will send Samuel to ask P.C. Northcott to stop in this evening. I will show him the notes and tell him about the flowerpot being dropped on the colonel's head, and inform him that an axe appears to be missing from our coal shed."

"And our unproductive search of the rooms?"

Cecily shrugged. "I can't see the point in telling him about that. No doubt the inspector will thoroughly disrupt the hotel and my guests, all in the interest of making a display of conducting an investigation, even if he feels it's unwarranted."

She shook her head in mock despair. "If this state of affairs continues much longer, Baxter, we shall have our guests finding somewhere else to enjoy their leisure hours. The entire object of the Pennyfoot is to provide a haven from the trials and tribulations of the everyday world. The very reason we are so successful is because the aristocracy can pursue their private pleasures without fear of being detected or disturbed."

"Yes, madam, I have to agree," Baxter said. "Yet we

cannot continue to expose our guests to the dangers of a possible murderer on the premises."

Cecily gazed up at James's portrait. "I just don't understand why Badgers End appears to attract not only the most affluent and prestigious guests in the country, but also the most devious scoundrels to walk the earth."

"It is a small village, madam, isolated on a lonely stretch of coast, and escapes the heavy jurisdiction of a city constabulary."

Cecily nodded. "Precisely. And I'm afraid the hotel itself is a perfect haven for the same reasons." She studied the still face of her dead husband. "Ah, James, what did you get us into when you bought a decrepit, lonely mansion and turned it into a hotel?"

"The Pennyfoot has brought a great deal of pleasure to a great many people, madam. Including myself, if I might say so. Had I not been hired to manage this hotel, I would not have had the very great pleasure of serving you."

Cecily smiled up at him, feeling the warmth of pleasure such words from him never failed to give her. "Thank you, Baxter. I am happy to have your support and your friendship. Now, as long as you are in such an excellent frame of mind, perhaps you wouldn't mind giving me one of your cigars?"

"I would mind very much, madam. Only as a concern about your health, of course. Since I have learned, however, that there is absolutely no point whatsoever in attempting to argue with you, I shall give in with good grace."

He wasn't exactly smiling as he lit the cigar for her, but the gleam in his eyes made her quite content.

CHAPTER
❈ 17 ❈

Samuel considered himself to be a reasonably even-tempered young man. He also regarded himself as being well versed in the wily ways of women. When it came to dealing with Doris Hoggins, however, even St. George himself would have had a problem dealing with that one.

It had been only that morning when he'd offered to take Doris to see the fireworks. She'd been smiling up at him with the bashful look on her face that he always found so appealing. He'd seen her eyes light up when he'd asked her to go with him, and the eager way she'd agreed. She'd seemed excited at the very thought of it.

Samuel kicked a lump of coal out of the way, watching it skitter across the kitchen yard until it hit the dustbin with a clatter. Now, just a few hours later, she'd acted as though he had leprosy. He couldn't believe it when he'd bumped into her in the hallway. Even her voice sounded different. She'd told him in no uncertain terms to bugger off and leave her alone.

Samuel shook his head, his gaze shifting moodily across the yard to where the door of the coal shed stood ajar. Doris must have left it open when she got the coal that morning.

Well, he was buggered if he was going to shut it for her. Let her get a nagging from Mrs. Chubb. Do her bloody good. She had far too much mouth on her, did Doris. And he, for one, wasn't going to stand for it anymore. She could go and boil in oil for all he cared.

He cast a glance at the shed as he passed, feeling a little guilty at leaving the door open. Halfway across the yard, he changed his mind and retraced his steps. He just couldn't deliberately let the girl get into trouble.

Besides, it was one of the rules of the hotel to shut all doors behind you, and Samuel Rawlins always tried to follow the rules. As his father had always told him, you got into a lot less trouble that way.

He reached the door of the shed and began to close the door, then paused as something in the corner caught his eye. It was a large sack, tied in the middle with a thick rope.

Samuel stared at it. It wasn't one of the coal sacks, because they were black, and this one was the usual light straw color. And the bulges inside it definitely weren't lumps of coal. They were too smooth and round.

He hesitated, his gaze riveted on the sack. He felt strangely reluctant to go into the shed. There was just something about that sack. It seemed to have patches of damp stains, for one thing. They were dark brown and mucky-looking.

He wondered if perhaps John the gardener had left the

sack there. But John never left anything in the coal shed. He had a big garden shed to keep his stuff in.

The more Samuel stared at that sack, the stronger was his revulsion. There was no way in the world he wanted to touch that thing, yet something told him he should look inside it, just in case. Taking a very long, deep breath, he braced himself to enter the shed.

Cecily glanced at herself in the mirror and tucked a stray strand of hair under the brim of her hat. She rather liked the hat, though it was a little plain compared to the monstrosities that Phoebe always wore. Or that most women wore nowadays.

It seemed that all women were competing to see who could wear the most fripperies on their hats, with the wider the brim the better. Cecily often wondered how a woman could hold up her head with all that weight resting on it.

Frowning, she tied a pale blue chiffon scarf under her chin. It amazed her how so many women allowed themselves to be dictated by fashion. There were a few rebels, of course, herself included. And Madeline. But then Madeline rarely conformed to any stricture of society, much less the fashion dictates.

Thinking about her friend did nothing to dispel Cecily's frown. Madeline could be in grave danger and must be warned. Yet that would leave a large gap in the preparations for the ball. There wasn't anyone in the hotel who could achieve with flowers the magic that Madeline appeared to produce so effortlessly.

It couldn't be helped, Cecily decided. If need be, she would handle the flowers herself. The most important thing was to safeguard her friend from any possible danger. And she could only hope, Cecily thought as she left her suite, that Colonel Fortescue would remain at the George and

Dragon, at least until the festivities began tomorrow. By
then she hoped this nightmare would be ended.

Reaching the foyer, Cecily caught sight of Doris about to
descend the kitchen stairs. To her surprise, the housemaid
had changed her uniform. She called the girl over, watching
her as she strode easily across the thick carpet.

Doris halted in front of her and dropped a small curtsy.

"I prefer that you wear black in the afternoon," Cecily
said, sending a quick glance over Doris's dark gray skirt and
blouse. "Though I seem to remember you wearing your
black dress this morning."

"Yes, mum, I was wearing the black this morning." Doris
looked pointedly at the grandfather clock as if indicating she
didn't have the time to stand around talking. "I spilled
something down the skirt and I had to change it."

"I see. Well, in future, please wear the gray in the
morning and the black in the afternoon." Cecily peered
closer at the girl's face. "Your cold sounds considerably
worse since this morning. Perhaps you should lie down after
all. I'll have Mrs. Chubb bring you a toddy."

"No!" Apparently aware that she'd sounded too abrupt,
Doris bobbed another quick curtsy. "Begging your pardon,
mum, but I have work to do, and I'm feeling quite well
enough, thank you."

Cecily sighed. For a young child, the housemaid was
remarkably stubborn. Obviously her cold was affecting her
temperament. "Very well. I was going to send you out to tell
Samuel I need the trap, but it's so damp out there today, I'll
do it myself. Please, Doris, do take care of your health. An
ounce of prevention is worth a pound of cure, you know."

"Yes, mum." Doris bobbed her head and rushed off to the
kitchen stairs before Cecily could say another word.

Shaking her head, Cecily crossed the foyer to the front
door. The walk around the hotel to the stables would clear

her head, she thought, as she stepped out under the gray skies. The brisk wind blowing in from the ocean almost took her breath away.

Whitecaps danced along the choppy waves, and the beach appeared to be deserted as she hurried down the white stone steps. The wind tugged at her hat, and she held onto it with one hand, thankful that she had it securely pinned.

She would have to make sure that Samuel closed the canopy before they set off for Madeline's cottage. Even so, it promised to be a chilly ride.

Once she turned the corner, the wall of the hotel sheltered her from the wind's greedy fingers. As she headed for the stable gates, Cecily glanced across the kitchen yard. To her astonishment, she saw Samuel hovering at the open door of the coal shed. He appeared to be staring at something inside.

Wondering what on earth captured his attention so securely, Cecily turned into the yard. It could be a fox trapped inside the shed, she thought, and she had no wish to disturb Samuel if he was attempting to coax it out.

Creeping up behind him, she stood on tiptoe to peer over his shoulder. She could see only the usual shovels and buckets, and in the corner that held Samuel's interest nothing but a bulky sack.

"What is it?" she whispered.

Samuel sprang in the air with such a shriek he startled her half out of her wits.

"Great heavens, Samuel!" she cried, leaping backward. "Whatever is the matter with you?"

Samuel's white face stared back at her, his eyes wide as if he'd just seen a dreadful apparition. He started to say something, then apparently changed his mind. He shot a hunted look at the shed, then a frenzied glance over his shoulder as if seeking help from somewhere.

"Really, Samuel," Cecily muttered, regaining her sense of humor, "do I look so awful?"

Finding his voice, Samuel said a little wildly, "No, mum. Sorry, mum, I was just . . . I didn't hear you come up on me . . . Is there something I can do for you?"

"Yes." Cecily straightened her hat and tied the scarf more securely. "You can tell me what it is that has you strung as tight as a violin." She sent a curious glance at the shed. "What were you staring at in there?"

Samuel shook his head so violently his hair fell across his forehead. Sweeping it away with his hand, he said feverishly, "It were nothing, mum, honest. I thought I saw something, that's all. 'Tweren't nothing more than me imagination, that it was."

Cecily continued to stare at him for a moment, while he shuffled his feet and did his best to meet her gaze squarely. Then she said quietly, "I trust you are not up to mischief, Samuel."

"Oh, no, mum, honest. Like I said, it were just me imagination playing tricks on me, that's all."

"Very well." Although less than satisfied, Cecily was in too much of a hurry to pursue the matter right then. "I want to go to Miss Pengrath's cottage, Samuel, right away. Can you have the trap ready for me?"

"Yes, mum." Samuel touched his forehead then, realizing he wasn't wearing a cap, pulled it from his pocket and dragged it on. "Won't take no more'n a jiffy to hitch it up. Did you want to wait inside while I bring it around the front?"

Feeling a fresh breeze whip around her shoulders, Cecily again caught at her hat. "Yes, I do believe I will. I'll wait for you at the door, Samuel."

"Yes, mum." Again the footman touched his cap, then sped off to the stables to hitch up the trap.

Cecily made her way back to the steps and climbed them, her mind still dwelling on Samuel's odd behavior. She couldn't imagine what it was Samuel thought he saw, but whatever it was that had caused him to jump like a startled hare, he was obviously reluctant to tell her about it.

She would ask him about it later, she decided as she stepped inside the warmth of the foyer. But right now she had other things on her mind. She wasn't sure how Madeline was going to take her warning, but no doubt it would be difficult for both of them. Madeline was sensitive about being regarded as a gypsy.

There was no doubt, however, that whoever was systematically ridding the world of female gypsies had included Madeline in his list, and Cecily was just not prepared to expose her friend to such a risk.

Now she had to convince Madeline that her life was in danger, and hope that the volatile woman would be sensible enough to recognize the fact and agree to stay away from the Pennyfoot until the murderer was apprehended.

Madeline was busily sewing button eyes on a teddy bear when Cecily arrived at the cottage a short while later. Leaving Samuel waiting outside for her, Cecily accepted her friend's offer of a pot of tea and her delicious fairy cakes.

The conversation remained on general topics while they shared the light snack, until Madeline put down her cup and saucer and settled herself more comfortably on the wide cushion she'd placed on the floor.

Madeline had room for only one chair in her cluttered sitting room. The rest of the space was taken up with boxes and baskets full of the exquisite handcrafts that were her main source of income.

Cecily never failed to find something new to exclaim over and usually purchased an item or two to keep as gifts, though invariably she would end up keeping them herself, unable to bear parting with them.

She sat now, fingering a pink silk crocheted shawl with a delicate lace edging into which tiny embroidered roses had been worked. "This is lovely," Cecily said, examining the fine handiwork. "This would go beautifully with that dusty rose gown I bought last spring."

"It would indeed." Madeline smiled at the compliment, then added, "But that's not why you have paid me this unexpected visit, is it? What is so important that it couldn't wait until I come to the hotel tomorrow?"

Cecily gave a rueful shake of her head. "I might have known you would see right through me." She paused long enough to reach into her pocket for the slip of paper she'd brought with her. "I'm afraid it isn't pleasant news."

Madeline watched her with a solemn expression, but said nothing.

"You remember, of course, the broken flowerpot in the hallway?"

"Of course. As a matter of fact, your aspidistra is doing rather well. I believe it will recover nicely, though it's a little early to tell."

Cecily had forgotten all about the plant. "Well, I'm happy to hear that," she said, wishing she didn't have to show Madeline the note.

"You mentioned the flowerpot?" Madeline prompted, and Cecily reluctantly nodded.

"Yes, I did. We . . . that is, Baxter and I, believe someone was trying to kill the colonel."

Madeline stared at her in amazement. "Good Lord," she said. "I know Colonel Fortescue can be irritating at times but I wouldn't have thought he deserved such an early grave."

"We believe that the same person who made an attempt

the colonel's life could be the man who is killing the
psies on Putney Downs."

Admittedly, Cecily thought as she watched the blood
ain from her friend's face, the statement had been rather
ld. Still, Madeline's reaction was rather dramatic. She
emed to have problems gaining her breath, and when she
ally spoke, her voice had a definite quiver to it.

"That man will burn in hell," she said fiercely.

"I agree," Cecily assured her, "but I want to show you
mething—"

"Are you telling me that miserable brute has been lurking
ound your hotel?" Madeline said after uttering a little
sp.

"I'm afraid so. I haven't called the police as yet, but I
end to send for P.C. Northcott this evening."

"It won't do any good." Madeline curled her arms around
r knees and stared sullenly at her feet. "You know how the
lice feel about gypsies. They are not going to waste their
ecious time on vagabond savages who defile the land and
al from the inhabitants. They'll just leave well enough
one, hoping the entire tribe is wiped out by this madman."

"Not if I can present them with enough evidence to
arrant a thorough investigation."

Madeline looked up in surprise. "You can do that?"

"I believe so." Cecily unfolded the note. "I've had several
tes pushed under my door that I believe were written by
e murderer. Also, an axe has disappeared several times
om the coal shed, each time apparently followed by a
urder."

"And it's put back again?"

Madeline sounded incredulous, and Cecily could quite
derstand why. "I know it sounds farfetched, and I must
mit I don't understand it myself, but there you are. The
e comes and goes with almost alarming regularity."

"And you think it's one of your guests?"

"I did think so. But Baxter and I searched the rooms of all the suspects and could find nothing to implicate any them."

Madeline gave her a wry smile. "I imagine Baxter ha something to say about that."

"He did indeed." Cecily looked down at the note in h hand. "I received this message last night, and in view what it says, I felt I should show it to you."

She watched Madeline's smile fade as she handed h friend the sheet of paper.

Madeline quickly scanned the words, then looked up, h gaze chilling. "I assume he is referring to me?"

"Yes, I'm afraid so," Cecily said, taking back the not "Under the circumstances, I think it might be better if yo do not come to the hotel tomorrow to work on the flower I can take them back with me tonight and I'll see what I ca do in the morning. I used to be quite a dab hand at arrangi James's precious roses."

"No," Madeline said firmly. "Absolutely not. I won't l that creature dictate to me where I do or do not go. Let hi try to kill me. I might just have a surprise or two up m sleeve for him."

"Madeline, I can't allow—"

"Cecily, dear, I appreciate your concern, I really do Madeline scrambled to her feet and held out her hand Cecily. "But my job is to transform that ballroom of you into a garden of flowers in time for the ball tomorrow nigh and I intend to do just that. And no one, particularly pernicious crackpot attempting to play God, is going to st me. Rest assured, Cecily, I shall be there tomorrow. An God help that fiend if he should dare to put in a appearance."

CHAPTER
❖18❖

cily returned to the Pennyfoot feeling most uneasy about
adeline's intention to work on the flower arrangements for
e ball. Climbing the steps of the hotel, she decided to ask
axter to keep an eye on her friend, just in case someone
ould attempt to harm her—though at this point it seemed
ghly unlikely that the murderer would risk being seen in
e hotel with an axe in his hand.

Still, the thought troubled her. So much so that she almost
n into Cyril Plunkett in the foyer. He stood in her path
ith the apparent intention of speaking to her, and she didn't
e him until the last minute.

"I do beg your pardon, Mr. Plunkett," Cecily exclaimed

as the little man skipped out of her way. "I'm afraid I w
wool-gathering."

"Quite all right, Mrs. Sinclair. It is quite dark in h
today. So difficult to see."

"It is indeed. I must tell Samuel to light the lamps an h
earlier. Now that the winter is drawing in, it grows dark
soon after lunch, the day is over before we know it."

Cyril Plunkett nodded, and Cecily smiled at him in
effort to put him at ease.

He really was quite a nervous little man. He clutch
the small leather bag in his arms as if afraid someone wo
steal it. His eyes darted everywhere but at her, and he s
several glances over his shoulder as if he expected somec
to come creeping up on him out of the shadows.

"I wanted to speak to you, Mrs. Sinclair. I won't
staying until the weekend, I'm afraid. I've had a messa
from the office, and they want me back in the city on Frid
so I'll be leaving tomorrow morning."

"Thank you for letting me know," Cecily said, glanc
past him at Baxter who had just appeared near the foot
the stairs. "I will see that your bill is made up in good tim

She caught Baxter's eye and winked at him, attempting
indicate that she wished to talk to him. His shock
expression almost made her laugh.

"Thank you, I'm sure." Cyril Plunkett fidgeted with
feet and sent a sideways glance toward the kitchen stairs.
must admit, Mrs. Sinclair, I shall be most relieved to ret
to London. Most relieved."

He ran a finger around the inside of his collar as if it w
too tight. "All these murders going on so close by. It rea
does make one feel jittery, you know. I find myself looki
over my shoulder all the time."

"I'm sorry, Mr. Plunkett." Cecily glanced at the grand
ther clock as it began to chime the Westminster chords.

o understand, but as I said before, you are quite safe here
t the hotel."

"I wish I could be certain of that." The salesman gave a
isible shudder. "I dread going to my room at night. I do not
eel safe until I have locked the door and bolted it. Even
hen, I do not feel secure."

"In that case," Cecily said, giving up her attempt to
ppease the man, "perhaps it is just as well your office has
alled you back. Now, if you will excuse me, I just have
ime to dress before dinner."

"Pardon?" Cyril Plunkett stared at the clock as it began to
hime the hour. "Goodness, I had no idea it was so late. I,
oo, must prepare for the evening meal. Please excuse me,
Mrs. Sinclair."

He backed away from her, almost tripped over Baxter,
mumbled an apology, then scrambled up the stairs without
a backward glance.

"I feel sorry for that poor man," Cecily remarked as she
oined Baxter at the foot of the stairs. "I'm quite sure he will
die of fright before he is very much older."

Baxter gave her one of his reproving looks. "If he doesn't
first expire from the shock of madam's audacity."

Cecily stared at him in mock surprise. "What did I do?"

Baxter leaned toward her and lowered his voice. "You
gave me a decidedly lascivious wink, madam. Most im-
proper."

"Lascivious?"

"Decidedly lascivious."

Cecily grinned. "Why, Baxter, you surprise me. I wouldn't
have thought you would understand the meaning of the word."

"What pains me, madam, is that you apparently know
what it means."

"Ah, but then, I read Sherlock Holmes."

She led the way down the hallway toward his office and paused at the door, waiting for him to open it for her.

"There are such words in the novels that you read?" he said, sounding disbelieving.

"There are indeed, Baxter." With a sigh Cecily sat herself down on the chair. "One receives quite an education when reading today's light novels. I have to say I thoroughly enjoy the experience."

"That explains from where you form your unconventional ideas. It would serve you better if you studied the works of more prosaic writers."

"Such as Dickens?" Cecily suggested innocently.

Baxter shuddered. "Such a vulgar man."

"But an excellent writer." She reached up and unpinned her hat. "I enjoy his books immensely. Though I must say he displayed an unfortunate attitude toward women."

Baxter sighed. "If I might be permitted to say, madam, according to your thinking, the vast majority of men display an unfortunate attitude toward women."

Keeping a serious expression, Cecily nodded in agreement. "Terrible, isn't it? No wonder women are having such a difficult time of it. I don't wonder they are rebelling in the streets." She paused with her hands still on her hat. "Is something wrong, Baxter?"

"You are not thinking of removing your hat in here, madam?"

"I most certainly am." She pulled it from her head with a flourish. "For heaven's sake, I'm not removing an article of clothing. It's just my hat."

"It makes me feel most uncomfortable, madam. It is rather an intimate gesture."

"So is lying together beneath a bed in a boudoir, Baxter, but I didn't hear you raising objections about that."

She felt sorry for him when his face flushed scarlet.

Madam, I implore you, do not breathe a word of that again. Someone could easily mistake my intentions—"

"Oh, piffle, Bax. You know very well I won't mention it to anyone. I haven't as yet heard any gossip, so perhaps Doris didn't even recognize us. After all, she saw little more than our feet."

"I really do wish you would refrain from taking such enormous risks," Baxter muttered, fingering his collar. "Not only with your reputation and mine, but also your life. As I am forced to point out on many an occasion, you may not always be quite so fortunate. I am deathly afraid that something will happen to harm you."

Cecily looked at him. "And you have given your promise to James, of course."

Baxter apparently realized he was treading on dangerous ground, for he adroitly changed the subject. "I overheard Mr. Plunkett in the hallway. He is leaving tomorrow?"

"Yes." Cecily laid the hat in her lap. "Thank you for reminding me. I had almost forgotten. Will you please have his bill made up by the morning? He didn't mention what time he wanted to leave, but I imagine it will be early."

Baxter nodded, seemingly relieved to be engaged in less provocative conversation. "I will see to it this afternoon, madam."

"The poor man seems terrified of being murdered in his bed, yet I can't help feeling that he is trying to avoid someone in particular. Most likely that ghastly Ellsworth Galloway." Cecily plucked at the ribbon on her hat. "I would much prefer that he were the one leaving tomorrow."

"If Cyril Plunkett is escaping from someone," Baxter said, opening the drawer of his desk, "I would think it more likely he is being harassed by Lady Belleville."

Cecily looked at him in surprise. "What makes you say that?"

"I saw them on the upper landing yesterday. Lad Belleville appeared to have Plunkett cornered and wa breathing in his face in a most disgusting manner."

"Really? I can't imagine what she sees in that droll litt man." Cecily laughed. "Obviously he must have son quality that has escaped me."

Stooped over the desk, Baxter wrote laboriously in th invoice book. "In my opinion, madam, if I may be so bol Lady Belleville should be committed to an asylum whe she can do no harm to anyone. It is obvious she is addled the brain."

"Baxter, why don't you sit down to write that bill," Cecil said impatiently. "You'll get a nasty crick in the neck tryin to write standing up."

"I prefer to stand, thank you," Baxter said, withou looking up.

Knowing it was useless to argue with him, Cecil watched his hand move slowly across the page in h impeccable script. "Lady Belleville does seem rather con fused at times," she remarked, "but I really don't think sh is dangerous to anyone, except perhaps herself."

"I wish I could agree with you," Baxter murmured. " nothing else, she is disruptive. Even Doris Hoggins threw fit of temper this afternoon."

"Because of Lady Belleville?"

"Yes, madam." He paused in his writing and looked up "From what I can understand, Lady Belleville ordered Dor to search for her missing bird. When Doris explained sh had duties to perform, the woman became quite belligere and threatening. Doris vented her temper on the kitche staff, much to Mrs. Chubb's annoyance."

"Oh, dear," Cecily murmured.

Baxter shook his head and resumed writing. "I was quit surprised. Doris is usually such a pleasant child."

"Yes," Cecily agreed absently. She had been listening with only half her attention. Her thoughts were on her encounter with Doris in the hallway earlier.

She could see the child in her mind's eye, standing sullenly in front of her, a look of pure rebellion on her thin face. Even the lighter texture of her dress failed to bring any life to her complexion, though it was a slight improvement on the stark black dress she had worn earlier.

Perhaps it was time, Cecily thought, to order new uniforms for the housemaids. One of the rules of etiquette she still followed was that the servants wear proper dress.

Although pale shades and even prints were considered correct for the mornings, protocol demanded that the maids wear black after noon. Since they owned only one light and one black, they should at least have a spare black in case of accidents.

Still thinking about Doris and her change of clothes, she watched Baxter finish writing out Cyril Plunkett's bill. "I'll have this sent up to his room right away," he said, tearing the sheet of paper from the book.

Cecily wasn't listening. Instead she rose and shocked Baxter by pounding on his desk with her fist.

"Madam?" he said, his eyebrows shooting skyward.

"I know who it is," Cecily said, with great satisfaction. "I can't imagine why I didn't think of it before."

"You know who is what?" Baxter asked patiently.

Cecily leaned both hands on the desk and tilted forward. In a low, deliberate tone, she said, "I know who is killing the Gypsies, Baxter. I know the identity of our murderer."

A short while later, Cecily sent for Samuel, who arrived breathless and looking extremely worried. Remembering the young man's agitation earlier that day, Cecily asked him if all was well.

"Just getting jumpy, I reckon, mum," Samuel sai
avoiding Cecily's gaze. "No wonder an' all, what with a
those women getting murdered. I'm just glad I don't have
go walking through them woods."

"Well, I'm afraid you will have to go out again, Samuel'
Cecily said, glancing at the grandfather clock in the foyer.
need you to take a message to P.C. Northcott, if you will

Samuel looked even more distressed. "Yes, mum. Rig
away."

Cecily handed him the sealed envelope. "Take care th
you hand this personally to the constable, and no one else

Samuel answered with a feverish nodding of his hea
"I'll make sure he gets it, mum, never fear."

He took the envelope from her and turned to leave.

"Samuel," Cecily said quietly, "are you sure somethin
isn't troubling you? We are all here to help, you know."

"Yes, mum. I mean, no, mum. I mean . . ." Samu
flicked her a nervous glance. "I'm fine, mum, honest. No
I'd better go and harness the mare." He touched his forehea
with his fingers, then dashed for the kitchen stairs an
clattered down them at top speed.

Deep in thought, Cecily climbed the stairs to her suite
Now she would have to find a way to deal with a murdere
That would take some thought and serious planning. All th
upheaval and distress was most tiring. If only it were a
over and summer was just around the corner instead of he
having to face the onslaught of winter. The smoke and du
of the coal fires irritated her throat, and the lack of fresh a
made her head feel like cotton wool at times.

How she missed the rose gardens and the pleasant strol
under a warm sky. The Esplanade always seemed so drear
and depressing without the throngs of seaside visitors.

The beach just wasn't the same without children racin
across the sands, building wobbly sand castles or laughin

a Punch-and-Judy show. Even the sea gulls seemed lonely the winter, swooping low over the cresting waves with ir dismal cries.

Somehow in the summer months she seemed to have ore stamina, more fortitude to deal with all the problems. d now she was faced with yet another problem, and one at could very well end in tragedy. It was not a happy night.

Reaching the door, she fit her key into the lock and turned The door slid over the sheet of paper lying on the carpet, aking it flutter in the draft.

Stooping, Cecily reached for it and picked it up. She aited until she was inside the room with the door locked fore opening it. The now familiar scrawl seemed to jump t at her. *Here comes a candle to light you to bed. Here mes a chopper to chop off your head. George.*

muel let himself out of the kitchen door and started to oss the yard. He deliberately kept his gaze averted from e coal shed, though he had a prickly feeling in the back of s neck as he passed by the door.

He hadn't been able to keep the vision of that sack out of s mind. If madam hadn't arrived when she did and spoken him, scaring him to kingdom come, he'd know by now hat was inside it.

Not that he wanted to know what was inside it. In fact, he anted nothing more than to forget about the darn thing together. Only he couldn't. And something told him he ouldn't be able to until he'd opened that sack and scovered what it held.

He hadn't breathed a word to anyone about what he'd en. If it was nothing more than rotting vegetables, he'd el like a fool. If it was something else, he couldn't think f anyone he'd want to open that thing. Unless it was Mr. axter. Or the bobbies.

The night breeze rustled a pile of dead leaves, makin
him jump. The moon was hidden by the thick bank of clou
that had covered the skies for the best part of the week. On
the glow from the lamplight at the kitchen windows cast so
shadows across the ground.

Tomorrow night would be Guy Fawkes, and the Espl
nade would be lit up from end to end with the bonfire on t
beach and hundreds of fireworks exploding in the dark sk

Tonight, however, all was still and silent, except for t
steady swish of the ocean breaking on the shore, the bree
rustling through the empty branches of the sycamore, a
the distant hoot of an owl from the woods on Putney Down

Thinking about those woods gave Samuel the co
shivers. He hunched his shoulders and thought once mo
about the sack waiting ominously for him in the dark corn
of the coal shed.

His fingers touched the gate that led to the stables, and t
note for the constable seemed to burn in his pocket. Let t
bobbies take care of it, he told himself. It was their job.

He swung the gate open and passed through. He coul
point out the sack and let the constable look inside.

He paused, his fingers gripping the top bar of the gat
His gaze seemed relentlessly drawn back to the dark outlir
of the shed. More than likely the constable wouldn't tell hir
what he found. Not unless it was rotten potatoes (
something, and Samuel's instincts told him it was somethin
a lot more sinister than that.

Samuel had an idea what was in that sack. And he wa
burning to know if he was right. He hesitated, thinkin
again about the note in his pocket. Then slowly he pushe
the gate open again and inched back into the yard.

Just one quick peek would tell him what he wanted t
know. Then he could scarper right down to the constable'
house and tell him what he'd seen.

He could just imagine telling the boys down at the pub what he'd found. That's if he was right about what was in that sack. And there was only one way to find out.

He reached the shed and tugged on the door handle. The door was jammed, and he had to haul on it to get it open. It came with a rush and a loud squeak, shuddering as it broke free from its restraint.

Samuel waited a moment or two but heard no movement from the kitchen. Reaching inside, he found the oil lamp that hung from the wall. On a shelf behind it lay the matches, and he struck one, shielding it with his hand until he had the wick alight.

Popping the glass cover back on, he waited for the glow to burn bright enough to cast a light across the shed floor. The sack huddled in the corner, waiting for him.

Holding the lamp above his head, Samuel swung it around, making sure that no one else watched him from the shadows. Then, with a sickening thud of his heart, he advanced toward the sack.

His hand trembled so much he could hardly untie the rope that bound it, but at last he had it free. Holding the lamp with one hand, he grasped the neck of the sack and pulled it open.

The movement disturbed the contents, and before he could move, something rolled out of the sack and landed against his foot.

Samuel took one look, then staggered outside into the fresh air, where he gave up everything he'd eaten at his last meal.

CHAPTER
✹19✹

The next morning, Madeline arrived at the Pennyfoot bright and early, pulling behind her the handcart loaded with bronze and dark red chrysanthemums. Huge sprays of bulrushes bobbed in the breeze as she parked the cart at the wall of the hotel. Leaving it there, she went inside to have a brief word with Cecily, then emerged a few minutes later to reclaim the cart.

The clouds appeared to be breaking up when she marched around the side of the hotel and through the garden gate. Approaching the ballroom from the rose garden, she eyed the shorn stalks of the rosebushes. John Thimble, the Pennyfoot's dedicated gardener, had performed his usual meticulous surgery on the shrubs. By next summer the roses would bloom in a glorious palette of color.

Madeline adored flowers. She and John shared a strong affinity for the mysteries of the plant world, though John approached his work with a less ethereal attitude.

Madeline used plants to heal pain and to stir emotions. With her flower arrangements she created picturesque beauty, designed to enchant the eye of the beholder and bring a sense of peace and love. Madeline was a child of the earth and believed that every living thing earned a place upon it.

She felt a certain sense of calm as she went along placing the flowers in the huge ornate pots that stood on either side of the stage. She arranged tall bulrushes at the back, spreading out at each side to provide a framework for the chrysanthemums. The white baby's breath filled in the spaces, and for depth she added sprays of cedar and pine.

She worked steadily, concentrating on the balance of color and shape, until she had filled the pots with almost identical arrangements. Finally satisfied, she stepped off the stage and backed away to the center of the dance floor to obtain a wider view of the entire creation.

The sun had not yet broken through the clouds, and shadows darkened the balconies around the ballroom. Massive stone pillars surrounded the dance floor, obstructing the view of the tables set against the walls.

Madeline's gaze was concentrated on the stage, and she did not see or hear the movement from the doorway on her left. But she sensed it.

She turned slowly, almost as if in a trance.

The figure stood directly in front of her, silhouetted against the French windows, looking taller somehow, more sturdy than she remembered, and infinitely evil.

Very slowly, Madeline looked down to where strong

fingers gripped the handle of the gleaming, deadly weapon that had been used too many times before. The missing axe.

"I don't flipping believe it," Gertie said, staring at the clock ticking away on the mantelpiece. "Every morning this week that blinking Doris has been late, but this time she's really gone and done it. Look at the bloody time!"

Mrs. Chubb lifted her head from the lump of bread dough she was kneading. "It is rather late," she said, sending a worried look at the clock. "Doris has had a bad cold for the last two days. Perhaps she's ill. I think you had better go and find out if she's all right."

"Strewth!" Gertie flung down the towel she'd been using to wipe the dishes and marched to the door. "As if I hadn't got enough on me bleeding plate, what with me belly-ache . . ."

"You got pains?" Mrs. Chubb asked sharply, but Gertie didn't have time to wait around to answer her.

She still had the dishes to finish and the silverware to polish, and her stomach was killing her, it was. And that bleeding lazy Doris was lying in her bed, snoring her head off, no doubt.

Tramping down the corridor to the housemaid's room, Gertie could feel her temper rising. Nobody liked to bloody get out of a warm bed on a blinking cold morning. Nobody hated hitting the ice-cold floorboards with bare feet worse than she did. But she could manage to get to work on time, even with her aches and pains, and there was no reason why Doris shouldn't, too.

Gertie paused for a moment as a stab of pain hit her low down in her belly. Gawd, that was a strong one. Took her breath away, it did. If the pains kept up, she'd have to sit down the rest of the day to do her work. She just hoped there wasn't anything wrong with the baby.

She waisted for the spasm to pass before continuing on down the corridor. Her back ached worse than ever these days. If only the baby would flipping hurry up and be born, maybe she could get back to feeling like a human being again, instead of a bloody sick elephant.

After what seemed like an eternity, she reached the door of Doris's room. She rapped sharply with her knuckles and yelled, "Doris? It's bleeding seven o'clock. Get your flipping arse out of that bed and into the kitchen. Good job you ain't in Buckingham Palace! They'd have you locked up in the Tower."

She waited, but could hear nothing from the other side of the door. Rapping again, she yelled once more, "Doris! What the flipping heck are you doing in there?"

Still no answer. Muttering to herself, Gertie tried the handle. Much to her surprise, the door opened.

She stuck her head inside the room and stared in disbelief at the huddled shape beneath the eiderdown. Flipping girl hadn't even budged.

Losing the last remnants of her patience, Gertie strode across the room and gave the figure a hefty slap on the rump. "Come on, you flipping twerp, up and at 'em. You've only got a cold, you ain't going to die. Look at me, I'm still on me feet, and I bet I hurt a lot worse than you do."

A muffled grunt came from the sleeping girl. The eiderdown was pulled up over her head, and Gertie leaned down to get her mouth as close as she could to where she judged Doris's ear to be.

Taking a deep breath, she yelled, "You want me to call the doctor?"

The figure jerked and shook her head violently.

"Then get the bleeding heck out of this bed, you hear me?"

The head nodded.

"I want to see you in the kitchen in ten minutes. If not, I'm sending Michel in to drag you out there. You hear that?"

Again Doris's head nodded.

Satisfied, Gertie crossed the room to the door, grumbling and muttering to herself about the lousy quality of help nowadays and how she had to do everything herself in order to get it done right.

Back down the hallway she trudged, wondering if she was ever going to feel normal again. If she'd known what she was in for, she would never have gone within a hundred miles of Ian Rossiter. Bleeding lumbering her with a baby and taking off to London to be back with his wife—he was the one what ought to be locked up in the Tower. In the darkest, deepest dungeon, that's what.

She was panting for breath by the time she reached the kitchen door. Doris would have to bleeding scramble if she was going to get to work in ten minutes. By the time she'd washed herself and done her hair, climbed into her clothes, and laced up her oxfords, she'd have to run like a bleeding hare to get to the kitchen.

Gertie smiled to herself as she pushed the door open. Do Doris bleeding good to run for a change. She crawled around like a bleeding slug most of the time.

Mrs. Chubb looked up as Gertie stomped into the kitchen. "Oh, there you are, duck. We was just wondering if you were all right."

"Course I'm all right. It's that blinking Doris you want to—"

Gertie stopped short, blinked, and blinked again. The figure at the sink stared back at her, looking as if she was about to wet her drawers.

Gertie stared at Doris in sheer disbelief. The girl was fully dressed, hair tucked neatly beneath her cap, her black

aced-up shoes peeking out from beneath the hem of her
lack dress.

"How the bloody hell did you get in here?" Gertie
emanded. "I just bleeding left you snoring in your bed."

"Now, Gertie," Mrs. Chubb began, then paused as Doris
uddenly burst into tears.

Gertie looked wildly at Mrs. Chubb, wondering if she
vas losing her mind. "She was in her bed," she said again,
er voice rising in her agitation. "I bleeding saw her. I
ouched her. I came straight back down the corridor, and
ere she is."

"It wasn't me," Doris wailed between sobs.

For a long moment both Mrs. Chubb and Gertie stared at
he weeping girl. Then Mrs. Chubb said faintly, "If it wasn't
ou, girl, then who was it?"

Doris gulped, held her breath, then lifted her tear-stained
ace. "It was my sister, Daisy."

"Daisy?" Mrs. Chubb folded her arms across her chest. "I
hink you'd better tell us what's going on here, then."

Doris gulped and sniffed, then wiped her wet hands on
er apron. "All right. There was only one job, you see. We
vanted to be together. We only had each other, since our
num and dad died—" A sob interrupted her words, and she
aught at her lip with her teeth.

Gertie felt a surge of sympathy for the little twit. She
new what it was like not to have proper parents.

"Anyway," Doris went on, her voice quivering on another
ob, "when we decided to run away from Aunt Beatrice,
ve made a promise that we would never be parted. But there
vas only this one job, so we sort of share it. Daisy did the
nornings, and I did the afternoons. Until she caught a cold,
hat is, then we switched over so she could sleep in. That
vay I wouldn't get too tired doing a whole day. I'm not as
trong as Daisy, and me back hurt so bad."

"Blimey," Gertie said in awe. "You mean there were two of you doing the work? No wonder you seemed different. But you must look exactly alike."

"We do," Doris said miserably. "We're twins."

"You live in the same room?" Mrs. Chubb said, sounding as if she couldn't believe her ears.

Doris nodded. "We sneak in food for each other, and we sleep in the same bed."

"Blimey, I bet that's bleeding uncomfortable," Gertie said with feeling. Since she'd grown a belly on her she hardly had room for herself in the narrow bed.

"It is. Especially when I have to sleep on me stomach because of me back."

"Mercy me." Mrs. Chubb threw her hands up in the air. "Whatever next?"

"We was only going to do it until Daisy could get a job somewhere close by. But there's no hotels near here, and none of the hotels in Wellercombe are hiring until the next season."

Doris started to cry again. "We just wanted to be together, that's all. We never meant no harm."

Gertie felt a strong urge to go over and give the girl a hug. Instead she gave Mrs. Chubb a look imploring her to do something.

"Well, it's not up to me," the housekeeper said, looking sternly at Doris. "I'll have to discuss this with madam, and it will be up to her to decide what to do with you."

"What do you think she'll say?" Gertie said anxiously. Doris might be a little twerp, but she was bleeding better than nothing. It was so blinking hard to find anyone to do the work. They all wanted to go to London nowadays and earn the big money.

"I don't know what she'll say, I'm sure," Mrs. Chubb said, "so we shall just have to wait and see. In the meantime, there is work to be done, and we'd better get on and do it. Meanwhile, I'll go to Doris's room and talk to her sister. I'm sure she knows by now that the two of you have been found out."

"Yes, Mrs. Chubb," Doris said, turning back to the sink with a loud sniff.

Gertie waited until the housekeeper had left the kitchen, then she went over to Doris and put an awkward arm across her shaking shoulders. "Come on, luv, cheer up. It ain't the end of the world, you know. Madam is really nice, and I'm sure she'll be able to sort things out. You'll see."

Doris turned her face up to Gertie and attempted a smile through her tears. "Thank you, Miss Brown. You've been really nice to me, and I'll miss you if I have to leave, honest I will."

Gertie didn't quite know what to say. She thought she'd been bleeding rough on the kid, and was feeling a bit ashamed of herself right now. Patting the thin shoulder, she said gruffly, "You'll be all right, you'll see. Madam won't let anything bad happen to you, I promise."

Doris nodded as if she didn't quite believe her.

"Any rate," Gertie said, grabbing a cloth to help the twit finish the washing up, "it must be nice having a twin sister. Stops you from getting lonely, like. I wish I had a sister to talk to sometimes."

Doris looked up shyly. "You can always talk to me. I like talking."

Gertie grinned. "So do I. Let's keep our fingers crossed that madam lets you both stay. Then we can all have a bloody good gossip." She felt quite pleased with herself when Doris finally managed to smile.

Madeline stood quite still in the middle of the dance floor and tried very hard not to look at the axe again. Instead she stared into the overbright eyes of the man in front of her and said pleasantly, "Good morning, Mr. Plunkett. It looks like being a nice day after all."

Cyril Plunkett's eyes narrowed to slits. "It is not going to be a nice day at all for you, I'm afraid. In fact, you will never have a nice day again. I'm going to chop off that pretty head of yours, so you had better take your last look at the world before you say goodbye to it."

Madeline met the cruel gaze without flinching. "I would like to know why you want to kill me. I think you owe me that, at least. I don't know you, and as far as I know, I have never harmed you in any way. I don't think I deserve to die by your hand."

Cyril laughed, a high-pitched cackle that seemed to rise and dance along the balconies, echoing high in the vaulted ceiling. The unearthly sound seemed to shiver in the air as he stared at Madeline with glittering eyes.

"You are a gypsy, and that is enough. You must be destroyed."

Madeline lifted her chin. "You still have not explained to me the reason. What have the gypsies done to you that you feel compelled to kill?"

"You are treacherous beings, unfeeling and cruel. I loved you once. You were everything to me. I spent every penny I had trying to show you how much I cared for you. And what did you do?"

"I did nothing," Madeline said gently. "You mistake me for someone else."

"You, she, what difference does it make? You are all tarred with the same brush. You are all the same. You took everything I offered you—jewelry, flowers, clothes, everything except my love."

He stepped toward her, shifting his grip on the axe with both hands. "Do you remember how you laughed at me when I tried to touch you? That laugh still haunts my nightmares. You told me how I disgusted you, that I wasn't fit to lick your boots."

"I'm sorry, but that wasn't me. You have been treated very badly, I can see that, but I should not be blamed for the ugly deeds of a stranger." Madeline shifted her gaze just long enough to look beyond his shoulder into the shadows along the circular wall of the ballroom.

"Is that why you killed all those women?" she asked, raising her voice just a fraction. "You want to kill all gypsies because of something one woman did to you? Is that fair?"

"Fair? *Fair?*" Again the maniacal laugh echoed chillingly throughout the ballroom. "All is fair in love and war, is that not so? You, a filthy, lowly gypsy, dare to tell me, a respectable, honest businessman, that I am not fit to lick your boots? Is that fair? I think not."

Cyril advanced once more, raising the axe in his hands. Madeline also raised her hands and pointed her fingers at the crazed man. "You may destroy me, you fool, but you will burn in hell for your crimes. I call upon the spirits of the underworld to take your soul and chain it forever, so you will wander in hell for all eternity."

Cyril appeared not to hear her. He advanced, axe raised, spitting words at her as he came. "Die, you heathen bastard, like the rest of them. I killed them all, and I will kill you, too. Then we will see who rots in hell."

CHAPTER

❖20❖

As Madeline continued to back slowly away, there was a rush of movement from behind the stage. Three burly police constables appeared, bounding across the floor, followed by the tall, lean figure of Inspector Cranshaw.

Watching the scene with Baxter from the shelter of the balcony, Cecily felt a vast rush of relief as they wrested the axe from the hands of Cyril Plunkett and wrestled him to the floor.

Cyril's high-pitched voice could be heard quite clearly above the muttered commands of the policemen. "It wasn't me," he cried over and over again. "It was George. I tried to stop him. I tried. He wouldn't listen. It was George. It wasn't me."

"Poor man," Cecily murmured when the policemen
ally had Cyril on his feet again. "I'm afraid he is quite
ranged. It will, perhaps, save him from the gallows."

Baxter nodded soberly. "Though I can't help feeling that
e poor devil would be better off. His life inside an asylum
ill be a living hell."

"Which is more or less what Madeline wished on him."
ecily leaned over the balcony rail to search the floor below
er. "Speaking of Madeline, I do hope she isn't shaken up.
e still has the tables to do, both here and in the dining
om."

"I saw her leave a moment ago. No doubt to take care of
e dining room before lunch is served."

"Yes, I imagine she would. Nothing seems to disturb her
r long." Cecily sighed. "This has not been a good week,
axter. I do hope nothing else happens to take our attention
vay from the festivities tonight. Our guests will be arriving
is afternoon, and it would be very nice to have nothing
ore to worry about than if the rooms are warm enough or
the beds are soft enough."

"I am quite sure everything will be in order, as always,
adam. The constables have caused quite a stir by their
esence, I'm afraid, but I have managed to satisfy every-
e's curiosity without giving away any word of the true
tuation."

Cecily gave him a warm smile. "Thank you, Baxter. You
e such a comfort, as always. Now I had better go down
d speak to the inspector. I understand he wants a word
ith me."

"Yes, madam." Baxter opened the door leading to the
airs and stood back, waiting for her to pass. "Will you
ed me to come with you?" he asked as she stepped out
to the corridor.

"No, thank you, Baxter. I know you have plenty to do

before tonight. Mrs. Chubb also wants a word with me,
I will talk to her after I've seen the inspector. Perhaps
can meet in the library after lunch to go over the last minu
details for the ball?"

"Of course, madam."

He seemed reluctant to leave her when they reached t
ground floor, but she assured him she could handle t
inspector.

"I will tell him exactly what he needs to know an
nothing more," she said, pausing outside the drawing roo
where the inspector awaited her. "Thank heavens I p
nothing in the note I gave Samuel that would indicate
might have known the identity of the killer beforehand."

"Very well, madam." He looked about to say somethir
more, but after a moment he turned instead and strode off
the direction of the dining room.

Cecily watched him go, then braced herself for t
meeting with Inspector Cranshaw.

The inspector's dour look warned her he was not to
pleased with her when she entered the room a moment late
"Once again, madam," he informed her in his usual fl
tone, "fortune appears to have smiled upon you. Had ye
not asked for our protection this morning, another traged
could well have taken place right inside your hotel."

"Providence, indeed, Inspector."

He eyed her with suspicion. "And you had no inkling th
man was a dangerous killer until this morning?"

"I only knew that my friend, Miss Pengrath, could be
serious danger, since so many members of the gypsies ha
been killed. Many people mistake Miss Pengrath for
gypsy, and I felt uneasy about her being exposed to possib
danger. When Samuel informed me he had found the remai
of those poor women, I decided to ask for protection."

"And it was sheer coincidence that the murderer ha
pened to be one of your guests."

"I must admit, finding that dreadful sack brought the ospect much closer to home. It made me dreadfully easy, I can assure you."

The inspector rocked back and forth on his heels, his rewd gaze seeming to penetrate her very thoughts. After a oment, much to her relief, he seemed satisfied.

He even answered some of Cecily's questions, much to r surprise. He was rarely so forthcoming. Though he did sue his usual warning to her about meddling in police fairs.

As she told Baxter later, the man seemed almost human, r once.

"Probably because he wasn't saddled with that idiot orthcott," Baxter muttered. He stood in his customary osition at the end of the table, his hands behind his back as e contemplated the rows of bookshelves.

"What did happen to Stan Northcott?" Cecily said, trying ot to think about the ghastly contents of the sack that had upset poor Samuel. "I expected to see him here this orning."

"I heard he had a cold in the nose. The man always was sniveling namby-pamby."

Well used to Baxter's contempt for the constable, Cecily niled. "Speaking of colds, I heard some very interesting ws from Mrs. Chubb. It's a matter we need to discuss." uickly she recounted what Mrs. Chubb had told her about oris and Daisy. Although Baxter appeared startled by the velation, he made no comment until she was finished. hen he said carefully, "What would you like me to do out it, madam?"

Cecily put her head on one side and looked at him. "What ould you do if you were in my shoes, Baxter?"

He pondered on the question for a moment, then said, "It ould appear that both girls do an adequate job, do they ot?"

"Adequate, yes. They have a lot to learn, but I think the
are willing to make the effort. Doris is a little weak
present, but she will regain her strength once she is eatin
proper meals. They have been living mostly on scraps fro
what I hear, sharing meals and scrounging what they ca
from the kitchen."

"And the other one? Daisy?"

Cecily shrugged. "According to Mrs. Chubb, Daisy
somewhat short-tempered, but she has had a lot to worr
about lately. Apparently she is the stronger of the two an
feels responsible for her sister. Mrs. Chubb feels that wit
the security of a job and a home, she will be less cantan
kerous, and will settle down before long."

"In that case, madam, I think we can afford to hire the
both. I find it commendable that they are determined to sta
together at all costs."

"I agree." She leaned back in her chair with a long sigl
Now that the excitement was over, she felt quite tired. "Wit
Gertie's baby due any day now, and Ethel no longer with u
we shall need the extra help."

"Precisely, madam."

"Good, I'm happy that we agree. I'll let Mrs. Chub
know this afternoon." Cecily sat in silence for a moment c
two, thinking over everything that had transpired tha
morning.

"You know, Baxter," she said softly after a long pause, "
can't help feeling sorry for Cyril. He is such a pathetic littl
man, and he must have been dreadfully hurt by that woma
That's why he killed those women, you know. In his min
he was killing the woman who'd scorned him."

"It is indeed sad, madam."

"He told the inspector," Cecily went on, "that he had t
keep killing her because she wouldn't stay dead. That's wh
he removed the heads. He didn't want to look at someor
else's head on the body he'd destroyed."

"How macabre." Baxter moved to the mantelpiece and ran his finger along it, as if testing for dust. "Tell me, madam, how did you guess that Cyril Plunkett was the murderer? He certainly didn't look the part, nor act it for that matter. He seemed quite a different person when he faced Miss Pengrath in the ballroom."

"Actually it was Doris, or was it Daisy?" She shook her head, then laughed. "It was both of them, I suppose. I saw Doris, or who I thought was Doris, wearing a different dress than she had that morning. She told me she'd changed it, and that started me thinking about the murderer's change of clothes."

Baxter gave her a sharp look. "The murderer's?"

Cecily nodded. "As I mentioned before, the murderer could hardly have mutilated those bodies without getting himself covered in their blood. I was so certain that it was one of the three persons whose rooms we searched, and yet we found not one speck of blood anywhere."

"True. But as I said, the killer could have discarded the clothing afterward."

"Which he most certainly did." Cecily paused as Baxter lifted his chin and studied the ceiling. She followed his gaze, but seeing nothing out of the ordinary, continued, "He could hardly come back to the hotel in that state, however. He couldn't take the chance of being seen on his way to his room. Which means he had to dispose of the clothes *before* he returned to the hotel, in which case he would need a change of clothes."

"Ah," said Baxter, directing his gaze along the picture rail above his head. "Cyril Plunkett."

"Not Cyril Plunkett. George." Cecily watched curiously as Baxter's gaze traveled around the room. "The inspector explained to me that in Cyril's mind he was two persons. The Cyril side of him couldn't bear what he was doing, so

he blamed the other person he called George. Which is why
he kept writing notes asking us to stop George from killing
those women."

"It sounds extremely complicated, madam."

"I agree. But I shall be seeing Dr. Prestwick at the ball
tonight, so I'll ask him to explain it further."

Baxter's chin dropped abruptly. "Oh?"

She finally had his attention, she thought with satisfac
tion. "Anyway, once I realized it was Cyril, I asked
Madeline if she were willing to take a risk, if it meant
apprehending the murderer. She agreed at once. I casually
mentioned to Cyril this morning that Madeline would be in
the ballroom all alone. He couldn't resist killing one more
gypsy. George did the rest."

"That was remarkably foolish of Miss Pengrath to take
such a risk," Baxter said sternly.

Cecily nodded. "Perhaps. But she was convinced, as
was, that the police would not pursue the case with any real
interest, and I had absolutely no proof. Merely conjecture on
my part, and you know how well the inspector would have
listened to that. He does not have a very high opinion of my
intelligence."

"Can you wonder at it," Baxter murmured, "after some of
your wild escapades?"

Ignoring him, Cecily went on, "Cyril Plunkett intended to
return to the city this morning. Once he moved out of the
jurisdiction of this constabulary, we would have had very
little hope of apprehending him. This seemed the only way."

"Well, all's well that ends well, I suppose. I just hope
Samuel recovers from the shock of finding the severed
heads."

Cecily shuddered. "I should imagine he would have
nightmares for weeks. I know—" She broke off, staring at

axter as once more he fastened his intent gaze on the
icture rail.

"Baxter," she said sharply, "what on earth are you staring
t?"

"Just a moment . . . ah!" He pointed to James's portrait.
Right there, madam. Look!"

For a moment her blood chilled as she stared at the
ortrait, wondering what he had seen. Then a tiny move-
ent caught her eye. There, on the corner of the golden
rame, sat a tiny, bright yellow bird.

"Great heavens," Cecily exclaimed, "Lady Belleville's
anary."

"My apologies to her," Baxter murmured. "She is not as
atty as I surmised, after all."

"You are like most men, Baxter," Cecily couldn't resist
aying. "All too quick to misjudge women. I fear you are
lmost as prejudiced as Ellsworth Galloway."

Baxter lowered his chin and rested his intent gaze on her
ace. "Not so," he said softly. "I have never misjudged you,
Cecily. I have always looked upon you with the utmost
dmiration and respect."

Reeling from the shock of his use of her first name,
Cecily managed to stammer, "Why, Baxter, I have always
dmired and respected you also."

She saw the expression on his dear, familiar face soften,
nd for a moment she detected such yearning there she
ched to hold out her arms to him. She stared into his eyes,
vhile time audibly passed, measured by the steady tick of
he clock.

Then he said, a trifle unsteadily, "I am honored to be in
our employ. In spite of your insistence on risking both my
eputation and my neck on many an occasion with your
oolhardy adventures, nevertheless I hope I may continue to
erve you for many years to come."

Swallowing her disappointment, as she had so many times before, Cecily said lightly, "I would hope so, too, Baxter. And come now, admit it. You would find life intolerably dull were it not for my adventures."

Again his eyes filled with longing, and he seemed to have trouble swallowing. "I would indeed. Cecily, I wonder—"

The sudden rap on the door made them both jump. Taking a moment to collect herself, Cecily called out, "Come in!"

She saw the flash of irritation on Baxter's face and rejoiced in it. Then she rose to her feet as Mrs. Chubb hurried into the room, wringing her hands. "We've sent for the doctor, mum, but we thought you'd like to know. It's Gertie's time. The baby is on the way."

Cecily almost laughed out loud at the excitement on the housekeeper's round face. "I'll come right away," she said, and followed the ecstatic woman to the door.

Looking back over her shoulder, she said, "I'll let you know when it's all over, Baxter."

"Thank you, madam." His face was as inscrutable as ever, but just before the door closed, she heard him mutter, "But did the wretch have to choose this moment to have her baby?"

Closing the door, Cecily met Mrs. Chubb's inquisitive gaze. Feeling her face warm, she said quickly, "Baxter is most likely concerned that Gertie will now miss the fireworks display."

She could tell that Mrs. Chubb wasn't entirely convinced, but it didn't really matter. Nothing mattered. Gertie was about to give birth to a brand-new baby, and suddenly life seemed so much brighter. Cherishing the memory of Baxter's voice murmuring her name, she hurried down the hallway to Gertie's room.